Sarvet & Livli

Sarvet & Livli

SARVET'S WANDERYAR

LIVLI'S GIFT

by J.M. Ney-Grimm

Wild
Unicorn

Sarvet's Wanderyar

and

Livli's Gift

are each also available

as separate volumes

Sarvet's
Wanderyar

To Wendy,
for her enthusiasm and encouragement

*T*ense and furious, Sarvet shook her mother's angry grip from her forearm. "I'll petition the lodge-meet for filial severance," she snapped, and then wished she'd swallowed the words, so hateful, too hateful to speak. And yet she'd spoken them.

The breeze swirling on the mountain slope picked up, nudging the springy branches of the three great pines at Sarvet's back and purring among their needles. Their scent infused the moving air.

Paiam's narrowed eyes widened an instant – in hurt? – flicked up to encompass the swaying tree tops behind her daughter, then went flat.

"You dare!" she breathed. "You're *my* daughter. Mine alone. And I'll see to it that you and every other mother in the lodge knows it too. You'll stay under my aegis till you're grown, young sister, even if I must declare you careless and remiss to do it!"

Oh!

Sarvet only thought she'd been mad before. "You never wanted me!" she accused.

Was it true? Or was she just aiming for Paiam's greatest vulnerability, aiming to hurt? Because under her own rage lay . . . desperation. Something needed to change. She just didn't know what, didn't know how. And didn't want to be facing it right now, facing her mother right now. It was Other-joy, and she wanted joy. For just a little longer. How had this day of celebration gone so wrong?

She'd woken to the pleasant consciousness that the morning of a fete-day brings. No chopping cabbage, digging potatoes, or long hours at the spinning wheel awaited her. The preparations for Other-joy were wholly different from normal chores, and this year the calling ritual would include three linking ceremonies!

She remembered smiling with anticipation, starting to push herself upright, then changing her mind to snuggle her cheek more deeply into her pillows. Light from the oil lanterns in the hallway was seeping through the chinks around her bednook shutters – Sister Teraisa must already be up – and Sarvet wanted to get up too. But not just yet. Her sheets were so soft, her blankets cozy, and the fur coverlet warm. She wriggled her toes in their bedsocks, ignoring the constraint in her right foot. There was something special to the first beginning of a day, all its promise ahead. She would savor it . . . and avoid a little longer the chilly moment when she doffed her nightcap and gown in order to dress.

She closed her eyes again and huddled her shoulders more securely under the bedclothes. Mmm. Because she was toasty from the neck down, the unheated air inside her bednook felt soft, refreshing even, on her cheek. *If only I could store warmth away like I store my sweaters on a shelf.* She would be shivering later, outdoors in the snow and the dark. Winter garb could do only so much. *If I could awake to Lodge-day instead of Other-joy this morning, would I?* She loved the clash of Other-joy's cold austerities with its equally warm and rich moments. But Other-joy was . . . complicated. Lodge-day was just fun. She'd spent it with her friend Amara last summer.

They'd greeted the men of Tukeva-lodge with traditional tossed thistle-silk streamers – a shower of crimson, gold, purple, amber, and blue pelted at the visitors as they approached the mother-lodge. Amara's father was a bear of a man, big and round and laughing, with a pillow of a beard. His hello hugs swooped Amara, Amara's mother Iteydet, Amara's aunt Enna, and Sarvet off their feet. His arms felt like tree limbs. Flexible ones. Only after his enthusiastic civility did Feljas gaze in puzzlement at Sarvet's face.

"But little Hilla never grew from belt high to chest high since Nerich!"

Amara broke into giggles. "Hilla's picnicking with her best friend, mapah! This is *my* best friend, of course. Sarvet."

"Then you'll excuse a mapah's zeal, little sister, won't you? I thought you were mine!" His eyes twinkled.

Sarvet found herself giggling along with Amara. "Of course," she answered. And knew a moment's wistfulness. *I wish he **were** my mapah.* But Ivvar would never visit Kaunis-lodge, even on the greater fete-days like Other-joy.

Feljas was more like a wixting-brother than a father. He claimed the very tip of the valley-rock for their picnic blanket, teased Enna unmercifully about the damage her long eyelashes would do to the hearts of unlinked brothers, juggled their luncheon pears in fancy patterns before passing them to each sister for eating, dropped kisses on Iteydet's cheek every fifth sentence, and pulled a sack of luxurious dried cherries from his capacious pocket for dessert. Then he fell asleep under Sarvet's amazed gaze.

Her expression must have conveyed her astonishment, because Iteydet ventured a laughing explanation. "He's always like this. Never stops until he *really* stops. In sleep. If I had to live with him day-in and day-out, like a sister, he'd wear on me."

But Hammarleeding women didn't live with their men. Sarvet had heard rumors that the Silmarish lowlanders did. Here in the mountains, sisters lived with sisters in the mother-lodges. And brothers lived with brothers in the father-lodges. As was proper.

Iteydet continued: "He'll wake again soon. And I'll be glad of it. It's not a proper fete-day without Feljas' jokes!"

He did wake. And proposed a game of tag combined with rolling down the mountain slope. Enna refused, but the sisters occupying three blankets near theirs were persuaded to join the fun, even including the normally staid Teraisa. Sarvet surprised herself when she abandoned keeping Enna company mere moments after her own plaintive refusal. Her limp was no disadvantage when rolling, not running, was the mode of movement.

The whole day had been like that: merry and easy and . . . loving. *Would* she trade Other-joy for Lodge-day? Yes! Well . . . maybe. Sarvet ducked her head down under the covers. No. *Other-joy is special.*

"Sarvet! Sarvet!"

The bright, excited voice of her friend Brionne sounded abruptly beside her bednook, followed immediately by the banging open of the foot shutter and Brionne herself bouncing in on the mattress. "Wake up! How can you still be sleeping? It's Other-joy!" Brionne's face was flushed and her eyes sparkled, but she was still in her nightclothes, for all her eagerness.

Sarvet clutched at the coverlet which Brionne's vigor had disarranged. The hall air was cold! "Stop," she protested halfheartedly. "Of course I wasn't asleep. Haven't you ever heard of a slow start to a day?" She hid a grin behind her hand, feigning a yawn.

"Arve!" Brionne's use of the old sweet-name was an unusual slip. She knew Sarvet was jealous of Amara (a year older than them both) and stretching away from childish things. Brionne must have believed the fake yawn.

"Girls!" Sister Teraisa's voice came low, but chiding. "Take it downstairs. Your neighbors are dreaming. Not everyone chooses to rise this early!"

Brionne pouted and lost some of her sparkle, but Sarvet couldn't resist giving her a reproving glance. *She* hadn't been the noisy one.

"I'm sorry, Sister Teraisa." Brionne was subdued, her surreptitious glance to her friend reproachful.

The Sister wasn't appeased, but she just shook her head, touched last finger to lip, and hurried away.

"Are you really going to stay here snoozing?" whispered Brionne. "If we attend first-calling, we'll get dried hoolinberries after. Come on, Sarvet, do get up!"

Sarvet relented. "I *am* up. But these covers stay put while you sit between me and the clothes in my cupboard. I'll move . . . when you do."

Brionne giggled, pulled a face, and slid out into the sleep-hall. Sarvet followed, wincing as her lame foot took her weight. It was always a little stiff right out of bed, even when she iced it in a bucket of snow before retiring. Of course, if she skipped the nightly icing, she couldn't walk at all until after Sister Evaia massaged the tightened tendons.

She rummaged through the shelf under her bednook, shivering, and pulled out her thickest wool stockings, felted boots, thistle-silk under garments, and her best sweater-tunic and hood in festive red. Brionne was ready first, as usual, garbed in her favorite forest green. Sarvet studied her friend. Her shiny, syrup-brown hair was so pretty. *I wish my hair were shiny instead of wooly.* But it wasn't. And . . . *who cares? It's Other-joy!*

Brionne searched the black sky through the clerestory windows above the bednooks for signs of dawn – none. She turned her head and smiled at Sarvet. "Ready?"

Sarvet nodded and pulled her hood over her ears. She was used to being slower. She knew her friends never thought about this difference anymore. But her palsied hip and twisted foot made the simplest tasks, even dressing, take longer. And she wished . . . the healing-call last year had worked instead of making things worse. *I won't think about that now. It's Other-joy, and I'm going to have fun!* She returned Brionne's smile, closed the cupboard door, and straightened.

The corridor was just wide enough for them to walk side by side. Brionne went slowly, not so that Sarvet – limping – could keep up, but because she knew Sister Teraisa would scold them for thumping, if they hurried. At least half the bednooks lining the passage on both sides still sheltered dreamers. First-calling was an optional rite on Other-joy, and many of the Sisters of Kaunis-lodge skipped its rigors.

Snow-washing the face and hands outside in the ritual of detachment followed by searching one's heart for deep wishes in the darkness of the unlit calling-hall held little appeal for many. But Sarvet found the cold, clear purity of it exhilarating, especially compared to the close, hot, tangled asceticism practiced by her mother. *But I won't think of that either.*

And she didn't. The bones of her hands ached with cold when she returned them to their mittens, and the skin of her face felt numb after its bath in the snow, but the stars overhead – pulsing like remote fire-beacons – seemed to herald newness, hope, and adventure. The Holy Caller's voice (praying Divine Sias for oneness of being, knowing where self ended and other began, and fluidity in engagement) sounded joyous and full of life.

I love this.

Back indoors, sitting on a bench in the calling-hall, she wondered what her heart-deep wishes for this year might be. *I hoped for healing last year. And that was a mistake. I wish I could have a wanderyar, like the boys in their father-lodges.* Why couldn't girls travel from mother-lodge to mother-lodge for a year? *I want wider horizons too! That was why I wished for healing.*

She spared a glance for Brionne, beside her, and was surprised to see a tear quivering on her eyelash. What did her friend want so passionately that it inspired grief? *I thought she was happy.* She always seemed so bubbly and energetic and content.

Later, nearer dawn, breaking their fast in the refecting-hall, Brionne was all blushing laughter. Had Sarvet really seen that tear? Her friend asked: "Can you imagine being a novitiate today?"

No, she couldn't.

"We will be, one day, you know."

"Not everyone choses the linking sacrament, Bri."

"So. Will you refuse? If Sister Valitte selects you?" Brionne directed a searching glance at her, then looked down.

"My mother did." Sarvet felt her face heating.

"Not her first time. You wouldn't be here, if she had." Brionne's smile grew serious. "Besides, don't you want to? It's supposed to be . . . nice."

"I don't know. I suppose I thought this" – she gestured at her leg – "meant I wouldn't be selected. I know my mother would prefer it that way." Sarvet shifted uncomfortably. Talk of brothers and linking and masculinity made her uneasy, but it was hard to avoid it on Other-joy. Especially once one was fifteen. She and Brionne would be meeting with Sister Kilti regularly soon, preparing for their own linking. It was rare that a sister under nineteen was chosen, but the women of the Kaunis-lodge liked every girl to be thoroughly ready.

"But . . . a birth injury couldn't be passed to your child!" Brionne looked startled. "You're not *vayatynt*, Arve!" The sweet-name again.

"No, but . . ." She didn't want to talk about her mother. Not today. And her mother was all tangled in this, although even she didn't understand how. "Bri, I haven't passed through my first blood yet." Another thing she was slow at. Both Brionne and Amara had reached that threshold before her. "I wish . . ."

Someone tapped her on the shoulder. "Sarvet! Brionne! Happy Other-joy!" Amara was glowing. The blue of her festival sweater-tunic and skirt always brought out the brilliance of her equally blue eyes, the richness of her smooth, chestnut curls. And her interruption was timely. The right words – *shun it*, the right *thoughts* – to get Bri onto another subject hadn't even begun to surface.

Amara walked around the end of the table to sit across from them. She looked enviously at their plates. The hoolinberries had been distributed to all the first-callers, but not yet eaten. "You lucky snow-pigs! Sister Tamma was generous!"

"You could have had some too, if you'd been willing to leave your dreams earlier," Brionne countered.

Amara tossed her head. "I needed my beauty sleep. Besides, I was up late." She snickered.

Sarvet felt her forehead wrinkling. Up late? Why?

"Sister Kilti remembered after all the oil lanterns were doused that I'd been ill the day she talked with the new witnesses about the secret rites." Of course Amara had to rub it in that *she* was a witness and *they* were not. "She rousted me out of my nook to explain it all. And she wasn't done until after the wixting-hour, mind you."

Sarvet plucked one of the hoolinberries deliberately from her plate and looked it over slowly, noting its fine crimson-purple color, its sweet floral scent.

Amara followed the fruit with her gaze all the way to Sarvet's lips. "Oh, can't I have one of yours? Please?"

A platter of pickled greens was making its way down the long table. Brionne seized it ostentatiously and flourished it under Amara's nose. "Gundru, Amara?"

"Oh, you!" But she laughed and served a healthy scoop of the slimy mass onto her plate. And then did likewise for her companions. "You know gundru's *so good* for you! I insist!"

Brionne giggled, and Sarvet found her friend's upbeat humor contagious. A chuckle escaped her lips, banishing the last of her tension. Of course, she actually liked gundru. Amara didn't, but she was being charitable about it.

"So!" Amara swallowed a bite of greens, grimaced, and continued, "Guess what Sister Kilti told me last night."

"What?" asked Brionne obligingly.

"There's another, *more* secret ritual within the secret rite!" Amara straightened and widened her eyes. "What do you think of *that*?!"

"After the blessing? Part of the communion?"

"Uh, huh."

"You'll get in trouble, if you tell us about it." Sarvet doubted that would stop Amara. And she *was* curious. What did happen during the communion that the witnesses witnessed? That she and Brionne – and all the other little girls, the "innocents" – would not? And what might this extra secret part be?

"Well, I'm not going to tell you *about* it. Just what it's called: the adoration! And only the Holy Caller attends."

"So all the witnesses file out? Just like the innocents do earlier?" That made Sarvet feel better. Amara would still not know everything. But what *was* the adoration? And the communion? She wished Amara *would* gossip about this.

"Yup. But Sister Kilti did tell me what happens! It sounds . . ." uncharacteristically, Amara trailed into silence. "Well, you'll find out next year."

"Next year!" Brionne burst out. "Amara Iteydet-spring! You have to say more than that!"

"No." Their friend's face grew solemn. "Sister Kilti made me see . . . that I could really ruin things for you, if I shared too much. So I won't."

"Hmh!" Sarvet looked at Brionne. They nodded at one another, and then turned back to Amara. Doubtful they could make the older girl disgorge more, but they could surely make her pay for telling only enough to tease! *Let's see, first I'll rag her about the spot on her face last week. Then I bet Brionne will bring up the time she walked in on Puheliet in the dump-buckets. And I can think of at least four more embarrassing moments. Excellent!*

Amara took it all in good part, but Sarvet refused to stop – or stop egging on Brionne – until Sister Piha directed everyone into the calling-hall for father-coming.

The sun was finally up, its light glowing dimly through the creamy leather window coverings, dispelling the shadows cast by the oil lanterns. Three candelabra on the sacred table held thickets of candles that would be lit at the start of the linking ceremonies. First this more contemplative interval must pass. Sister Piha was calling on Sias to guide their meditations on the active principle. Mother

Johtaia gave a homily, reminding her listeners that chastity should not be prudery. The Holy Caller chanted the *Calling Song* and then commended the gathered sisters to silence and reflection. Sarvet closed her eyes obediently.

So what about this much vaunted "active principle"? Surely it was just doing things. And why was it always coupled with brothers? Sarvet was sure the men and boys of Tukeva-lodge were active. They must have to clean and cook and knit and herd-lure just like the women and girls did here. And the brothers ran a sawmill in the valley. But the sisters of Nottkia-lodge ran a tannery. Surely the mother-lodges were every bit as "active" as the father-lodges.

And yet . . . there was something different about the fathers. And the brothers. Not so much the babes who still lived with their mothers at Kaunis-lodge, but the big boys who'd transferred to Tukeva. And the men. It wasn't just that they were taller and broader and had such deep voices. There was an . . . *energy* to them that was . . . powerful . . . compelling . . . exciting? Sarvet shivered. *This is what Brionne was trying to talk about earlier, wasn't it? I wanted to shut her up.* Sarvet still didn't want to think about it. And yet she did.

What was her first experience of fathers? She didn't really need to ask that question. She knew the answer. *I'm just delaying.* She'd been little, really little. *How many years did I have then. Maybe five?* It was one of her earliest memories. She was sitting in a clump of alpine flowers making a chain from the blooms, carefully selecting all the pink ones, when a shadow fell over her. She'd looked up to see . . . a father looming against the sky. He seemed as tall as the clouds, and his bearded face scared her.

"Sarvet?" His voice was gentle and his eyes kind.

He knelt so that she wouldn't have to crane her neck to look at him. "Do you remember me?"

She didn't, but her fear ebbed. He looked nice.

"I'm Ivvar, your mother's linking-brother."

She still didn't remember him, but she held up her flower chain to show him. It was nearly done.

"Beautiful," he told he. "Would you make one for me?"

And she did, a yellow one, not pink.

He'd just draped it around his neck and was thanking Sarvet when her mother arrived, hot and bothered and annoyed. "You shouldn't be here," Paiam declared.

"I've a right." His voice was equable, but he stayed seated on the grass.

Paiam went on to argue with him. Sarvet couldn't recall the words, but Paiam's rage seemed to cover another feeling. *She would have been crying, except that Paiam never cries.*

Sarvet did remember the end of it. While Paiam stood by in fury, Ivvar had taken his daughter kindly in his arms and kissed her forehead. His lips were warm and dry. "Goodbye, little Sarvet. I'll love you forever."

"You're going?" He'd been a fun play fellow. It seemed a shame to lose him just when she'd found him.

"Yes, I'll be living at Rakas, not Tukeva, now. The brothers of Rakas visit a different mother-lodge."

"Oh." She'd been placid then, accepting his farewell. Now . . . now she felt differently. *Paiam drove him away, shun her! I could have been like Amara and Brionne, seeing my own father several times each year, if it hadn't been for her.* With a small shake of her shoulders, Sarvet opened her eyes.

Her mother was seated on the bench in front of her, a little to the right. She had the same expression on her face that Sarvet felt leaving her own features: faint distaste mingled with longing. Sarvet winced. *I don't want to be like her.* She looked away. Brionne, on one side, was staring at the floor and wiggling her foot, bored. Amara, to the left, was rapt, lids closed on some private exultation. Sister Mieha, one of the novitiates, positively glowed. Whatever *she* was contemplating was . . . inspiring. Sarvet looked away, embarrassed, and caught Brionne doing the same. Her friend stifled a giggle. *I'm ready for this to be over.*

Sister Piha brought the meditation to an end with the deep, low hail of the alpenhorn. Sarvet filed out quietly to the porch with all her lodge-sisters. The overcast from the evening before had dissipated, but the day was merely breezy, not gusty. The snowy slope of their mountain, as well as the peaks across the valley, sparkled under the wintery sun.

The brothers of Tukeva-lodge were close, winding up the path below the smokehouse. They were singing, fitting the rhythm of their steps to that of their glad voices. Sarvet craned from side to side, trying to peer around Brionne. Ivvar would not be among them. He never had been in all these years. But . . . was Nial somewhere in that long line of men and boys? *Shun it!* She couldn't *see.* Then Brionne made room for her at the rail, and she had a clear view. There were Gunnar and Eetu, Nial's friends. But where was Nial himself? She bit her lip. Was he still away on his wanderyar? *It's been more than twelve months. He left before last Other-joy. I thought the wanderyar lasted exactly a year.* But he wasn't there. Could something have happened to him? Out in the wide world beyond the Fiordhammars?

Brionne started bouncing on her heels. "I see him! I see him!" she squealed, and then clapped a hand to her mouth. *Nial?* Sarvet grabbed her arm. It really wouldn't do, if Brionne hurtled down the porch steps to greet the brothers on the path. *They're* supposed to approach *us.* But where did Brionne see Nial?

"Sarvet, Vaino is back!"

Oh. Not Nial. Sarvet sagged. She'd really hoped . . . not just to see her brother-friend, but to talk with him about some of the things that confused her so. He didn't have to live with Paiam – she deliberately used her birth-mother's *name* rather than her kinship – the way Sarvet's lodge-sisters did. He wouldn't alternate between pained silences and feeble excuses. But she wasn't to have the benefit of his thinking. He hadn't yet returned to his father-lodge.

She stopped paying attention. The ritual greeting between Mother Johtaia and Father Biejan, the symbolic offering of pannkuja to each brother as he stepped onto the porch, and the formal presentation of the sister-novitiates to the brother-novices all passed her by.

She emerged from her disappointment in the calling-hall. The candelabra had been lit. Waves of heat rolled out from the fires in the twin hearths beyond the sacred table. Sister Valitte had already pronounced the blessing on the prospective linkings. The disrobing was about to begin.

Each brother-novice bowed to his bride, gently took her hands and turned them palm up. She, in turn, slowly unbuttoned his sweater-tunic. The men were hot from their climb and the warmth of the fires. Getting out from under the thick wool must be a relief, thought Sarvet. *Why do they have to stay in it until now?*

The removal of garments was a deliberate act, considerate, almost a courtship. Sarvet glanced at Brionne again. She was fidgeting, eager for the dismissal of the innocents that would come soon. But a rising tension swept over the witnesses who would stay. What would they witness? Sarvet felt a tingling in her core. She wished she could stay. She also wished she were bored like Brionne, like she had been last year at this point. She wished Nial were here, sitting with the other brothers across the aisle on the benches there.

Then the sister-initiates were standing in their thistle-silk shifts, and the brother-novices were down to their smocks and braies. Sister Piha intoned the dismissal, and Sarvet found herself in the gallery amidst a cluster of girls and boys her age and younger. Brionne, assigned several toddlers for watching, gathered her charges and herded them toward the nursery-hall.

Sarvet turned toward the front portal. She felt hot and prickly and irritable. *I'm not a witness, not a child-minder, not a goatherd, not a kitchen maid. Does Sister Aidnu think that just because I'm lame I can't do any chores that require standing?* It was true she couldn't run after a straying youngster or goat, but even Paiam – *Mother* – urged her to exercise each day.

Someone behind her jostled her elbow as she paused before the coat pegs. The next instant she was engulfed in an energetic, comprehensive embrace and swept off her feet. "Sarvet! There you are!" It was Nial. But, goodness, a Nial much taller, much broader, and *bearded*! She was laughing and hugging him back. *He's here! He's here!*

"Sarvet, where can we go to talk? I have so much to tell you!"

They ended up under the pines behind the lodge, the spot she'd imagined occupying alone. *He's here! But why am I so happy?* She didn't know. She didn't care. It just was so.

"Shouldn't you be in the calling-hall?" she probed. "Or do you have to be older to witness, when you're a brother?" He must be – she calculated – nineteen. She would witness three communion celebrations by that age.

"The father-lodges in the south celebrate Other-joy a month earlier," he explained easily. "I've already been through the whole rigamarole this year. Besides . . . banging open the door amidst communion? Father Biejan would never forgive me."

She giggled.

So he'd witnessed. Her eyes fell. What did he think about the secrets Amara had spoken of? He seemed pretty casual and unconstrained about it all. She looked up again. He was surveying her. "You've grown . . . pretty, Sarvet. In these fifteen months since Ionaber year. Taller, too." He smiled. She felt herself flushing. How did he stay so calm? Seem so grown up? Is that what a wanderyar did? *I want one!*

"You've changed too," she ventured. His black curls – wooly like hers – were the same, and his hazel eyes. But the rest! She wouldn't have known him. Except she did. "I . . . feel a little strange," she confessed.

He laughed. "I feel a bit strange myself. I keep tripping over my own feet, when I'm not careful. Ilggai" – his father – "says I grew so fast my limbs forgot how to find each other." He settled back against the most massive tree bole. "Just this morning, emerging from my tent, I managed to catch both front guy-lines and bring the whole thing down."

"Is that why you were late?" She couldn't really believe the mishap. He didn't seem clumsy. In fact, he seemed more at ease in his body than ever before.

"Oh, no. It took me no time at all to get it back up. The true problem was young Oavan."

"Oavan?" She still felt strangely shy, reluctant to pelt him with either questions or tales of her own doings. *He must think I've grown stupid . . . as well as . . . did he really say I was pretty?*

She managed another glance at him. He showed no signs of anything except enjoying her company.

"Oavan's just arrived from his foster-change," Nial explained. "He's little – just thirty months – and he misses his mother."

"And?" she tilted her head.

Nial grinned. "And he's spirited. And spoiled. And when he was presented with travel tack and fried jerky for breakfast – instead of his usual pannkuja and cloudberries – he threw the father of all tantrums. He was still screaming and writhing when it was time to start for Kaunis-lodge, so I volunteered to stay behind with him. He calmed down soon enough once we were the only ones in camp. But I figured I'd better get some food into him before I carried him here, or there'd just be trouble again." He leaned forward to wink at her, clasp her hand, then let it go. "Ilggai vows he should have sent me off on my wanderyar sooner. He complains: 'If I'd known you'd mind the foster-babes, tromp the wool-bales, and mend the roof with enthusiasm instead of groans . . . you'd have gone at thirteen!'" Even she knew that boys didn't set out until they were fifteen, and many waited for sixteen or seventeen.

"So . . . what did you see? In your wanderyar? Where did you travel first?" She wanted simply to hear his voice, but the tale of his adventures proved enthralling. He'd left the Fiordhammars as soon as he got far enough north to skirt the settled lands of the Silmaren vales and head west to lumber territory. The saw mills were very like those of the Hammarfolk, just larger, but the people dwelt in treehouses or cabins up on stilts.

"And they live man and woman together!" he told her. "Linked for all their years, not just the month of a sweet-moon, as we are." That sounded bizarre. How could the women bear to leave their sisters? And the man his brothers?

"Did you talk with them?"

"I stayed with a family that needed a 'boot-boy,' because their oldest son was laid up with a broken foot."

She felt her eyes widening. "Were they nice?"

"Oh, Sarvet!" The boyish tone was back in his voice. "I wish you could meet them. Them . . . and all the other friendly folk I encountered. It really is a big world out there. Big . . . and wonderful!"

She wished she could too. Why *couldn't* girls have wanderyars? They *should*.

Nial had continued west from the lumber country, all the way over the Tahdenfiall peaks into Tromme-land, where the Trummor-folk built towering totem poles painted in garish reds and oranges and blues, and bathed by sitting naked in piping hot steam huts. Finally he'd circled east again, passing through the ruins of a Ghriana delving on his return trip over the mountains.

"There was the strangest pool there." His gaze had gone distant. "It showed me waking dreams of . . . I hardly know what." Would he say? Find words for the strangeness? Somehow she wanted to know.

"There was a Fatherly Caller . . . he looked a lot like me . . . but he had your eyes . . . and he was older. He was searching ancient hieroglyphs in a natural sandstone maze open to the sky." Nial twitched himself free of this vision and relayed more of his journey. "Have you heard of the Reindeer People?"

Sarvet shook her head no.

"They're on a perpetual wanderyar, traveling from grazing glade to grazing glade, always seeking fresh moss for their herds. They beat wide, flat drums – as wide as they are tall – to frighten away the Deathwind Woman. And they eat fried bone-marrow, blood sausage, and blood pancakes."

She swallowed down an incipient nausea. "Did you . . . ?"

"It was good. Really." He smiled. "But, you know the oddest thing, Sarvet? The really oddest thing was coming home again. I expected to discover astonishing things on my wanderyar. And I did. But home looks pretty astonishing, too."

He paused, studying the sky. It was blue and clear, but its stillness had become breezy, and a line of cumulous was visible beyond the farther peaks.

"I'd thought the Hammarlending tradition was *the* way to live. That other ways were wrong. And some of them might be, but the ones I saw are just as normal as ours.

"In fact" – he sat up abruptly to be sure of her attention – "some of the wrong ways might be right here in our own lodges!" He sounded indignant.

Now, there was a startling idea. But she didn't feel startled. *I'd say my own mother's way is one of those wrong ones.* "What do you mean?" she asked.

"Rakas-lodge was my first stop back in the Fiordhammars. They would have seemed perverse before my wanderyar, but" – he grinned – "after? . . . well, not so much. Their sister-clan is Iloiset-lodge, and the two chalets are so close they share the same smokehouse, spring-house, and byre! Pretty unusual for us, but remarkably like the Silmarish, the Trummors, and the Reindeer People. They even have the linking sacrament more than thrice a year at Other-joy and Mother's Bounty and Long-dark."

His mouth tightened. "It was Jakkiat-lodge that bothered me. They don't have a sister-clan. They don't celebrate Other-joy. And they believe women are vessels of evil.

"The brothers seemed . . . inflexible, joyless . . . even mean. Not all, but . . . too many. And they seem wronger than Rakas-clan and Iloiset-clan." He shook his head again. Smiled. "Never mind. The Jakkiat-brothers might have problems, but most folks are splendid! My travels were fabulous! And it's good to be home."

He took her hand again, this time holding onto it. His fingers were warm and strong. "But what about you? You've let me talk on forever. I wanted to tell you . . . well, all that and more, but I didn't mean to hog the whole conversation." He studied her face. His own changed. "What's wrong, Sarvet?"

How did he know? She'd been smiling, enjoying the marvels he related, not thinking about . . . things she didn't want to think about. But she'd wanted to consult him, and here he was, evincing warm concern for her. Perhaps it was time to think about . . . stuff.

She'd tell him. Well, not everything. Her mother's tears in the night before the Evener sheep-luring, Paiam's ceaseless prayers to the Divine Mother, and her wistful longing for the ancient days when sisters were said to birth daughters without linking seemed . . . too perverse, too private to put words to. But there were plenty of more normal grievances. Where to start? Maybe with yesterday's spat?

"I know I'm lame," she began abruptly, "and that there are things I can't do well enough to do at all. Like taking the goats up to the high pastures or hauling hay bales in the byre. But I'm strong, and a lot of the chores . . . well, it might hurt some to see me moving in halting jerks, but I *can* do it."

Nial nodded – thank Sias *without* any pity on his face, just listening – and allowed her to free her hand for gesturing.

"But *Paiam* has decided that just about any task that requires more than sitting is too much for me. So she petitioned Sister Aidnu to excuse me from kitchen duty, milking, and gardening. Without even asking *me* about it." Sarvet could hear the outrage creeping past her determination to talk calmly. "Maturely," as her mother – *Paiam* – would say.

"The byre-sister and the green-sister know me well enough that . . . well, they evaded promising her anything and checked with me. So I'm still taking my turn at milking and weeding and wilding.

But when I reported to the kitchens yestermorn, Cook Unni simply dismissed me!"

"Umh . . ." Nial grimaced. "Surely your lodge-mother?"

"She asked me if I liked cooking. And . . . I don't really. So then she explained that if I were longing to chop cabbages and mix pannkuja, she'd overrule my mother, but since I wasn't she preferred to honor Paiam's vulnerability." Sarvet vented a grunt of frustration. "I'm fifteen, for Sias' sake! Nearly sixteen! I'll be old enough to witness in five weeks! And Paiam may be vulnerable, but this is *my* life, not hers!"

"You need a wanderyar." Nial shrugged. "Oh, I know that . . . isn't possible. Girls don't. But that's part of why boys get one. Fathers have a hard time seeing that their sons aren't young ones anymore. And . . ." – he hesitated, then continued – "the boys usually can't see that while they can do *most* things, they aren't yet able to manage *everything*. Of course, by the time they finish their traveling, they *can*!" He grinned, taking the sting out the implication that she wasn't yet fully grown.

"Speaking from experience?" she asked, feeling the corners of her mouth turn up. Maybe things weren't so desperate. At least Nial understood.

"Of course! Ilggai was still trying to tell me when to get up and when to go to sleep last year."

"Oh! Paiam does that too! And when to go to branching-hall for daily postures, and to be thorough about my dawn-sequence while I'm at it. But to make sure Brionne carries the full milk buckets for me and not to go farther than the ice-rock when I'm wilding for nettles. Urgh!"

"It's irksome," Nial agreed. "But, Sarvet, there's something more that's bothering you, isn't there?"

She nodded and felt tears prick her eyes. "Brionne's mother is a lot the same way, just . . . not quite so bad." She swallowed, trying to swallow down the sudden grief in her throat, then burst out: "I understand why Paiam overprotects me, but I wish she wouldn't! Why can't she see all the things I *can* do? All the clever ways I get around the things that might stop me, but don't?"

Nial slid over to her tree trunk and put an arm around her shoulders, wordless.

She turned in the loose circle of his embrace to demand fiercely: "You don't see me as broken, do you?"

She felt the tremor of his stifled laugh – reassuring her again that he didn't pity her. "Of course not! Sarvet, your mother can't possibly see you so! You're a capable young woman who's dealt well and thoroughly with a challenging physical impediment. Paiam should be proud of you!"

Sarvet untwisted herself and leaned against his solid torso, relaxing. "I don't think she is, somehow."

"Really?" Nial looked startled.

"Just yesterday, when she was scolding me for being three skeins short of my spinning quota – I'd spent too much time in the byre and then in the branching-hall – she broke off criticizing and suddenly started apologizing to me for . . . for being too fond of her linking-novice." Sarvet felt herself blushing. She hadn't meant to share this. Too embarrassing! "Paiam believes I suffered my birth injury because she loved my . . . father. That if she'd hated poor Ivvar, I'd be sound and whole." She stared fixedly at the pine needles under her felted boots. Maybe she should have kept safely to talk about Nial's wanderyar. He couldn't help her. And airing this wound . . . oh, Sias! what if Paiam were right?

"Sarvet . . ."

He waited until she finally looked up. His eyes were serious, caring, but not patronizing. "You're not broken. Hear me?"

She nodded, felt another sob rising in her throat, and swallowed angrily.

"And your mother loving your father has nothing to do with your lameness. It doesn't work like that."

"I didn't think it did." She sighed. "It's just . . . that Paiam can be so . . . I don't know."

"Yeah. I know. Your mother is . . . I don't know either."

Sarvet gave a shaky laugh. Nial might know a lot, but he still didn't know everything. Thank Sias!

"But, Sarvet, you're the one with the right ideas in this. Hold fast to that! She can't limit you forever. And then . . . it *will* be your life. Make sure you're ready to live it your way, not hers." His lips tightened. "Promise?"

She nodded, feeling an answering determination rising in her.

Then Nial stiffened and muttered . . . something. Had he cursed? Maybe not, because his next words seemed less agitated than those following an oath should be. "Good. You can do it, you know."

She nodded again.

"Good," he repeated. "Because Paiam just rounded the corner of the lodge, and she's headed our way. She looks . . . steamed," he added.

"Has she seen us?" Maybe Paiam was merely fetching an extra measure of water from the spring house. The break in the weather – certainly a temporary thing – meant the stream was releasing a trickle of moisture, and spring water tasted nicer than melted snow.

"Yes."

"Shun it!" Sarvet often preferred to avoid her mother these days, but this had to be the ultimate in moments she didn't want Paiam intruding on. "Let's hide!"

"Um. I don't think that'll work." She could feel Nial chuckling. His ability to see the humor of her involuntary suggestion bolstered her courage. She turned her head.

Her mother hadn't stopped even to put a coat on. Of course, it was warm for Falnary, and the sisters' sweater-tunics and shoulder-hoods kept the cold out, but the anger prompting Paiam's haste was clear in the stomp of her feet and the jerk of her elbows. Her energy brought her up with her daughter in a very few moments.

"Good nooning, Nial Ilggai-spring," Paiam ground out. The words were courteous, but her tone was not. "I need a few words with Sarvet." Her curt gesture invited Nial to leave.

He returned the greeting, but ignored her invitation. "I'd say you need solace and an smidgeon of serenity before you attempt those words," he observed.

The advice did not go down well. Paiam's nostrils grew pinched and white with the force of her inhalation. "I know very well what I need, and it isn't your opinion or your presence, Tukeva-lodger. Now, go!"

He did stand, drawing Sarvet up with him. Paiam had stopped a little downhill from them, so this put their heads above hers. Nial addressed Sarvet: "What would you prefer? Will my staying help or not?"

His refusal to acknowledge Paiam's authority, along with the sight of his hand holding Sarvet's, seemed to enrage a woman already enraged to her utmost. She abruptly transferred her attention to her real target.

"What are you doing here like this? Neglecting your chores and canoodling like an novitiate. How dare you! Get back to the lodge this instant, young sister, and into the spinning room where you belong."

Except Sarvet didn't belong there. The noontide dinner came next, and no one was doing any but rock-sure necessities on Other-joy. Certainly not spinning. She put her chin up, finding – maturity? – in the firm clasp of Nial's fingers. "Nial is our guest," she reminded her mother, "and my friend. I'd planned to attend him in the refecting-hall." With her steady gaze she dared Paiam to continue scolding.

But Paiam needed no dare. "Guest or no, *you* will be attending no one! You'll catch up on the skeins you left undone yesterday, Sarvet *Ivvar-spring*, if I have to get Mother Johtaia herself to rule so!"

The fight devolved from there, with Nial on the sidelines, opening and closing his hands in uncertainty about what to do. This conflict was beyond him! Paiam went so far as to seize her daughter's arm, and Sarvet lost her Nial-gifted cool. She was screaming a threat to petition for a fosterer and jerking at her mother's clutching grasp, while Paiam jerked back and promised a curfew lasting until Nerich. Mother Johtaia's voice, unusually stern, interrupted them. "Sisters! Paiam! Sarvet! Stop!"

They did stop. Sarvet felt like someone had doused her with cold rain. Welcome rain. Her throat was hot and scraped. She curtsied to her lodge-mother, noticing that Paiam managed the obeisance just as awkwardly as her daughter.

Mother Johtaia nodded to Nial. "I'll sort this, Brother. Perhaps you'd care to join your lodge-mates for dinner." She smiled. "Not to worry. I'll send Sarvet out to your table presently."

Apparently that was sufficiently reassuring, because Nial ceased shifting from foot to foot as though he might sling Sarvet over his shoulder and physically carry her away from her maternal attacker. "You alright?" he asked her.

She was shaking, but she trusted Mother Johtaia. "This might take a while," she answered obliquely. Would he catch her unasked worry?

"I'll be there. And sip sweetleaf tea while you dine, if it takes a *long* while."

A sigh puffed out of her. She nodded and watched him lope effortlessly – so effortlessly – down the slope toward the lodge. The clouds were thickening above the distant peaks visible beyond the nearer ridge. The air smelled like snow.

Mother Johtaia surveyed Paiam for a long moment. Sarvet's mother was scrubbing her hair back from her face. The long, wooly ropes were youthfully dark, but her reddened eyes were . . . old? Sarvet squelched the nascent pity rising in her. *I can't start making allowances for her the way everybody else does, or she'll swallow me whole.* She gritted her teeth.

"Come, Sisters." Mother Johtaia's voice turned matter-of-fact. "The sooner we settle this, the better."

"I'll deal with my daughter myself, thank you." Paiam straightened her shoulders, pulled the cowl of her hood back up, and conspicuously dug her heels into the pine needles.

Johtaia's left eyebrow flew up, but her expression remained warm. "You may tell me so in my counsel-haven." And her authority held, because Paiam did follow.

Sarvet eluded her mother's reaching hand. The snow beyond the shelter of the pines wasn't deep, and she didn't need help. Paiam shrugged and desisted. They accomplished the short walk to the back porch in silence.

Johtaia's counsel-haven was a cozy room near the back door. All its chairs featured armrests and patterned, red wool cushions, with knitted afghans tossed over their backs. The fire in its small hearth had been newly fed, and Sister Kemra placed a tray with a steaming teapot and three mugs on the table before she left them.

Mother Johtaia poured out and got straight to the point. "This isn't the first time, Paiam." She tilted her head. "Care to tell me about it?"

"No." Sarvet's mother flushed. Her tone was curt.

"Very well. I'll ask your daughter."

Paiam drew in a sharp breath. "I *am* her birth-mother."

"Yes, and I am her lodge-mother. I owe a duty to each of you." Johtaia smiled. "Come, Paiam, let me in on this."

Paiam's list of her daughter's offenses was accurate in so far as the facts went. Sarvet did speed through her spinning. She hated the hand loom, a new implement to be learned. She lost herself in the legends recorded on the scrolls Sister Piha lent her. And she spent more time out of doors than Paiam considered proper. But the interpretation that went with them: disobedience, rebellion, lack of cooperation, and insistence on having her own way?! *She wants to control me completely. Any time I stray from her strict orders, I'm defiant.* Sarvet clamped down on her impulse to argue. Mother Johtaia's swift, sidelong glance meant Paiam might not have this all her way.

"I think you love your daughter very much."

Huh? How in the north did Mother Johtaia translate "she's contrary and unruly" into "you love your daughter very much"?

But Paiam gulped, nodded, and abruptly buried her face in her hands.

Huh. So "contrary, unruly" did apparently mean "love her." But it wasn't reasonable. *Her love is strangling me!*

Johtaia was still focused on her mother. Her voice grew gentler still. "What is it that worries you so?"

Paiam's face emerged from her palms, tear-streaked. Her reply was a whisper: "That she'll get hurt."

Johtaia folded her upper lip over her lower, stifled a sigh. "It hurts when someone we love gets hurt, yes."

"I'm not going to let it happen!" Paiam's voice was low, but fierce.

Johtaia nodded. "Let's hear what Sarvet has to say. Can you listen, Paiam?"

Sarvet watched her mother's openness retreat at this reminder that her daughter *was* present. "I think I know what she'll say, but perhaps you don't."

"Let's pretend that neither one of us knows. Because . . . perhaps . . . we don't. Will you try, Paiam?"

Sarvet's mother nodded.

"Good." Johtaia turned to Sarvet. "What happened after the blessing? When you left the calling-hall?"

Sarvet wriggled her shoulders. Surely talking about Nial was the wrong thing to do. But . . . if Mother Johtaia thought she should risk it . . . well, she would.

"I was disappointed, because I was expecting Nial to be back from his wanderyar, and I thought he wasn't."

Paiam's face looked wooden, but Sarvet turned her eyes back to Mother Johtaia and went on. "I was angry about . . . yestermorn" – the lodge-mother nodded, so she understood the reference – "and I wanted to be alone to think about it. But then Nial came after all! And I thought it might help to talk to him about it." She stared at her tea, not wanting to see Paiam's condemnation. "And it did help! Or, at least, it did until . . ." she trailed off. Mother Johtaia must have had a clear view of their conflict while she traversed the slope from the lodge to the pines.

"How long have you known Nial, Sarvet?"

Now she's using her gentle tone on me! But maybe some of it would rub off on Paiam. "We were really little when we met. He'd gotten separated from his minder and was scared. So Sister Lempea, who was minding me, just added him to the group. He taught us how to play leap-squirrel." She smiled at the memory.

"So he's an old and good friend."

"Yes. He is." She'd never put it quite that way to herself, somehow. She saw him only thrice each year – at Other-joy, Long-light, and Giving-day – but she shared her thoughts with him more than with . . . anyone. *Brionne and I do things together. And we both enjoy Amara's liveliness, her jokes, her singing. But I'm closer to Nial. Huh.*

Mother Johtaia addressed Paiam again. "Nial is a kind and reliable young man, but I think this friendship bothers you a lot."

Paiam's hands jerked. "Sisters shouldn't *be* friends with brothers," she grated.

Mother Johtaia looked surprised. *How could she not know?* Sarvet pushed the afghan she'd pulled over her knees off her lap. The hot tea had warmed her up. *I guess Mother has kept her – fear? – of men secret.*

"Why not, Paiam?"

"*Sarvet* shouldn't be," Paiam corrected herself.

The lodge-mother merely tilted her head.

"Only loss and pain and sorrow will come of it. *I* know! And I *am* her mother, Johtaia." So, Paiam wasn't saying her real objection. Sarvet sighed softly. *Why did I hope she might? It wouldn't change anything.* Except . . . maybe it would have, if her mother would take someone other than her daughter into her confidence.

"I won't force you to share your heart's keys, Paiam, but Sarvet is in her wixting years. The guiding of her is now shared between you and me and other sisters with authority." Johtaia met Paiam's eyes straightly. Would Paiam acknowledge her prerogative? Yes, she dipped her gaze.

"And I think Sarvet will benefit from my support. That *is* my charge."

"What is your ruling?" Paiam remained angry, but not defiant.

Mother Johtaia smiled. *Amazing how she could be sympathetic to both contestants when sisters were at odds. Or even when she disagreed with one. Or both!* "I will have more than a single ruling, but this is the first." She returned her attention to Sarvet. "Brothers and sisters do well to be friends. I think you already know this, and that is well. But now I pronounce Nial to be other-brother to you as well. You may trust in your trust for him."

Oh! Sarvet had never dreamed so far ahead as to imagine who her linking-brother might be. In fact, she'd imagined she'd never have one – just as she'd told Brionne. But now Nial would be one of the choices offered her . . . when the time came. It felt strange. Very strange, but right. Her heart lightened inside her.

Paiam's nostrils were white again, but she said nothing. Mother Johtaia was well within her warrant.

"This pleases you?" Johtaia's gaze on Sarvet was loving.

Sarvet managed a nod. She was too happy, too surprised, for words.

"Good. But before I make my second ruling, I have another question for you." She interrupted herself to pour more tea for everyone. "Sarvet, it can be scary to dream big dreams. There are real dangers. What if you let yourself know a wish that you can't live without, once you know it?

"But the rewards of dreaming big are often worth the risk. Without dreams, we settle for far less than we need to." Johtaia paused, checking to be sure Sarvet understood her. (Or to give Paiam a chance to prepare for what came next?) Sarvet nodded, quelling an unlikely hope. *Can she mean –? Is it possible –?*

"So, Sarvet, I'd like you to do some big dreaming. What if you could change anything? What if you could do anything? What if you had all the support you needed to try something amazing?

"Think on those ideas.

"And then dare to dream. How might your life be different? What new experiences might this year bring? What is your deepest desire?"

Sarvet studied the lodge-mother's face. Johtaia was in earnest. This was real. Sarvet could ask something bold, something outside of convention, something unheard of – and be heard. *Did* she dare?

"Tell me," invited the lodge-mother.

"I want a wanderyar," Sarvet announced sturdily. "Just like the brothers. Where I travel from lodge to lodge – mother-lodge to mother-lodge – or even farther, if that seems right."

"No!" Paiam jerked to her feet, spilling tea from the mug clutched in her right hand. "This is absurd!" She rounded on Mother Johtaia. "Now, see what comes of encouraging her! I told you!"

The lodge-mother was nonplussed. She swallowed, then spoke. "I'll admit I'd envisioned something a little more within bounds. A visit to Siajotti-lodge" – where the sisters maintained and added to a repository of scrolls recording Hammarleeding traditions and legends – "or the request for a fosterer. Or even" – Johtaia pinned Paiam with a stern stare – "an interval of ritual restraint to allow her mother to cool. But this . . ."

Sarvet's neck bent. So, her answer had been too daring. The lodge-mother had wanted something bold, but conventional and with precedent, for all her fine words. Perhaps Johtaia had thought she'd meant them, but . . . Sarvet felt thoroughly let down. And yet . . . *shun it! I won't give up!* That little moment of belief – *maybe I can have this* – was infectious. She lifted her head.

"You said to dream big. And I have. I want a wanderyar. Will you not support me?"

Johtaia looked like she'd been punched in the stomach, but before she could find words for dialog, Paiam jumped into her silence. "That's enough, young sister! Even were you a brother, your lameness must keep you home. Request a fosterer if you want, shun it! Demand a restraint, if you must. I don't care at this point. But here you will stay, and that's that!"

Mother Johtaia recovered herself. "Paiam, wait. That was a surprise, yes. And I agree with you that it isn't practical, but let's talk this through. It's not fair to encourage Sarvet to name her desire and then summarily refuse to grant it.

"Sarvet, let's explore what's behind and beneath this wish of yours. Surely there is a less extreme solution that will satisfy your heart."

I don't think so. But what would Johtaia do now? She was in a predicament as much as Sarvet was. Having exposed a wixting-sister to the irrational wrath of her mother, how would she make good on her duty to both? Or would she?

Paiam reseated herself rigidly and mopped at the spilled tea with a tea towel.

Mother Johtaia pursued her point. "Tell me more about what a wanderyar would do for you."

Sarvet lifted her chin. "I'd see new places and new people. I'd encounter folks who wouldn't always be focusing on my weakness and my limits. I'd do for myself, and discover that I *could* do for myself. I'd be a woman, not a girl, when I got back." *And I wouldn't have to fight Paiam every step of the way, because she wouldn't be there.* The most important point of all.

"Hmm, yes, I see."

Maybe she did, but Sarvet doubted it. *I've never doubted the lodge-mother before.* She felt dizzy.

"But, Sarvet, surely a visit to Siajotti-lodge would do all that."

In a small way, yes. But Sarvet wanted the big way. Especially now that she'd tasted the idea. "I've been to Siajotti. Their scrolls . . . opened vast horizons in my mind. But I want horizons that challenge . . . my body!"

"Oh, Sarvet . . ."

Now Sarvet was mad. "Don't you see?! You're doing it too! Deciding for yourself where I am able and where I am not! I want to *fail* sometimes, shun you!"

The lodge-mother was beyond nonplussed this time; she was stunned.

Paiam, sensing that Johtaia had swung to her side in the dispute, spoke more reasonably for the first time since confronting Sarvet under the pines. "When Nial had his wanderyar, he wasn't risking serious injury or worse. You would be. Elder sisters must safeguard younger ones, as well as supporting their drive toward independence. The answer is no, Sarvet."

"Indeed, Paiam is correct in this." Johtaia reclaimed her authority once more. "But, Paiam, something must be done. You don't want your daughter hurt, but *you* are hurting her. Surely you see this."

"Wixting girls are always difficult. I can bear the burden."

"But let's make it easier on you both. I think a sojourn at Siajotti is in order for the short term, while we ponder the long term. The difficulties between you are . . . complex. We'll not solve them in a week, and certainly not in an hour. But you both need some relief now. And a meal!" Johtaia managed a twinkle.

"Sarvet, go get some dinner, child. And then do your packing. I'll send you off tomorrow morning with Sister Kasikira. Paiam, bide a moment with me here, if you will. I'll ask Kemra to bring us food."

Sarvet fled to the branching-hall. No one would think to look for her there. Or hear her, the way they might if she sought refuge in her bednook. The dim, raftered space was cold and empty. She pulled a bolster and two meditation quilts from a cupboard, then curled herself in a nest under a window. One corner of its hide covering had worked loose. Placing her chin on the sill, she could see out. The conifers in the grove behind the hall, long-trunked and thickly planted, showed little snow on the needle carpet between them. The overcast had returned while she debated with her lodge-mother and her birth-mother; the cheery light of direct sun absent, segued into chilly aloofness. She felt blank, hollow.

Johtaia hadn't devised a solution, and there was additional loss in that. *I'd always thought her infallible.* Even today, when Paiam attacked me, I was so sure our lodge-mother would sort things out. Even when she made them worse, there in her counsel-haven, I thought she'd retrieve it all. *But she hadn't.* The proposed journey to Siajotti was no use. The scroll-sisters had been thoroughly indoctrinated by Paiam on earlier visits in how to over-protect Sarvet. All that would happen was that when Sarvet returned, Johtaia would appoint a fosterer. *And I don't want that.* Yes, it would get Paiam off her back. Yes, it would assure her some freedom from Paiam's suffocating concern. But it would also make her birth-mother not her mother. *Her bossing me is the only connection we have left.*

I don't want freedom forced out of Paiam. I want her to grant it. I want her to change. And no one can give me that, except Paiam herself.

Except, she can't either. She doesn't know how.

Pain stabbed through Sarvet's numbness. *Why does she have to be so impossible? So unyielding? So . . . afraid?* Hot tears sprang onto Sarvet's cold cheeks, and hot sobs crowded her throat. *Her fear makes me afraid, and if I get any smaller I'll disappear.*

She cried for a while.

The wind picked up outside, swirling a few flakes dropped by the clouds. Sarvet's raw emotion moderated, gave way to thinking. *I know why she's afraid.* She told me last year, at the same time she explained first blood. She said: Don't have a child, Sarvet. Your heart will break, when she suffers.

But she's wrong! She's wrong! It's not my limp that broke her heart. It's her refusal to accept that what I *have* is so much greater than what I *lost*. And her refusal takes even more away.

Sarvet mused on the failed healing-call that came soon after that talk with her mother. Sister Piha had chanted the entire day-long supplication, while Sister Evaia massaged the diseased joints with blessed and sacred anointing oil. Brionne had insisted on attending and prayed from dawn to dusk. *That's what she was crying about this morning.* Sarvet was suddenly sure. *She was crying, because I am still lame.* Awe pervaded her. To have such loyalty in a friend and not quite realize it. Oh, Brionne!

But the supplication, the intense massage, the prayers, and the attempt to forcibly realign her hip and ankle had been worse than useless. Something had given way within the palsied flesh, and she had been months regaining the ability to walk. Even now, her limp was worse than it had been last year.

But she wasn't going to feel sorry for herself. The lesson wasn't that trying always fails. The lesson was: don't chase after past losses. *Try something new.*

And that is what I wanted to do: take what I *do* have and use it to try something new; many things new! Go meet all the strange people and customs and places in the big and wondrous place our north-lands are. The north-lands that Nial described so vividly. And I still want that. Only I can't have it.

She felt more resigned than desperate.

I suppose I should go scrounge something from the kitchens. Dinner must be long done. She straightened within her cocoon of quilts.

"Oh, Sias! What must Nial be thinking! I never came to him as Mother Johtaia promised."

She jumped to her feet, wincing as the sudden jolt to her stiffened hip and foot brought pain. Ow! She bundled the quilts onto their shelf in the cupboard, shoved the bolster onto its, then lurched onto the porch. On the slope beyond the lodge, brothers and sisters were tossing snowballs at one another, but the rising ground between the lodge and the branching-hall held only one hurrying figure: Nial.

She waited for him.

"Sarvet!" He came leaping up the steps and gripped her shoulders. "What happened? I finally went to your lodge-mother. But why didn't you come eat?" He folded her close, then stepped back to scrutinize her. "You've been crying." He touched a gentle finger to her cheek. "Did the lodge-mother fail your trust?"

"No. Or, rather, yes. But . . . Nial, will you help me?" *Would* he help her? Her thoughts flitted to other times he'd supported her. Every Ionaber during Death-joy, he went aside with her to the Zele-chapel to kneel in meditation, telling over his prayer beads in time with hers, joining his voice to hers in the chant: *we arrive on the waters of birth; we depart across the river of death.* His own choice would surely have been the clapping game preferred by most. Few were the years when he and she were not the sole occupants of Zele's sacred space.

(Paiam defied custom and sequestered herself alone at the shrine she kept in her room.)

The laughter of the jumping, spinning celebrants in the adjacent calling-hall was loud, along with their chorused claps and the thump of their feet. The words of their song were eerie – *when will I die?* (clap) *when I am young?* (clap) *at life's end?* (clap) *when I am old?* (clap) *when I am ancient?* (clap) *when tomorrow comes?* (clap) – but their tone, merry. The rattle of their flung pebbles sounded an insistent staccato for living, defying the lassitude of dying. Wouldn't Nial rather be leaping and laughing? She'd almost chosen so last year, but the dry quiet of the chapel drew her. And . . . the daring defiance of death, seizing revelry in its very teeth, scared her. But Nial remained steadfast each year. *Would* he help her now? With this?

Nial looked confused. "Of course, I'll help you. That's what I offered; but what do you need help *with*?"

She drew in her breath. "I'm going on a wanderyar, and I want you to get me a tent and a pack and a bedroll."

Nial's hands dropped to his sides. Then he gripped her shoulders again, giving her a little shake. "You can't! Mother Johtaia never gave you permission for that?"

"No." Her voice sounded forlorn in her ears. *None of that. I'm not waiting on anyone's permission any more.* She lifted her chin and straightened. Her voice came out stronger. "But I'm giving *myself* permission."

Nial was starting to smile. "How can you do that?"

Her lips curved to match his. "But, Nial, anyone can do that any time. I'm *going*."

"Okay." He tipped his head to one side. "And not planning to seek my permission either, huh?"

"Of course not."

He let his hands fall again, but only to abandon his skeptical demeanor. "I think you'll need trail food and coin as well."

"Oh." Her shoulders fell. She could probably find hard tack and jerky in the pantry, but how would she abscond with it through the busy kitchens? And the lowlander Silmarish did use coin, she remembered, but the Hammarleedings did not. Traveling from from mother-lodge to mother-lodge would not work, since she went without her lodge-mother's permission. *I need coins, if I leave the Fiordhammars.*

"Sarvet, don't worry. I've got both."

"Oh!"

"And I will help you . . . but . . . can you tell me a little more? More than just you're going? A wanderyar . . . takes preparing, too. Not just going."

"Like linking." Suddenly she felt less embarrassed about linking and communion and adoration – whatever those last two involved. Was it because Nial was now her other-brother?

"Like linking," he confirmed.

"And I don't have any." Somehow she knew he wasn't objecting. This wasn't a prelude to an effort to stop her. *No, he's gong to prepare me . . . as best he can.*

"No, you don't." He hesitated. *Was* he going to stop her? Surely not. Or was his belief in her strength only strong if she didn't test it? He continued: "But with the right supplies – my supplies – you'll be fine. The Silmarish and the Sammiad and the Trummor-folk like wanderers. They'll help you along. And you'll find how to pay your way." His grin dawned. "Come on!"

Would it really be this easy?

Not quite. But it wasn't Nial who would stand in her way. He led her to the path around the grazing bluff – thus avoiding the slope immediately below Kaunis-lodge where the brothers and sisters threw snowballs – and along to the empty brother-camp.

"You'll need my lightest gear," he remarked. "Luckily, I had a notion of trekking to the Tunkahorn on my way home."

"Do you mind –"

"Not a bit." He stopped rummaging in his tent and turned back to face her. Looking up from his knees, he grew suddenly serious. "This is your moment, Sarvet. Like a bird on the wing, you're meant to soar. And I'm going to give you the wrist toss you need for it. It's about time someone did."

"I'm not –"

"Only a fool would think you broken or a burden or dependent." He was fierce. "Never apologize, Sarvet! You're strong and creative and able. Always remember that."

She felt shaken by his vehemence, but a wild exultation rose in her. Her words emerged calm, despite it. "I love you, Nial Ilggai-spring."

He took both her hands in his, turned them over, brushed a light kiss in each palm. "And I love you."

"Is it allowed?"

"Didn't Mother Johtaia just make me your other-brother?"

A short laugh blew out of her. "How did you know?"

"Father Biejan made you my other-sister and . . . I hoped." His eyes were deep and tinged with awe.

"I'm not old enough."

"No. Not yet." He drew her head down, and his lips touched her forehead.

"And I'm still taking my wanderyar!"

A chuckle shook him. "You wouldn't be Sarvet else."

Her scowl became a grin.

Once she was equipped, Nial surveyed her. Following his cue, she inventoried herself: rucksack, bivy, and sleep-sack all of thistle-silk – the latter quilted; oiled ground cloth, water canteen, mess kit, tinder wheel and tinder store; jerky, hard tack, and powdered kerin-herb; snow-shoes, poles, ice-hammer. "I need my coat and gaiters and over-mittens."

"I can get them."

And he did. Plus a small pouch of dried cloudberries and alp pinyons. Her stomach was grateful, since she'd missed the noon meal.

"You must go down, not up, Sarvet. Peak ascensions require a group effort."

"You were headed to the Tunkahorn," she reminded him.

"The valley trail, not the highlands."

"Mmm. Well, I want the lowlands anyway. I want to meet all those interesting people you talked of."

"You will!" His eyes lit. "You will. And Sarvet . . . Sias keep you."

"And you." The formal parting seemed right somehow: not a denial of the new connection she felt for him, but an affirmation – and an acknowledgment of postponement.

She looked back when she reached the valley-rock.

He stood silhouetted against the sky, distant already, but watching for the last sight of her. She waved, waited for his answering salute, and stepped around the curving descent.

I'm away!

And she was. It would be dusk before she could turn onto the Ulko-polku, the trail leading away from Hammarleeding ground toward the Silmarish lowlanders. *But I'm not making camp until then.* The gentler slopes should afford a better spot for pitching her bivy and . . . she craved newness.

When the mountain slopes darkened, and only the clear sky reflecting on the snow allowed her to see, her desire for newness muted to mere stubbornness rather than eager anticipation. A grinding ache pulsed in her right hip, and she narrowly missed tangling her right snowshoe in the left on too many of her limping right steps. Going down was always more painful than climbing. A small level cranny between two half-buried boulders tempted her. Then she spotted the turn-off for the Ulko-polku. *I'll stop as soon as I come to the treeline.* The pine grove sheltering the Kaunis-lodge was an anomaly. All the slopes below it were turf-covered until this lower elevation. *Nial said not to camp directly under any tree branches, but a clearing amongst the pines would be pleasant and safe.*

But it was the trees that were her undoing. With their protection came shadows. She never saw the thin, whippy branch lying across a steep stretch of the trail. An invisible hand seemed to grab her left ankle, wrench her snowshoe sideways, and pitch her downhill with stunning force.

She awoke to burning numbness in her left cheek where it pressed the snow, a bone-deep throbbing in her right hip, and a scary wrongness in her right ankle. Her stomach sickened under the pain, and she hovered on the edge of the black pit from which she'd emerged. *I could die here.* She didn't feel cold – except for the one cheek. Whether it was because of her layered clothing or because pain drove out chill, she didn't know. *I have to move.* But she couldn't somehow. She could feel all her limbs, guessed that with enough will exerted, they would move, but the pain sapped her strength. *I will move. I will move!*

And still she lay unmoving.

A feathery coldness dusted her right cheek. The snowfall she'd smelled earlier had arrived. Her body felt heavy and cooler. She lifted her head a fraction and was surprised by her relief from the icy grating of the half-melted snow against her frozen skin. Her arms were trapped under her torso, and she wriggled them free, then pushed upward. The movement jolted her hip and leg, shooting pain through the entire limb. Her hands slipped, and she found her face planted once more in snow as she grabbed for the source of agony.

When she tried again, she pushed up only enough to free her face and creep herself forward a hand span. *If I could just get to a flatter bit of ground.* The steepness of the trail thwarted her care. Even the minute downhill momentum from inching forward was sufficient to carry her onward in a slippery rush. The bumpy ride provoked a fresh staccato of pain, whiting out all thought.

Coherence returned slowly. *Downhill isn't working. I can't control my descent.* Was there some way to go up instead? She checked her surroundings. Her slide down the trail had brought her to a wider place in the way. Could she reverse herself? Painstakingly she worked herself sideways, learning with each stabbing error how to use her arms and left leg without jolting her right leg. Several times she gave up, but the instinct for survival eventually prevailed after each defeat. Having her head uphill made breathing easier; having her feet downhill increased the intensity of the shrill torment in her ankle.

She lay gasping. Her snowshoes had detached in her fall, her poles, escaped from her grasp; but she wouldn't be standing in any case. *I'll get there crawling,* she told herself, waiting for readiness. It didn't come, but she began her ascent without it: dig in the good foot, push with the good leg, pull with the supporting arms, gasp at the stab of pain brought by movement. One push-pull after another. She didn't stop when she reached the turn-off for home. *If I stop, I might never start again.* Her face was slick with sweat – the result of exertion and pain combined – and her clothes felt warm and soggy. Push-pull, up, flinch. Push-pull, up, flinch.

The snowfall had stopped by the time she reached the fork in the trail below the valley-rock. She halted. *Why am I resting? This is it! I've made it. Turn right. I'm almost home.* Paiam's tense face and voice swam in her memory: Don't have a child, Sarvet. Your heart will break. Your heart will break. Your heart will break.

She wrenched herself violently to the left, stifling her scream at the hot agony this produced. Push-pull, up, *aagh!* Push-pull, up, *ungh! I won't go back! I won't!* Anywhere were better than home.

She lost all sense of time, of place, of self. She was a swirl of hurting, of disorientation, of fury, of stubborn striving ever upward. Another flurry of snowfall came and went. The overcast cleared, but she barely noticed. The stars of the wixting hours pulsed in all their grandeur and glory, heralding promise and hope. Sarvet struggled onward, oblivious.

When she found herself lying on flat turf, an eon later, she faltered. What if flat gave way to down? *I won't go down. I won't go back.* And where had the snow gone? Inching forward on short, resilient grasses and mosses was so much easier than tackling the slippery incline of snow and ice. Where *was* she? She lifted her face.

The moon had set, but starshine illumined the alpine meadow stretching away from her. Black, spangled sky swung dizzily around her, fringed at its lower hem by white ridges in the distance, across great valleys. She'd never climbed so high before. Had anyone in Kaunis-lodge? But where did she go now? There seemed no up accessible, save for an eagle.

As she paused, panting and unwilling to admit defeat, a kind womanly voice sounded in . . . not her ears, but her mind. "Thee must be braver still, brave climber."

What?

Sarvet jerked her gaze to the right. *Had* the silent behest come from her right?

Ah! *There* was up: at the meadow's rim a sheer precipice, black in the night, rose to yet unseen heights, perhaps the peak of this mighty uplift of earth. Could she find a trail, however steep, by which to continue her journey? She renewed her struggle to move. The pain seemed sharper after the brief hiatus, and she was . . . more weary. *I will move.*

But she didn't.

Instead she gazed at the night sky. There was Livli the Skier on the horizon, and the Great Chalice. If it were spring, the sun would be rising. Being winter, the stars reigned supreme, still promising . . . *more than I will ever receive.* She didn't feel defeated, just . . . accepting? *Maybe I've already received . . . enough? Hunh?*

A flutter of movement over the reach of the wide valleys drew her attention. What was it? Eagles and peregrines hunted at dawn and dusk, when the rock doves were active. Sarvet narrowed her eyes. Something winged. Some *three* things winged, yes, but white and gauzy. She pushed upward on her arms to see better, gasping at a stab of extra pain. Not birds . . . no. And big, far bigger than she had first suspected. Were they –? Could they be –? Her lips parted. *Oh!*

The pegasi! The fierce winged horses who defended the sacred precincts of Duoja's immortal spring and who attacked Lagon's demons in the ancient War of the Lodestones. She'd thought them creatures of legend only, but here they soared, strangely transparent and indefinite at their edges – yet real, for all that – riding the air toward her. She stared transfixed.

Nearer and nearer they flew, magnificent wings outstretched, hooves trammeling the breeze in preparation for landing. Then they were down, furling their vast eery wings, galloping across the greensward toward her. Their churning transparent legs shook the ground, their half-seen nostrils flared with aggression, and their pace brought them upon her in an instant. *Will I be trampled?* The lead pegasus gave a ringing neigh and reared to a stop, his muscled forelegs thumping into the grasses beside Sarvet's tense hands.

"You intrude, bold dreamer." The stallion's voice – unheard by the ears, like the mare's earlier – was deep and challenging. "If you've defiance, proclaim it; if a gift, offer it; if a boon sought, beg it. But you may not merely wait on fate here."

Sarvet was shaking, half in awed wonder, half in shock at the thunderous approach of the three steeds. She swallowed, suddenly aware of her dry mouth and throat. Could she form speech?

"For shame, cloud strider." The mare's voice, still kind, bore reproof. "This be no hero, nor foe, nor pretender. She's a true pilgrim, though she knoweth it not, and a small one at that, a mere filly." The pegasus to the right – dancing-friend? – stepped delicately forward. "Canst thee speak, valiant seeker?"

Sarvet found her voice. "No. He's right." She swallowed again. "I do beg a boon."

"Indeed, bright traveler. Yet thee needst no challenge. Be welcome and speak thy prayer."

Sarvet swallowed a third time. Unlike Mother Johtaia, these creatures out of legend would not fail her. Was she ready for the challenges success might bring? Was she ready to ask a second time for the scariest wish of all?

"Grant me health." Her voice wavered. "Grant me vibrant health and steady steps. If you will."

The mare on the left – wind-caller? – eased closer. Her "voice" was lighter – older? – than those of the other two. "Dost thee understand the price of thy request, sweet mountain-child? There is always a cost to any striving."

"I know." Somehow, she did know. And, although she didn't know what cloud strider and dancing-friend and wind-caller would ask of her, she suspected it would be nothing so simple as a barter or trade of help for service or coin. "What must I give?"

Wind-caller's answer stirred her tired hurting limbs like a call to arms. "You must surrender your most cherished defenses, embrace your greatest fears, relinquish the self you are for the one you would become. Will you do this?"

That was comprehensive. Sarvet swallowed yet again before whispering: "I will." And then her arms collapsed, her vision dimmed, and her cheek – turned just in time – pressed damp turf.

Dancing-friend's velvet lips whiffled over Sarvet's jawline. "Hast tried thee too hard, strong seeker! One more effort from thee, and thou shalt rest. Canst thee dare it?"

Sarvet tried to nod, but doubted her head moved at all.

Dancing-friend seemed to intuit her unuttered yes. "Shalt kneel to thee, and then thee must place thine right hand upon my cannon bone."

There was an interval of . . . maneuvering or something. Sarvet scarcely knew. Then a presence and a warmth lay close by her side. She raised her right hand, felt something solid under her palm, and pressed against it.

"Good, valiant trier! Canst thee leap?"

Leap! She'd not have managed that before the failed healing last year!

"The merest intention is enough," dancing-friend assured her.

Sarvet managed to twitch her left foot. And found herself seated on a warm, solid horse back between a blur of wings, unfurling to free dancing-friend's flanks for Sarvet's legs and re-folding to cover them. The dramatic change in position sent an agonizing lancet of pain through Sarvet's hip. She did not fall, but she did slump forward against dancing-friend's mane in a haze of exhaustion.

The pegasus rocked her way to standing in the way of equines. It should have jolted her rider, sending limp Sarvet to grass, but somehow it didn't. Dancing-friend's back and neck felt rock-stabile even as she tipped this way and that. *I am cradled,* thought Sarvet dozily, *like a babe in arms.*

Dimly she sensed the pegasus turning, walking, moving under the stars. The night's sheeny light dimmed – were they passing under a rock arch? – then a warmer glow replaced it.

"Thee must exert thyself once more, brave pilgrim."

"Mmm?" Sarvet felt too sleepy to do anything. Was it the dangerous sleepiness brought on by cold? She almost didn't care. Besides, it was warm here on the pegasus' back inside this grotto.

"Needst not move from mine back, but thy skin must be free of garments."

Even this peculiar request left Sarvet unperturbed. "Mmm."

"Thee climbed a mountain one-legged, little sleeper. Must touch that courage enough to undress now."

Lassitude still claimed her, but Sarvet found her fingers wriggling out of over-mittens and under-gloves, seeking her coat toggles amidst dancing-friend's mane. She let her clothing simply slide down dancing-friend's flanks to the grotto floor. The gaiter and boot on her right foot were hard. *Will I fall?* Somehow she didn't, despite the awkward way she dangled over one side, picking at the laces and attempting to ease the gear off her swollen ankle without jarring it. Renewed pain pierced her hip, but she didn't even slip. *Is there some magic between the wings of a pegasus?* Falling never seemed remotely possible through all the shedding of her layers, including the tricky business of removing her under-trews.

It felt odd to be naked and warm. Even in summer, Kaunis-lodge was filled with cool air, and the switch between nightclothes and day clothes was a chilly proposition. Dancing-friend's hide was smooth as thistle-silk against Sarvet's bare thighs and buttocks. The pegasus was moving again, picking her way down a gentle slope. A generous pool of still water, glimmering in the golden light of the grotto, startled Sarvet awake.

"I can't swim!"

But dancing-friend had already entered the tarn in a gentle surge, and the warm water covered Sarvet's legs, rose to her waist.

"Shalt bear thee up, earth-child. Fear not."

The water was deep, over Sarvet's head if she'd been standing on her own feet, but aback a pegasus she was safe. Dancing-friend waded deeper, and the water reached Sarvet's chest.

"Mayest sleep now, dreaming doer. Thou hast reached haven at last." Dancing-friend's translucent wings lifted up out of the water, apparently (and unexpectedly) dry, screening most of the grotto from Sarvet's view.

But Sarvet was enthralled by the caress of the warm water against her skin, the soothing weight of it on her sore body, the ease of her perch on the pegasus amidst the dangers of deepness. She stretched her arms to embrace the ripples when they reached her shoulders, dipped her face to taste them with her tongue: slightly salt, slightly eggy.

"Mmm."

"Is it well, sweet receiver?"

"Yes," she murmured. "Yes." *I've never been this relaxed,* she realized, *ever.* Always, through all her memory, she'd been tense.

Resisting pain, resisting being an invalid, resisting favors, resisting . . . *Paiam*. Abruptly she was tense again.

"Let it go," suggested dancing-friend.

But if I let go . . . Paiam will win.

"Oh?"

"I'll never grow up. I'll be her baby forever, her child, her dependent. Spinning and weaving in that close room under her eye, never digging, never hiking, never rolling down the slope. Always working, always trapped!" She felt sobs choking her throat. "I want to be free!"

"Here is freedom." Dancing-friend's words were soft.

"No, it's not! It's danger. Letting go is letting her *in*, and I won't!" Sarvet's tension was growing, and with it came increasing pain. Her right hip and foot were throbbing again, her ankle under assault by sharp wrongness.

Dancing-friend continued moving gently through the water. "What are your dreams for yourself, beloved?"

Oh.

Beyond her wanderyar, she hadn't truly had any. Sarvet's tension ebbed. She thought. What *did* she want for herself? There were decades ahead of her, and wandering for all of them . . . well, she wouldn't see much of Nial.

Nial. Nial was part of her future. She wanted . . . communion with him . . . adoration with him . . . *babies* with him. Terror shot through her, banishing her returning relaxation. My heart will *break*. My *heart* will break. *My heart will break.*

Oh.

She *was* her mother's child.

For all her resistance to Paiam's narrowness, some portion of it had crept within her, nestling in a dark and sacred place, rooting within her soul. She was scared to expand, scared to claim the fullness of bounty available in a life, scared to expect fun, scared to expect pleasure. *I snatch when chance presents an opportunity, but I don't seek any out.* I'm a beggar at the gates of living, just like my mother, and . . . *I do not have to be!*

Her ribs shuddered and hot tears wet her cheeks. She was crying, feeling all her lost moments, feeling the pinch of her own choice of limitation: different from her mother's shrinking, but equally narrow.

She is hot and cramped and tangled, but I am cold and barren and spare. I don't want either; I don't want either. Oh, Mother, Mother.

She was crying more easily now, chest loose in its sobs, throat open.

"We are here," came dancing-friend's whisper.

And they were. Sarvet could feel the cloud strider and wind-caller in her mind along with dancing-friend, wordless yet present, strong and loving and . . . calm. *They trust me,* she realized in surprise. They recognize this battle, and . . . *they have faith I will* win *it,* whatever winning it may be. Her sobs were slowing, stopping. She felt . . . no, not empty. She felt . . . open, clear . . . free! I *am* free. I can . . . make a different choice.

Oh!

I can expand. I can be . . . big! I can grow up. And have a baby. *Babies!* And I can do more. Maybe I'll have more than one wanderyar. Maybe I'll search the oldest scrolls in Siajotti-lodge and discover more legends – like the pegasi – that are true. Maybe I'll invent a cure for other girls like me who suffer a birth injury. And boys too. Maybe I'll be a hero! Maybe I'll claim my birthright! Maybe . . . I will *live.*

She put her chin up and let the last residual morsels of holding, gripping, and *resisting* go. With it went the armor holding her utter weariness at bay. Sarvet slumped.

"Well done, brave warrior! Well done!" The pegasi's praise carried the force of a shout, in spite of their gentleness.

She found herself smiling, snuggling her cheek in dancing-friend's silken mane.

"Be at peace, pegasus-friend. Be peaceful."

She slept then, vaguely aware of being shifted after an interval from dancing-friend's back to that of wind-caller, and later still to the cloud strider's. They carried her outside and packed her leg and hip and foot in snow at the edge of their grassy meadow, then returned her to the grotto for more watery warmth. She roused only partially for the different measures of the circuit, just enough to make the effort of will that seemed to replace efforts of limb. Hot to warm to cold to hot; friend to caller to strider to friend; inside to outside to inside.

She awoke properly on wind-caller's back in the grotto. Dancing-friend was nudging Sarvet's shoulder with her nose. "Must drink and sup, victorious one."

Sarvet sat up and looked around her. Wind-caller was bedded on a drift of golden moss. Other mats of the fuzzy stuff dotted the grotto floor, and they all glowed. *So that's where the light came from.* She spotted her pack buried under the pile of her doffed clothes and started to dismount.

Dancing-friend stopped her. "Not yet, dreaming healer! Thy foot wilt be ready in time,.but must rest a while." Once assured that Sarvet would stay put, the pegasus picked her way around the grotto's pool, gripped a pack strap between her teeth, and hoisted the pack from the piled clothing.

Draining her canteen, Sarvet discovered the unexpected extent of her thirst and wished for more. How could she get a refill, if she were not allowed to walk? And from where? The hot water that soothed her hurts held little appeal for drinking.

"Sup first," instructed wind-caller.

Just as water recalled her thirst, so jerky and hardtack recalled hunger. The dense, resistant texture of the food made for a lot of chewing when she wanted to gobble. Perhaps it was as well that she was forced to go slow.

Refilling her canteen proved involved, but not insupportable. Wind-caller stood with the same rocking motions used by her companions, then carried Sarvet through a curving tunnel that connected the grotto to the outside. It was a gusty day, the wind chasing mare's tail clouds across the endless sky, yielding a rapid flicker of shadow and sun across the meadow. The flanking mountains peaked far below this high sanctuary, and the flower-studded lawn felt like the uttermost top of the world. The magical warm stillness between the pegasus wings held both breeze and chill at bay. Sarvet felt winter's sting only when she stretched out her arm to the snowbank at the meadow's edge, scooping the icy crystals into the wide mouth of her vessel. Dipping the filled canteen in the warm water of the grotto's pool melted the snow just enough to create a refreshing, slushy drink.

Then the healing circuit devised by the pegasi resumed: warm water bath while riding followed by snowpack out of doors. After a third visit to the pool, wind-caller added a new therapy. Sarvet was permitted to recline on a bed of moss while the pegasus healers brushed her injured leg with their wings. It was bewildering to *see* the insubstantiality of their pinions, yet *feel* the real brush of silken feathers against her skin; although little less confusing than the clash of the senses produced by riding their firm backs while seeing the gauziness of their bodies.

A pleasant tickling within Sarvet's foot, ankle, and hip joint distracted her from the conflict between sight and touch. She resisted it initially, just as she'd resisted the warmth of the grotto bath. Physical pleasure just led to physical pain when she over-reached the capabilities of her palsied limb. *I won't.*

"'Tis thy future, beloved."

Oh. She drew in a deep breath, released it. *I will.*

And she did.

With her surrender, the tingling grew stronger. She tensed again, and the sensation edged over into pain. She gasped. Immediately the pins-and-needles softened to the easier tickling.

"Stronger heals best. Canst bear it, dear heart?"

"I'll try, but –" Could she? It was hard to welcome . . . not discomfort really, but intensity.

"Be soft."

Yes, staying loose was critical. Could she manage it? The tickle became a tingle became pins-and-needles, became a vibrating buzz. *I can do it! I can bear this! I can welcome this!*

It didn't go on for very long. They returned her to the pool and then the snow pack before the next short session of intensity. Water, wings, snow, water. Eat and drink. Water, wings, snow, water. Sometimes the sky was blue and cloud-swept for the outside visit, others black and star-spangled. She might have grown bored – the healing was every bit as repetitious as weaving or spinning – except she'd never experienced anything like this before. With each repetition, she felt strength and health increasing in her once-palsied limb. And with each repetition, she embraced *being* – not resisting – a little bit more.

One day, they let her stand on her own feet. She felt . . . crooked. *Have I forgotten how to straighten?* Then she realized: this was a new kind of straight. *I don't have to pull with my left side muscles, stretch with my right ones. I'm straight . . . and tall . . . without effort.* She cried again. *I'm not lame anymore.*

It wasn't quite that simple. She had to learn all over again how to walk. First at the shallower edges of the pool with a pegasus on each side for support, later in the flattest part of the meadow. And there were exercises, leg lifts and toe presses and such, both in the water and out. She was eager for it all. Moving this new body of hers was . . . hard work . . . yet effortless, just like Nial loping easily down the slope from the branching hall to the lodge. *My body was made to do all this!* It amazed her.

Amidst the wonder, she knew one flash of unease. "This feels so good," she told friend-dancer. "How could I bear it, if I were injured again?"

The pegasus seemed to smile. "Loss always hurts. And loss after other losses . . . be more fearful. Thee knowest more. But . . . beautiful climber, thee also knowest the answer."

"I do?" Sarvet let the calmness that seemed to pool somewhere beneath all her new experiences flow through her thoughts. Yes, she did know. "Receiving a gift is dangerous, but barring out risk in fear . . . is the greater loss."

"Yes."

When Sarvet was running and jumping and tumbling in the meadow, the cloud strider approached her. "It is time. Art healed."

She knew it was true. She was whole and healthy. And suddenly eager to do . . . whatever she would do next. *I've had my adventure, but there are more awaiting me!*

She rinsed her clothing in the grotto pool and hung it to dry from jagged spurs in the rock walls. She packed her rucksack, noticing that the jerky pouch was empty and the hardtack down to three pieces. It *was* time to go. She dressed. Her thistle-silk under garments were as soft as the hides of the pegasi, but their touch all over her body felt strange. She'd grown used to nakedness.

She'd imagined hiking down the way by which she'd come, but the pegasi had other ideas. "The blizzards of late winter lingered in the upper reaches. Thee wouldst require skis, intrepid walker!" Wind-caller whickered gently. "And . . . we should enjoy thy company a small time more."

Her flight home was magnificent. The cloud strider bore her. His back was solid and safe, as usual, but the entire world stretched out below them, a vast tapestry of snowy ranges, green valleys, and the far-off blue lowlands reaching to the line of the horizon. The pegasi climbed higher at first. Sarvet caught a glimpse of a small, brownish dot mid-slope on a neighboring mountain. "There!" And then they wheeled and spiraled down, down and down.

They landed in a clearing in the pine grove above the branching-hall, and Sarvet leapt to the ground. Now that the moment of parting had arrived . . . she didn't want to. "Will I . . . ever see you again?"

"Shalt dwell in our hearts forever, splendid one," wind-caller told her.

"Then . . . this *is* goodbye?"

"Even at parting, true friends never part." Friend-dancer nosed her one last time.

Sarvet gathered the courage to say what she really meant. "I love you."

"And we, thee," answered the cloud rider. "But know this, brave climber: thee mayst visit us whenever thine heart knows the time is ripe. We wilt not always await you in our meadow on the Maara-mount, but when we do, shalt welcome thee."

Their leap into the sky was like a lightning strike in reverse. The power of it made Sarvet wonder that their hoofs had not kicked a portal open to the crystal caverns that were said to lie in the Fiordhammars' roots. She watched the winged horses soar out over the valley, then turn and circle ever upward into endless blue. They were gone.

She looked down. A small spring was flowing from a shallow, rock-lined cavity. She laughed. No portal to the underworld, but . . . perhaps . . . a flow of healing water? She dabbled her fingers in it: warm.

The first Kaunis-sisters she saw were her friends, Brionne and Amara, leading Timbilio – the little goat kid born out of season in late Sombry – away from the milking byre. Had he escaped from the makeshift stall in the garden shed *again*? Whatever his fault, he was feeling frisky. Amara's clutch on his collar came loose as he bucked and twisted. Brionne's swipe for him missed and put her in prime position to receive Timbilio's whirling butt to her seat. She jolted to her hands and knees, cursing: "Shun it!" Amara was no help, collapsing in giggles.

Sarvet stepped briskly forward, capturing the escapee as he attempted to dash past her with a well-timed grab for his ear. The goat grew docile under this persuasion, and she led him away from the branching-hall steps. Amara finally stopped laughing and looked up. Brionne stopped cursing and looked up. Both girls' mouths dropped open.

Brionne was the first to recover. "Sarvet!" she shrieked, leaping to her feet and hurtling into Sarvet's arms. "You're alive, you're back, you're tall! Oh, Sarvet, oh, Sarvet!" Then she burst into tears.

Luckily Amara was more collected in her response, since Sarvet's grasp on Timbilio's ear slackened upon Brionne's tumultuous arrival. Amara secured the frolicking goat by his collar and remarked, "Nial was frantic, but I thought he was being silly."

Brionne lifted her red face out of Sarvet's shoulder long enough to retort, "It might have been nothing that sent him looking, but he was right to be scared! You know the tracks he found. Sarvet had fallen! And been hurt! She *crawled* back to the valley-rock. And then lost herself in the snowfall."

"I don't think so. I mean, look. She's fine. In fact . . ." Amara's voice trailed off. Apparently her preference for pretending the calmness of a grown sister failed under the unusual circumstance confronting her. And her indifference was certainly feigned. "Sarvet, what happened? You're . . . different!"

Sarvet smiled. "Come on! Let's get Timbilio here penned before he hustles you under the porch steps with his antics." Her friend was being jerked across the damp turf of the slope – the snow always melted here first – by the goat's jigging.

Amara's feigned composure cracked. "But you have to explain! Where've you been? Why did you go? *Were* you hurt? Tell us . . . oh, tell us everything!"

"Of course! But not –" This time she was the one stopping in mid sentence. What was Nial doing here? For it was unmistakeably Nial racing up the mountain from below the lodge. Surely the brothers of Tukeva-lodge had returned home – a month ago? or more? But it was Nial.

She awaited him, close to the spot where she'd awaited him before and with a similar intention, and yet how differently: she was full, not empty; she was confident, not desperate; and she would act openly, not in secret. Real strength had no need of secrecy.

"Sarvet! Sarvet!" Nial's embrace was more vigorous even than his mad dash upward. He lifted her off her feet, crushed her to him, spun around thrice, dabbed kisses all over her face, and then held her close, tenderly, as though she might break.

His chest felt good under her cheek, but she wanted to see his face. He let her go when she stepped back a bit. And his face was worth seeing: awe, love, and joy exalted his features. Was it truly for her return?

"I knew you were well!" he exclaimed. "More than well!" He looked her over in turn. "Sarvet, you're just the way I always saw you in my mind's eye . . . but never did see you in my fleshly eye. You're healed!"

She nodded.

"In more than your hip and foot."

She reached for his hand. "I'm healed in every way, Nial."

His excitement was moderating, mellowing into a steady joy much like her own.

Amara's laughter, happy rather than amused this time, broke the moment. And Timbilio jumped free. Again. Sarvet led the chase, just because she could, marveling at the way she too could now run all over this slope. It was exhilarating.

Once the goat was finally penned, she asked, "Will you come with me?"

Nial was too elated to be wary, but she could tell he thought twice before answering. He knew her well enough to suspect . . . something.

"I'd like you to hear what I will tell Mother Johtaia," she reassured him.

Someone must have caught sight of her through a lodge window – a few of the hide panels were off to let the warmish Nerich day inside – because Mother Johtaia evinced no surprise when the four of them crowded into her counsel-haven. Sister Kemra had kerin-tea and capricole savories ready, and four chairs arranged before the one in which the lodge-mother sat.

Johtaia arose, nodding to Amara, Brionne, and Nial, and took Sarvet's hands. Her smile was rueful. "I owe you an apology, Sarvet Kaunis-daughter."

Interesting. Sarvet tipped her head to one side. *I hadn't expected her to own it.*

"My solution wasn't . . . a solution. I take it you found a better one?"

Sarvet told her story. Nial had long since confessed its prelude: her determination to *take* a wanderyar – since one would not be given her – and his clandestine help. She gathered he'd felt misgivings within moments of her departure, resisted them for a while, then finally come after her. And been scared silly when he found evidence of her tumble and lost her tracks in the fresh snowfall. All the brothers of Tukeva-lodge had joined the Kaunis-sisters in searching through the night.

"I did fall," she confirmed. "And I did make it all the way back to the valley-rock. But . . . I couldn't bear to crawl back inside the husk I'd left behind."

Mother Johtaia nodded. Amara wrinkled her brows in puzzlement. Brionne and Nial looked guilty. Surely they didn't imagine her difficulties were *their* fault? Or maybe they did. It was easy to imagine you could have done more for a friend in need. Especially when looking back. It was usually more confusing at the time.

"I found *pegasi* on the mountain top. Pegasi!" she told them.

Nial's and Brionne's mouths dropped open. Mother Johtaia looked . . . wistful? Was it possible . . . she'd had her own experience with winged horses? There was knowingness to the far-off look in her eyes. Only Amara exclaimed, "No! There are no such! Not really." But Amara's disbelief faded as Sarvet continued her tale. She found it hard to describe her inner experiences. The outer events were easier to relate: the warm water, the snow packs, the labor of the exercises.

"It sounds awful!" sympathized Amara. "You poor thing! Were you very lonely and bored?"

Lonely! She'd never been so companioned in her life. *I must be doing a more wretched job of telling this than I thought. Amara doesn't get it at all!* But Johtaia looked as if she understood. And Nial's and Brionne's faces reflected wonder.

The lodge-mother didn't leave them long for contemplation of Sarvet's adventure. It was, after all, her job to be practical. "I'm glad it ended well, Sarvet. You do know it might not have."

Oh, yes. Sarvet nodded soberly. She would not have made it back down the mountain, if the pegasi had not been present to succor her at its top.

"Father Biejan and I have been talking these four sevendays."

"Are the Tukeva-fathers still here?" So that's why Nial was not long gone home.

"No. Nial's been tenting on their campsite alone." Mother Johtaia smiled wryly. "Biejan forbore to order, and I . . . well, I hadn't the heart to persuade."

Nial blushed.

"But Biejan agrees with me that some girls need a wanderyar as much or more than any boy." Johtaia paused. "You were right, Sarvet. And I was wrong."

"You mean Sarvet gets to have *more* adventures?" burst out Amara. Apparently she'd forgotten her earlier judgement of Sarvet's enterprise as boring and lonely. "That's not fair! I think she should be punished, not rewarded!"

Johtaia cast Amara a reproving glance, then continued with her own agenda. "But a girl embarking on a wanderyar needs *training* for it, as I think you have proved. In future, candidates will attend the ramble-class in Tukeva-lodge *before* they travel." Johtaia turned her gaze on Amara a moment. "That does include you, Amara, if you truly wish for adventure. Such undertakings *are* frequently uncomfortable." Then the lodge-mother's attention was back on Sarvet. "If you still desire a wanderyar, it is yours."

Sarvet laughed. When you weren't ready, things could be so difficult. And when you were . . . barriers folded like . . . Brionne going down at Timbilio's buffet. "I hadn't planned on asking you this time. I was just going to *tell* you. But yes, I am going."

Johtaia's laugh mirrored Sarvet's: delight and confidence at its heart. "*After* the ramble-class, I trust."

Sarvet grew serious. "I'd like the ramble-class, but may I join the one now in progress? I'm not waiting until you manage to organize a girls' class."

Johtaia was taken aback. Then she laughed again and shook her head. "I'm never quite prepared for you, am I, Sarvet?" She sighed. "Well, I needn't make the same mistake twice. If Biejan approves it, then you have my consent as well."

Amara groaned – a muted groan – and Brionne gasped. Even Sarvet herself wondered if maybe she'd been a bit *too* bold. *Where will I sleep in Tukeva-lodge?* Surely they wouldn't put her in a bednook in the boys' sleep-hall.

Nial was ahead of them. "My lodge-father has already cleared the callers' spare box-room for Sarvet's use. And moved one of the portable nooks into it. She can come to us today." His gaze, warm and proud, turned to Sarvet. "If it please you!"

"I'd like that!" Indeed, she'd hoped to depart today. Even after a month of intense change, she still felt . . . allergic to Kaunis-lodge. She wanted to sleep somewhere else.

Mother Johtaia moved swiftly to necessities. "You'd better pack another satchel, child." Her gaze sized up Sarvet's rucksack. "You'll want more than the clothes you stand up in." She hesitated. "I'll tell Paiam, if you like, but . . ."

Sarvet overrode this. "No, I can do it." Her voice sounded quiet, but firm in her ears. "I want to do it."

"Would you like me to come with you?"

"Yes, but . . . for her. Not me. I think –" Sarvet wasn't sure what her intuition was telling her, but she suspected Paiam needed . . . something. At least her birth-mother wouldn't be able to hide this further grief caused by her daughter. And she might try, if there were no witnesses. But just one. "Amara, Brionne . . . Nial –"

Nial understood before she requested or explained. "It's a private moment."

Johtaia nodded. "I feel sure you girls have a few chores still waiting . . ." Brionne nodded, conscience-stricken, and scrambled up to go finish her lodge tasks. Amara went with her, reluctantly. "Nial, you may make yourself comfortable here, if you wish."

Sarvet and Johtaia found Paiam at the small spinning wheel in her sitting room. Sarvet could see her birth-mother clamping down on her immediate impulse to leap from her seat. Paiam's jaw clenched. "So! You're not dead in a blizzard."

Johtaia was taken aback once more. *What is it about me and my mother?* Sarvet felt unsurprised. Paiam had been fighting her vulnerabilities for so long, she'd likely forgotten how to feel relief.

"I'm healed . . . Mother."

"At what cost?" grated Paiam.

Sarvet remembered wind-caller's words. "I've given up all my defenses, faced my worst fears, and let go of who I was."

"Then you're not my daughter." Paiam's voice was harsh. "I wouldn't have you, if you begged me."

Johtaia's consternation ripened to shock. "Sister! Think what you're saying!"

"I'm leaving, Mother." Sarvet felt sad, but not for herself. *If only my healing might have salved Paiam's wounds as well.* But each person had, apparently, to work out her own salvation.

"Did you think I didn't know?" Where Paiam's eyes the least bit shiny? Her teeth gripped her lip in anger.

"I wanted to say farewell, Mother."

"Well, you've said it." Paiam started her spinning wheel again.

"I love you."

Paiam opened her lips, shut them, and shook her head. "Long partings never prosper. Go."

Sarvet turned in the doorway and walked away. After a dismayed moment, Johtaia followed her.

"I *am* sorry, Sarvet. If I'd realized . . . well, I think I should have told her myself."

Sarvet smiled. "No. I knew how it would be. And I wanted to do it."

Her parting from her friends was more satisfactory. Amara gave her a small bound sheaf of pages and a stylus. "Write it all down, Sarvet," she urged. "I don't think I'm brave enough to go on a wanderyar! The only one I'll have will be by imagining yours. I want to hear *everything!*"

Brionne clung to her in an anxious hug. "Promise you'll come back, Sarvet," she whispered. "I know it's exciting out there, but . . . please come back."

"This is home," Sarvet reassured her. "And I'll be ready for home . . . after a year . . . or two . . . or three!"

"Oh, Sarvet! Three years?"

"Maybe. But not four, I promise. I want a wanderyar, not a new lodge-family. I'm Hammarleeding," she declared. And she was. But this wanderyar felt . . . essential.

The ramble-class would be the beginning. What Hammar-sister had ever guested in a father-lodge before? Except, really, her wanderyar began with the inner journey in the sanctuary of the pegasi. And would never end – despite her promise to Brionne – even when she returned home. She did intend to return home, to Kaunis-lodge. *I'll be traveling through time, through life, through the great adventure of being. And that never needs to stop.* Is that what Nial learned on his wanderyar?

Nial, of course, went with her on this first leg of the journey. He *was* going home.

*T*hree years later, Sarvet strode along the Ulko-polku, arms swinging and shoulders loose. She'd lightened her pack at the Tukeva-sawmill; no need to bring camping gear and coin back to Kaunis-lodge. The brothers would see that the next wanderleeding out got them. She drew a deep breath in through her nose: the mystic scent of the pines mingled with warmer aromas of risa-turf and starflowers. She'd not yet reached the familiar landmarks of the Vrea-vale, cradled by Maara-mount and Valtava-scarp and the Tunkahorn, but the alpine valleys and their towering snow-capped peaks were all around her. *I'm home!* And she was ready to be home. The world was a fascinating, enthralling place, but . . . she craved the pleasures of staying put now. And the place where she wanted to settle was at her origin. She knew some wanderleedings *didn't* come home. But for Sarvet, her birthplace in the Fiordhammars was the right spot.

What will I tell them, once I'm home? There was so much! She'd travelled south. Nial's adventures beckoned her fancy, but her heart whispered of making her own discoveries, and she'd not traced his steps after all. Amara would hate the first bit on the fishing boat. Sarvet glanced down at her right wrist. The scar from the spinefish would likely fade over the years, but never entirely disappear. But she'd loved the waves and the salt breeze and the energy of the sailors and fishers. Once her stomach got used to the constant surge of the water.

Brionne would like lady-chapels of Fiorish. But that tale wouldn't do for the first burst of news and greeting. The sweet healing of the baby born with the malkin-lip needed a more private telling. And she wasn't sure she could share the other miracles she'd witnessed in those sacred spaces. *I wouldn't have believed my own eyes, if I hadn't experienced my own miracle on the Maara-mount.*

And her visit with her father – Ivvar – at Rakas-lodge, was too intimate, too lovely and special, to share at all.

But she could certainly talk about the many cowherds of Erice, as well as the spiceflower fields on that island. The rose plantations of Frisange and Sarvet's work in the distillery where the rose-attar was made would interest Sister Evaia, although her apprenticeship to the antiphoner in Imsterfeldt would be the biggest draw for the healer. Odd how Sarvet's earlier experiences in her wanderyar – Merovessic fish, miracles on the Isle of Fiorish, spiceflowers, and rose-attar – had fitted her perfectly for Maittresse Saussen's purposes.

But what would she tell Nial? Everything. *When* would she tell Nial? *Maybe I'll turn right instead of left at the Vrea-way and go straight to Tukeva-lodge.* She'd been missing Nial with an almost physical ache for the past half year. But when she reached the path toward home she turned left. She wanted to test herself in her native milieu. *Have I truly grown enough to face Paiam?* Her birth-mother seemed a small figure in her memory after three years away. Would she loom larger in Kaunis-lodge? *I hope not. I want to settle there, and I can't do it, if I can't keep my own perspective in Paiam's presence.* But she felt strong. *I'm ready. I know I am.*

Around the bulk of the valley-rock, a surprising sight met her gaze. The father-camp was filled with a flock of tents, along with milling men and boys. What were the Tukeva-brothers doing here now?

Then she caught a glimpse of one Tukeva-brother in particular, at the same time he saw her.

"Nial!"

"Sarvet!"

She didn't await him this time. Nor did he await her. She shed her rucksack just before she stepped into his arms.

"Sarvet, lovely Sarvet, oh, Sarvet," he murmured, folding her close and kissing her hair. He was still the taller. He'd shot upwards more while she was away; but she'd grown too. She lifted her face.

His lips were warm, urgent. A delicious tingling – it had scared her when she was fifteen – rose through her body. Her own lips parted. *Nial, oh, Nial!*

She'd never received the linking-lessons from Sister Kilti, but Maittresse Saussen had discovered her ignorance and pressed several informative Cambers-scrolls upon her. She stopped her fingers from from opening Nial's sweater toggles with an effort. *We can't celebrate an adoration right here on the edge of the father-camp!*

Nial released her, panting. His eyes were bright and dark. "Do you know what day it is?"

She shook her head, wondering.

"It's the skip-span, and Other-joy is late this year."

So that's why the fathers are here!

"Sarvet" – Nial knelt before her, taking her hands in his – "Will you commune with me?" His eyes held something more than love. It was a pledge . . . like the one that Cambers men and women made to one another . . . but that wasn't part of Hammarleeding culture. Nial wanted to adore her forever. And she –?

Sarvet knelt in turn and pressed his fingers. "Always," she breathed. "This Other-joy and the next and the next. Until our very last."

He kissed her palms. She nipped his thumb.

And they both joined the father-procession when it started up the hill for Kaunis-lodge. *Poor Johtaia,* thought Sarvet irrelevantly, *she'll be just as shocked by my method of homecoming as she was by my wish to leave in the first place.* She smiled at Nial smiling back at her.

On the lodge-porch, Sarvet accepted symbolic pannkuja from an astonished Sister Unni. *If I'm going to be a tradition-breaker, I may as well break them thoroughly,* she decided. Besides, she was hungry.

Johtaia had not yet seen Sarvet in the crowd. The lodge-mother began the presentations of the sister-novitiates to the brother-novices. This year there were five couples, and one of those were Brionne and Vaino. Vaino knelt and kissed Brionne's hands. Brionne flushed. She looked happy and starry-eyed.

Sarvet stepped forward with Nial for the lodge-mother's blessing. Mother Johtaia's face registered just the surprise Sarvet was expecting. Then she laughed and shook her head. "Welcome home, Sarvet!" And she really meant it. But couldn't forebear remarking: "I suppose a quiet return on an ordinary day would never have been right for you!" Leaving her formal role aside for a moment, she moved to embrace her prodigal daughter and kissed Sarvet on the cheek. Her voice grew wry. "I take it you wish to celebrate a linking with Nial?"

"Yes, I do."

Johtaia smiled, nodded, and returned to the ritual words. "Sisters of Kaunis and brothers of Tukeva, I call on you to search your hearts. Two of our body have discovered without sanction their desire to share a linking-moon. Is there a brother who will speak for Nial Ilggai-spring and his descent lines? Is he fit to adore a woman?"

Father Biejan came forward. "I speak for him."

"It is well," Johtaia intoned. "Is there a sister who will speak for Sarvet Paiam-spring and her decent lines? Is she fit to be adored?"

Sarvet held her breath. *Would* anyone speak for her? It had to be a once-linked (or more) sister who knew Sarvet's genealogy. She searched the congregation of women clustered on the porch. Where were the green-sister and the byre-sister? Surely they would speak for her. But no one was moving forward.

Several of the sisters near the front portal shifted; three moved aside. The long silence hung. Then Sarvet's birth-mother stepped forth.

She looked different. What was this difference? Her clothes were the same drab sepia Paiam had worn for years. She was just as tall and angular as always. And her face was serious. But not . . . tense. Was that peace in her expression?

Paiam's gaze met Sarvet's and . . . softened? She smiled, a slow smile that reached all the way to her eyes and beyond. She walked to Johtaia's side, claiming the traditional honor for a novitiate's birth-mother. "*I* speak for Sarvet. She is beautiful and whole. She is fully fit to be adored . . . *and to adore!*" All through her declaration Paiam gazed with love and pride upon her child, now grown to womanhood.

Sarvet's eyes grew damp and her vision blurred. *She's healed . . . and free of some darkness that's ridden her ever since my birth.* Paiam's heart was whole.

THE END

Livli's Gift

For my mother,
with love, respect, and admiration

And for Paty,
whose liking for the Hammarleedings
encouraged me to tell Livli's story

*L*ivli rerolled the scroll carefully, returned it to its pigeonhole, and sighed. The whisper of her breath sounded loud in the quiet space, as had the crackle of the brittle parchment and the faint click of the closing cabinet door.

The tale of *The Princess and the Griffon* did not have the reference she was looking for. Neither had *The Lindworm's Eyrie* nor *Triton's Egg*.

"Why am I bothering," she murmured. "It's a wild *gos* chase."

But she knew why she was bothering. She really, really wanted the information in whatever tale it was.

"I wish I could remember."

But she couldn't remember.

Of course, she could ask her birth-mother. Sarvet would undoubtedly reel off an entire list of the folktales she'd told her children at bedtime. *But I don't want her to know . . . what I'm thinking about right now.*

Livli sighed again and shifted uncomfortably. Having to pee so often was for the birds. *I just got back from the dump-buckets! I'm not traipsing through all three of those long corridors again.* At least not right away.

Instead she straightened and moved over to the windows.

The view was incredible. Not so much for its scope – a vista across a snowy valley brushed by clumps of dark pines, bounded by granite cliffs, and presided over by tall mountain peaks was ordinary in Hammarleeding enclaves – but for its wavy presence through glass while Livli stood indoors within warmth. The scroll-lodge of Siajotti was richly supported by all the sister-lodges and brother-lodges, and a library needed good lighting. So Siajotti had glass in its windows rather than hide coverings. And the scroll repository itself had *big* windows.

A coal fell in the tile stove that stood in the corner between the windows. The building creaked. The day was abnormally still, with no wind to mask the smaller sounds.

Livli paced from one end of the windowed wall to the other and back, her footfalls soft against age-darkened pine boards.

That lost scroll wasn't her only problem. *What am I going to do about Thoivra?*

She traced one of the circular muntins holding the small glass panes – it was cool to her touch – and bit her lip. Focus, she reminded herself. One thing at a time. Scroll first.

I need to look somewhere else, but where?

None of the parchments on prayer, ritual, superstition, or even birth described the rite she sought. *If it even exists.*

She turned again to scan the placards on each cabinet door: Mind-tenets. Being-truth.

Surely not.

Sacred Doctrines, then Calling Lore. *No.*

A faint fragrance of beeswax mingled with the mellow smell from the basket of pearwood beside the stove and the more acrid odor of vinegar used to clean the glass-fronted cabinets.

Mathema and Ingenia. *Definitely not. It's got to be in Folktales within Gathering Lore, if it's anywhere at all.*

Unless . . . *could* it be in Sagas? But she'd tried that, and Sagas was full of epic tales of battles and warriors from ancient days.

Her eyes traveled on.

Healing Arts occupied three massive cabinets to the right of the scroll-hall's doorway. Could the story be in there? It seemed unlikely.

Her stomach growled. This morning's sausages, with which she'd broken her fast, were a distant memory of savory satisfaction.

As Livli studied the leftmost cabinet – Folktales – a Siajotti-sister stepped through the adjacent doorway and paused. Ibba wasn't young precisely, more a matronly sort, but she was a good bit younger than most of those with direct responsibility for the scrolls. And she was much more sympathetic for ills of the flesh than the rest of her older cohort.

Those old crones have forgotten what it's like to be without *aches and pains,* thought Livli irreverently.

But Ibba's face looked concerned. Did the Scroll Guild need both tables again? *I suppose I should take a break anyway.*

Ibba pushed a chair up to the window where Livli stood. "Still no luck?" she asked, gesturing Livli to sit.

Livli sank onto the hard wooden seat – *I should have brought a cushion, like I did yesterday* – and shook her head. "I was sure I'd find it with the rest of the children's tales, but I've looked at every last one of those and it isn't there."

"Let me search for a while." Ibba smiled. "It'll be a nice change from mending torn parchments and replacing worm-eaten rods. Imagine . . . actually *reading* scrolls instead of just repairing and organizing them."

Livli felt the frown leaving her face. "Do you think the one I'm looking for is among those being restored?"

"It's possible. I've been checking as I work." Ibba tilted her head to one side. She hesitated, then went ahead. "Sister Moija has brought a fresh pot of kerin-tea to your chamber, and I think you should put your feet up."

Livli opened her lips, closed them, then said simply, "Thanks."

Had her hunger remained quiescent or her bladder, less insistent, she might have resisted Ibba's care, stubbornly chasing her goal. As it was . . . she went. At least Siajotti never ran out of sawdust, and the sawdust really did keep odor at bay in the dump-buckets.

In her room, she saw the tray with the teapot also held a platter of cream cheese dainties rolled in smoked chevon. Her stomach growled again. She'd grown so used to nausea the past three months that, now it was past, she tended to forget her appetite was back.

She pushed her chair a touch farther from the tile stove – *my metabolism's so high these days, I'm never cold* – and settled into the purple wool cushion. The matching footstool was exactly the right height for ease, and the kerin-tea bore the hint of sweetness that meant it hadn't steeped too long.

Mmm. It was so peaceful here.

The memory of her departure from home intruded on her quietude. *There* was an unpeaceful scene: Thoivra shrieking and shaking her finger at a horrified brother.

Poor skinny Issat had no idea he wasn't welcome in the foyer of Kaunis-lodge. He figured he was walking with Livli for the first leg of his journey to Tukeva. And she was going out the front door. Why shouldn't he?

Thoivra told him why. *This is the lodge, not the spa. Get out!*

Ugh! I don't want to think about Thoivra right now. I want to enjoy *not* being in the same place she is. *Enjoy my break from the bustle of the spa. Enjoy Siajotti's tranquility.*

Although her earliest memory of Siajotti-lodge was the reverse of serene.

She eased her shoulders, took a sip of tea, and allowed reverie to claim her.

Livli had been only five, but Sarvet decided her daughter would enjoy the children's scrolls at Siajotti. They had such fine illustrations. And Sarvet's research project would likely take two weeks, longer than most birth-mothers cared to be apart from their girl-children. (She'd felt no qualms about leaving baby Gaiju with Sister Brionne. He was newly weaned. And . . . he was a boy.) Besides, Livli was a cooperative little person.

Sarvet's reasoning was no doubt sound, and all would have gone just as she imagined except that Livli's father also happened to be at Siajotti.

Or perhaps Sarvet knew Nial intended to visit the scroll-hall.

Hammarleeding men lived apart in the brother-lodges, while the women congregated in the sister-lodges. But Sarvet sought her mate's company more often than did most of her sisters.

Whatever the reason for the timing, Nial brought Livli's two older brothers with him. Davvad hoped to find information on the ice-men of Tuisilund before he departed on his wanderyar. As for Harral . . . well, it was time he paid heed to something besides skiing and wrestling and rock-climbing.

Davvad was old enough to know better, but the three siblings were used to reunions at the brother-lodge. Livli still loved visiting there. Tukeva had its quiet places, but the brothers were a boisterous lot. Their rhythms were so different from those of Kaunis-lodge: stamping dances before supper, jovial shouts filling the corridors, and everywhere the bursting energy of men and boys.

Odd to think that in her birth-mother's girlhood none of the Kaunis-sisters had ever been to Tukeva. Now such visits were commonplace.

Anyway, the enthusiasms of Tukeva had invaded Siajotti in the persons of Davvad and Harral. Besides, the ring of tiny walled gardens surrounding the scroll-lodge positively invited a game of hide-bide-and-slide. Which then morphed into swooshing down the bannisters of the magnificent staircase connecting the sleep-halls to the public rooms. Which morphed again into an all-new creation combining elements of every active game ever played by Hammarleedings with energy to burn.

The scroll-sisters had been kind about the glass herb-house damaged by the three of them.

And about the pillows ruined in the bannister runs.

And about the tray of savories accidentally knocked to the floor.

Apparently they enjoyed the novelty and the joyousness of the childish bustle. Especially when the culprits were so genuinely abashed at their misdeeds. And willing to make amends. Livli still remembered the replacement crewelwork on those pillows. She hadn't been good at crewelwork, but she'd surpassed herself out of sheer guilt.

And Harral had discovered his love of healing roots as he replanted the herb-house. While Davvad learned that in spite of his hatred for run-of-the-mill cooking, he enjoyed concocting delicacies.

The sisters were less forgiving of the scroll torn in the scuffle. And Sarvet and Nial made sure that future encounters between the siblings occurred anywhere but at Siajotti!

Livli drained the last of her kerin-tea, thought about leaving the last chevon dainty – *surely I needn't eat this much* – and then gave in to its lure. Yum!

Her thoughts returned to her older brothers.

I miss Davvad and Harral.

She didn't get to see them nearly as often as she had while growing up. Although she'd visited them many more times than most girls visited their sweet-brothers. *I wish boy children didn't leave the sister-lodge to live with their fathers at two years of age. And I wish . . .* She didn't finish the thought.

If wishes were llamas, then sisters would trek. *I'd better get on with my scroll search.*

After another trip to the dump-buckets.

Sister Ibba had found nothing, although she'd checked all the remaining scrolls in Sagas. "Just in case," she explained. "You did say it was a story, didn't you? Not a folk tradition?"

"Yes, a children's tale, I thought." Livli wasn't surprised it wasn't in Sagas. That's why she'd stopped a third of the way through.

"Maybe you should try Tongues. Sarvet speaks Istrian doesn't she? Maybe she brought the tale back herself from her wanderyar."

"Oh! Yes! Ibba, you're a prodigy!"

Ibba smiled ruefully. "If I'm so prodigious, why didn't I think of it sooner?"

"Never mind. Thank you! I'm going to dive right in."

But the tale wasn't in Tongues. Nor was it in Calling Lore or Sacred Doctrines – long shots both, but Livli was getting desperate.

In the end, three days later, she did scour both Ingenia and Mathema.

And found it.

The Lindworm and the Queen.

It had been misfiled within the subcategory of treatises on geometria, of all things!

Hands trembling, she took it to the nearest table and set it on the worn surface. The day was sunny, and light flooded through the windows. She sat with her back to the view. The sun on the snow was blinding, but she had to arrange herself to avoid casting a shadow on the scroll.

Once upon a time there was a queen who longed for a child. As she sat in her garden weeping, an old crone approached her and asked her what the matter was. "Oh, no one can help me," sobbed the queen.

Yes, this was that old story her birth-mother had recited at bedtime, along with other more favorite ones, before Livli had outgrown fairy tales.

Livli studied the parchment a moment more, and then retrieved paper and a stylus from the cupboard with writing supplies for Siajotti-visitors.

I will need notes.

She spent the afternoon recording the information that had been so hard to come by. After supper, she begged two blown-glass cloches and a few seeds of aegis-rockfoil from the Siajotti's green-sister.

The next morning she traveled home.

Livli had hoped to do her planting immediately. It was Nerich, just past the Spring Evener, and cold for delicate seedlings. But wind had scoured the snow from the ground, and Siajotti's cloches would protect her rockfoil plants.

She was eager to try the powers of the ritual used by the fairy tale queen.

Would it work for her as well?

She'd have to wait to find out.

Well, she'd have to wait in any case. Her baby wouldn't be born until summer, late in Jubiante. But she'd have to wait even to discover if she felt . . . different . . . after getting the rockfoil in the ground.

Two injuries, one invalid, and two contagions had all arrived at the Kaunis-spa last night. Livli usually focused on helping convalescents return to normal living, but the healers needed extra hands today.

She took a moment to check with Kaunis' green-mother, reserving a spot in the herb garden, and then placed her pair of cloches in a corner sheltered by a neighboring boulder. The earth was damp, but not soggy, and not as cold as she'd expected. She hilled a little soil up the sides of the glass bells. They were heavy, but the winds of the Fiordhammars were strong. They could tumble even goat kids down the mountain slopes sometimes. This garden nook was sheltered and sunny. The cloches would warm the earth before she planted her seeds. Maybe it was as well that she couldn't do it today.

"Did you hear the brouhaha about Brother Aitan and young Ristlinna?" asked the green-mother.

Livli frowned, shaking her head. More trouble? She'd broken her fast with only a handful of sisters, quiet at dawn in the refecting-hall. Who knew what this week's gossip covered?

"Aitan came to bid his birth-mother farewell before he embarked on his wanderyar."

"That's Thoivra's son, right?" Hmm. *Thoivra* again. "I thought they were estranged?"

"They might be again. After this."

Livli lifted a brow in inquiry.

"Ristlinna went off with him to the valley-rock *alone*."

"So?"

The green-mother snorted. "You know Thoivra. 'Don't come back,' to her son. 'Your daughter needs a taste of of the osier switch' to Ristlinna's mother. And on and on. I'd laugh, if it weren't for the sisters giving a serious listen to her notions."

Yah, that was the problem. Thoivra did have listeners.

"Poor Juudet didn't know what to do. She wanted to scold – worried about Aitan's enthusiasm for his wanderyar infecting Ristlinna – but felt bound to defend her daughter against Thoivra's accusations of stolen kisses and such. As though Ristlinna sees Aitan, a mere stripling, as anything but a sweet-brother," scoffed Kirsta.

"Anything come of it all?" asked Livli. Thoivra kept agitating for new rules. Or old rules to be reclaimed and used. Old rules that seemed better left behind, in Livli's opinion.

"For a wonder, no. Seagga insisted that children were best guided by their mothers and fathers, not lodge rulings, and that Thoivra could discipline her son, but could not ban him from Kaunis."

Surprised, Livli felt a laugh puff from her. The lodge-mother rarely exhibited such decision.

"Unexpected, no?" agreed Kirsta.

Livli nodded and washed her hands under the pump at the green-shed.

Then she hurried uphill toward the bath-hall. It was a graceful wooden building located within the pine grove some way past the branching-hall. Shallow terraces surrounded it, since the hot springs emerged in an uncharacteristically level bit of the mountain's flank. Pine needles on the path through the grove muffled Livli's footsteps, and her soft ankle boots made little noise on the flagstones of the terraces, but her slight weight was enough to echo on the wooden boards when she stepped up onto the deck.

Inside, in the foyer, Sister Hibma looked flustered. "Thank Sias you're here! Mother Gaddja was threatening to make me accompany Cuuji into the hot spring! And I know I'd drop her. Or trip and fall on her. Or something."

Livli couldn't help laughing. Gentle laughter. "I knew we were busy, but that busy?"

Hibma's eyes grew teary. "It's just that she's a baby, and she cries so. Her birth-mother feels so badly that the boneset-sister at her lodge was away when the child's arm was broken. So it wasn't set properly. And then the journey here was too difficult for some months and . . . well, nobody wants to make the little thing wait a moment longer. Even when a crushed hand and a paralysis in far more danger are waiting."

Livli kicked her boots off. "I'd best not linger then."

The warm water felt unexpectedly good. The hike from Siajotti to Kaunis had tired her more than usual, and her feet ached. Were the loose tendons of pregnancy arriving already? She'd have to ask Sister Marja.

Since Cuuji was a baby, she'd be sticking to the cooler regions of the hot spring. Which was good. Too much heat could be dangerous to her own baby.

My own baby. It still seemed unreal, especially now the nausea had passed. Except . . . she did feel *different* somehow. *I suppose I'll believe it when my belly starts to round.* In the meantime, she could enjoy this visiting baby who needed healing help.

Cuuji was cute, a plump moppet with springy red curls, and once in the hot spring she stopped crying. Livli sat in one of the rock scoops at the edge and held the little girl on her lap, letting her play and splash. No need to work the damaged arm at this stage. Several days of relaxing the muscles and ligaments would be necessary before Sister Gaddja could assess the limb and then create a treatment plan. Cuuji wasn't really a baby. She'd learned to walk a few months ago (late due to balance problems from the injured arm), and once she was fully comfortable in her new surroundings, she hopped off Livli's knees with a splash to exercise her new talent.

"Yiy! Cuuji!"

Luckily she was an early swimmer. Iloiset-lodge, Cuuji's home, was on a lake.

"Come back here, you!" Livli surged after her. The water got rapidly hotter toward the pool's middle.

"Go! Go!" crowed Cuuji.

"Oh, no. I'll get you some cups, Cuuji. But you must stay put."

"Me swim!"

"At home, you do. Not here."

Cuuji was docile under Livli's retrieval, despite the youngster's enthusiasm for a one-armed swim. Livli waded to the steps towing her patient, hoisted Cuuji to her hip, and climbed out onto the flagstone paving that edged the hot spring. The shelf holding towels and therapy tools included children's toys amongst its contents. She hadn't thought Cuuji would be ready for them this soon. It was a good sign for the little one's future.

"Bir! Bir!" Cuuji screeched excitedly in Livli's ear.

Livli paused at the window. Siajotti's not the only lodge with glass, she mused. Of course, this was the bath-hall, not the lodge proper. The healers needed to be able to see every bit as much as the scholars perusing scrolls. And since healers and patients in the hot spring went naked, the glass kept heat in the air. Hide coverings would deteriorate in moistness. Thus glass. Ha!

Livli scrutinized the clustered pines outside, wavy in the ripples of the round window panes, but couldn't see what Cuuji was pointing at. "What kind of bird?"

"Li' bir!"

"O-oh. I see." She didn't, but she did notice a slight tightening in Cuuji's shoulder. She needed to get her back in the water or she'd be whimpering again soon. "Which cup would you like first? The big one? Or this little one?"

"Li' one!"

"Okay! Here you go." Both were birch bark, wouldn't break if dropped on stone, and would float if released in water.

She worked with Cuuji all day, giving the toddler to her birth-mother for nursing and meals (and to eat and drink herself), alternating between sessions in the hot spring and gentle massage in one of the warmest closets.

Mother Gaddja managed to find a moment to check Cuuji just before supper.

The healer joined them in the water, sighing. "Let me see this little one," she said, holding a small north-bear carved of heartwood toward the baby.

Cuuji was tired, leaning back against Livli, but she cooed and reached. Gaddja let her have the bear and probed Cuuji's shoulder, her strong fingers gentle, exploring the lie of the land under the skin: collar bone, scapula, down along the humerus. "Hmm."

"She's moving it a lot more easily than she was this morning," Livli observed. "When I first got her, she kept the whole limb tightly clenched to her ribs."

Gaddja nodded. "Her arm's not as bad as I feared." Her lips crimped slightly.

"But the break adhered crookedly?"

"It's far from straight, but . . . the ligament and tendon involvement is much less than it should be. Which is excellent."

"I'm wondering . . . should I stay up with her through the night? We've placed oil lanterns in here before."

Gaddja's attention shifted abruptly from Cuuji to Livli. "Worried the stiffness will return?"

Livli nodded. "You know it will."

"Yes, I know."

"Don't you care?" Livli knew it was a nonsensical question even as she asked it. Gaddja wouldn't be a healer, if she didn't care, and care passionately. But . . . how could she be so calm?

That's why I focus on convalescents. Because I can't *stay calm.*

"Cuuji is little, but she's tougher than you think, Livli. Yes, she's going to have more pain, and you want to spare her that. But you can't. We can't. And healing *is* sufficient. Kaunis-spa cannot offer freedom from suffering, but we do offer healing. Healing *is* gift enough."

Livli sighed. She knew this. It was just harder to accept when faced with a darling tot who would be wailing by the wixting hours. Although it would be Cuuji's birth-mother who would have to deal with that, not Livli.

"How are the lung fever patients doing?"

"They'll live." Gaddja's voice was curt. "You'd think they would have had the sense to come in from the cold after falling in the beck, instead of continuing on the track of the frost leopard, but I suppose the Sundin-brothers are just as keen to pursue their calling as we are in ours. And" – now she was merely grudging – "there are too many lodges in these parts to let the creature keep hunting our flocks. Once the *onderneming* start on goats, it's only a matter of time before they try shepherd for dessert. But . . . the brothers might not have gotten lung fever, if they'd simply put on dry clothes."

"What about the mangled phalanges? And the . . . strained back?"

"Hegon gets to keep the hand. Isku . . . we'll see."

So they'd weathered the influx of newly hurt and newly injured. And Cuuji hadn't been bumped until tomorrow, because Livli had returned to take up the slack. It had been a good day.

"You're all in, Livli."

Livli nodded. She was tired. Not as tired as she'd been in the first months of her pregnancy, but tired enough.

"Go eat," instructed Gaddja. "Cuuji will be here in the morning for you, and you'll ease her then. Hold to that, and get some rest. I'll take the babe to her mother."

Livli woke before the sun was up the next day. And the sun was up early in these first days of spring. But she'd fallen into sodden sleep immediately after dinner and visited the dump-buckets only twice in the night, barely opening her eyes to navigate the corridor from her bednook.

She felt rested.

Although her bladder was bursting. And her stomach ravenous.

She took care of these pressing issues promptly, so promptly that dawn was just breaking as she emerged from the refecting-hall. The sky was pale pink over the Ita-range. The thin skimming of cloud overhead would soon burn off.

I'll plant my aegis-foil now, she decided. *If I wait much longer . . . it can't possibly work.*

Would it even work now?

I won't think about that. It had to work.

The ground under the cloches was cool, but pliable. Planting *would* be possible.

It seemed too easy, now that her search amongst the scrolls was done. She dented the soil with her fingertip – three small dimples clustered here, four over there – dropped a seed in each depression, sprinkled earth over all, and patted.

Then she fetched the watering can with the finest rose, sprinkled her plantings, and replaced the cloches. She fingered one of the vent holes located on their tops. It wouldn't let enough heat out once Nerich passed to Thyaril, but for now she need only remove the cloches when she watered each morning.

I've done it!

Did she feel different? Lighter? It was hard to tell.

I want a girl. A girl like Cuuji. Only I won't let her arm get broken. And if our bonesetter is away, I'll walk from one end of the Fiordhammars to the other to find one.

Except Kaunis-lodge had a group of healers, and they never went away. Their patients came to them.

My baby will be safer. Kaunis is the safest place to be in all Silmaren.

She scrutinized the soil under her cloches. Then laughed at herself.

You'd think I was six years and planting my first spikenard, checking to see if it had sprouted mere moments after touching earth!

What a miracle it had been when the first green peeped from underground. Six had been a good year. She hadn't minded when it was time for Sarvet to give her little brother Gaiju to Nial. She still felt guilty when she remembered that she'd been relieved. He'd been such a fussy baby. And she was tired of sharing her birth-mother with him.

Sarvet had taken Livli with her when she went to live in the moon-cabins.

Nial was there, of course. Livli spent a blissful six months hiking with Nial, playing leap-squirrel with Nial, being spoiled by Nial. Her father had always been better at splitting his attention between children than was Sarvet. Livli grew jealous only at the end of the passing-moons when Gaiju got to go home to Tukeva-lodge with Nial. Gaiju didn't appreciate his good fortune. He screamed from his father's shoulder until their path turned round an out-thrust shoulder of the mountain.

Parting with Jorgan had been much, much harder.

Livli had been ten, and was used to minding this little brother every afternoon. He was never fussy, just fun. He often asked for *her* instead of Sarvet to tell his bedtime story.

Jorgan was on his wanderyar now.

The stories he'll have when he returns! I can't wait.

She missed him.

And she wanted a girl baby, not a boy. Saying goodbye at thirty months to *her* son would be . . . impossible.

Cuuji's arm had stiffened as expected. It hurt Livli's heart to see the baby holding it close against her torso while tears rolled down her cheeks. She reached her good arm out as soon as she saw Livli. "I 'ur! I 'ur!" she sobbed. "Wawa?"

Livli cradled her. "Yes, the water will make you feel better." She paused to reassure Cuuji's mother. "The mornings will get better after a few days."

The sister nodded, obviously shaken. "Yes, Mother Gaddja said. It's just harder to see her in pain after seeing her without it yesterday. But go! I don't want to delay you one moment more!"

Livli nodded, removed her robe and hung it on a hook, then carried Cuuji to the steps into the hot spring. The currents seemed slightly warmer than before. Their temperature did vary, with a predictable cycle lasting roughly eight days. Today was right on schedule. And the moist warmth helped Cuuji so much that Gaddja assessed her arm mid-afternoon.

"That's a marvel. There simply aren't any adhesions. There should be. I couldn't believe it when I didn't detect any yesterday, but they're just not there." Gaddja smiled and leaned back.

"So . . . ?" *What did that mean for treatment?* It sounded good, but . . .

"She'll be spared the manual breaking the adhesions loose and the ice packs after. You can start directly with mobility and range of motion right here in the warm."

Livli sighed her relief. "I'm so glad. Do you know if the replacements for the floats that went walking with our last child patient are finished yet? I'd like to have her reaching for a ball tomorrow. She'll be ready, based on what I've seen her do today."

"Ask Hibma." Gaddja didn't linger. "I've got to return to the lung fevers. Both the Sundin boys are approaching crisis. Oh, they'll make it," she added. "But they need close attention."

Cuuji improved rapidly over the next three days, reaching ever farther with her arm for interesting toys, then catching a tossed ball-float, then paddling round the edges of the hot spring using *both* arms.

She was elated at being allowed to venture off Livli's lap. "Me swim! Me swim!" she crowed.

After an eight-day, she was moving both arms when she walked on dry land. Another eight-day saw her running well and swinging excitedly from pine boughs.

She was ready to go home.

Livli gave instructions to her mother about continued massage and exercises for Cuuji in the lake at Iloiset-lodge. It was hard to say farewell. She'd gotten fond of the little one.

In six moons, I'll have a little girl just like her. Well . . . like her own self, but just as precious.

Livli rubbed her belly. Was it finally rounding? She was eager to have something besides her ravenous appetite and her need for a nap mid-afternoon to show that she was expecting a baby.

The aegis-foil sprouts had emerged the day after Cuuji swam.

They boasted three pairs of leaves apiece by the time the tot departed for Iloiset-lodge. The leaves would likely be large enough for the folk ritual in two more eight-days!

When would the blossoms come?

Livli might have found it hard to concentrate on anything but her plants were it not for the fascination of returning disabled folk to health.

I do like my vocation.

Hegon, his hand bandaged, but past any danger of infection, set off for Rakas-lodge the same day that Cuuji and her birth-mother left for Iloiset. Rakas and Iloiset shared a mountain flank – unique among the Hammar-lodges in their close physical proximity – so the three of them could hike together.

Hegon would be returning to Kaunis-spa once his superficial lacerations were healed. He would need intensive work under Livli to regain the full use of his fingers.

Isku's paralysis had cleared abruptly three days prior. Gaddja speculated that his fall down the cliff face had not severed the vital spinal *styrke* as she'd feared, but merely bruised it so badly that the swelling blocked its flow. They were keeping him for observation, and Livli would start him on exercises to strengthen his entire torso once they were sure he would not relapse.

The Sundin-brothers were agitating to get out of their bednooks.

They had regained their feet, just not for long. Livli was sure they'd have taken off on their leopard hunt, if only they had the strength. Both were so weak that one brief amble around the bath-hall terraces sent each back to his nook in their cabin for more sleep. Steffi, the younger one, was especially impatient with his convalescence.

"That beast's still on the prowl! And the boys are in the high meadows now with the goats." The herd-girls were too, but it was natural a brother would be more aware of the doings in the father-lodges. "It's not safe for them."

"It's Thyaril, Steffi," Livli reminded him. "The flocks can't stay in the byres any longer. And if the goats go, the shepherds must too."

His face was exasperated. "Of course. But we've never sent them with a known killer on the loose! It's not right!"

"Won't Sundin-lodge assign someone else to the hunt?"

"Hirvie. Or Avvu." His voice was scornful. "Metsasta and I are the predator hunters. The leaf-brothers can't match the *onderneming*. In fact, you'll probably have them on your hands here when the frost leopard starts hunting *them*."

She sympathized, but her tone grew tart. *She'd* had to learn to stop for food and sleep when treating her patients. Steffi would have to learn that he must stop hunting when he became ill. "I suggest you just heal harder then," she told him. "Go take another nap."

He had the grace to laugh. "Yah. But I don't like it."

Well, she didn't like it either. But they'd just have to trust that Hirvie and Avvu were more able than Steffi thought them.

His face took on a quizzical look. "Who was that witch poking her nose in our cabin this morning?" he asked. "She had more questions than a vervet, and she didn't much like our answers."

"One of the nurses?" It didn't sound like Bija or Janina.

"I haven't seen her before," Steffi persisted. "Round face, sour expression. 'How long have you been here? When do you leave? Why did you get lung fever anyway?'"

"Thoivra." Livli shook her head. Apparently disrupting the lodge wasn't enough for that conservative matron. Now she was attempting the spa.

But I'll put a stop to it.

"Just an interfering busybody. I'll see she doesn't bother you again."

Steffi laughed. "Oh, I think I saw to that. Told her if she didn't understand lung fever she didn't belong here. And if she did, why was she asking?" He wrinkled his nose. "She went off in a huff."

The corner of Livli's mouth twitched up. *Good.*

A few days later, the last gasp of cold weather brought an unseasonable storm down from the northwest, a windy blizzard dropping snow enough to top Livli's head. The goats had to return to their byres, while the Kaunis-sisters tramped snowshoe paths between lodge and spring-house and branching-hall and bath-hall.

Two days after, the strong vernal sun had melted everything on their south-facing slope, but a thundering avalanche roared down the flanks of the Tunkahorn across the valley.

At sunset, under a sky stained clear yellow with tinges of lavender, one of the Rakas-brothers' rescue dogs brought in a buried traveler.

No Hammarleedings were missing from their lodges, but one of the Rakas-alpenhunds had whined insistently to go out. When the brothers capitulated, the dog hunted the bottom runout of the avalanche debris.

Her instinct proved quite right.

The rescued man was clearly not Hammarleeding. His hair was wooly, like that of many mountain-folk, but pale blond, and his skin, less tanned. His blue tunic was fashioned from boiled wool rather than knitted of goat hair, and beads, not crewel-work, formed its decorations. His outer cloak was not the pelt of a north-bear or feral sheep or frost leopard along with the helmet-hood created from the creature's head; instead he wore a more fitted garment sewn from reindeer leather.

Livli saw the unconscious stranger carried in by the Rakas-lodgers.

She'd been lingering in the foyer of the bath-hall, chatting with Hibma about which patients might depart for home on the morrow, when a sudden bustle outside on the terrace made her look up. The doors flew open and four Rakas-brothers marched inside, the rescued foreigner slung on a blanket between them. His bearded face was dark with cold, and his breath came and went unevenly.

Emergent healing was not Livli's expertise, but even she knew that this patient needed warmth right away, or they'd lose him.

"Help me get him undressed! Fast!" she commanded.

Hibma dashed for the store shelves, dashed back to dump four wool blankets down beside Livli, and then ran to fill six sheep bladders with water from the hot spring. Gaddja returned from checking the Sundin-brothers, took one glance at their new arrival, and pitched in. She spread all four blankets on the massage table in the closet Livli had been using (warm from its tile stove, still lit) and then turned to helping Hibma with the bladders.

Livli directed the Rakas-rescuers to transfer their now-naked patient to the padded table. She wrapped the first blanket around him and packed all six filled bladders against his covered feet, torso, and arms. Then she covered him with the remaining blankets. His color was improving already, and his breathing had steadied.

Gaddja examined his skull and neck. "No head blow," she murmured. "No injury to the spinal *styrke*. We'll have to wait on assessing for other injuries until he's warmer, but there's hope." She turned her attention to the rescue posse. "Was he unconscious when you first found him?" she asked, ushering them back into the foyer. Nodding at Livli, she closed the door to keep heat in and noise out.

Good. She'll get more of a patient history out of them than Hibma could.

Livli settled down to watch the stranger. He looked younger than he had when he first came through the doors to the bath-hall. *I bet he's older than Harral, but not so old as Davvad. Maybe twenty-nine?*

He was well-muscled, almost burly, except for a slight wasting in his left arm. What had caused the muscles to shrink there? It looked recent, as though the left arm had matched the right a year ago.

She would ask him about it when he awoke.

This did not occur before Gaddja returned however. The mother-healer tested the warmth in the closet, then touched the inside of her wrist against the man's pressure points and found him no longer chilled. She unwrapped his blankets. His clothes had protected him from abrasion and laceration, but bruises bloomed on both shins, the left thigh, the left hip, and the left arm.

Livli drew in a sharp breath. There might be bone breaks under any and all of those purple marks.

"Looks like the avalanche tumbled him into a still-standing tree," remarked Gaddja. "It's likely why the alpenhund could find him: a lot of snow rushed past while he was hung up; the bulk was beyond him instead of on top of him. He was lucky."

"I suppose lowlanders wouldn't know to avoid steep, snowy slopes in early spring. He is a lowlander, isn't he?"

Gaddja paused in her gentle probing of the injuries to glance sharply at Livli. "He's a man of the Reindeer People. Have you never seen one before?"

Livli shook her head. The golden paleness of him was fascinating. A few Hammarleedings sported red hair, but most were brunette or black-headed.

"We don't receive them often here in Kaunis-spa. They range farther north, in the territories the Silmarish lowlanders call Misstrand and Norgosstrand. But a shaman of Minmahal-tribe visited us . . . oh . . . a year ago? She was an interesting lady – believed a supernatural Deathwind Woman caused contagions by spitting – but her knowledge of anatomy and disease was spot on, for all that. We compared notes." Gaddja was re-wrapping the Reindeer man. He would chill without blankets, even in this hot closet. "Where were you then? Last Bricember year?"

"Siajotti, I think." Actually, she knew, just didn't want to admit it to Gaddja. She'd originally begun to research the notions held by her birth-mother's mother, Paiam, about boy-babies and girl-babies then. And only given it up – switching to the search for the folk tale – when the lore in the Being-truth scrolls grew utterly contradictory.

"Too bad. You'd have liked her. Conversation with the lady was an education. Despite her Deathwind Woman fixation. What was her name? Paghet? Paglunet? Paglunai? Something like that."

"How long was she here?"

"Just an eight-day. The tribe had consecrated her oldest disciple, but Pagluna worried that a complex case would strain the girl's powers." Gaddja straightened. "No true breaks in this gentleman's bones. A chance the shin's cracked, however. I'll tell Bija – she and Janina are attending tonight, aren't they?" – Livli nodded – "to keep an ice pack on it, as well as filling the hot water bladders regularly." She stepped toward the door, noticed that Livli was still seated, and paused. "Nothing more we can do for him now, you know. Bija will get some kvass into him as soon as he can swallow."

Livli shrugged.

Why am I so reluctant to leave? Surely wanting to see the color of his eyes is . . . ridiculous.

She rose, stood staring down at him for a moment, then followed Gaddja out. They would miss supper if they didn't hurry. *And I am hungry.* Her stomach growled.

The Reindeer man was conscious next morning, but not coherent. He'd developed a raging fever in the night which produced its characteristic delirium. And he spoke in a language foreign to Livli.

Gaddja said it was Tao-wika – "the tongue of the people" – and that she had learned a few words from the Reindeer shaman. Evidently she'd learned more than a few, because her instructions to the patient produced good compliance from him. He swallowed kvass and broth and willow bark tea on command, patiently endured being laved with cool water, and obediently kept to his bed.

Livli made a point of memorizing the vocabulary she heard Gaddja using.

Tubig meant water, *paliguan* meant bath, and *sabaw* meant broth.

My birth-mother never limited herself to just the Aidinkieli, her tongue of origin.

Sarvet spoke the Istrian of the Giralliyan Empire, the Hammish of Silmaren's lowlanders, the Florish used by all the peoples around the Merovessic Sea, and the Pavese of Pavelle and Cambers.

I want that breadth of knowledge too! Suddenly the dead and ancient languages Livli had acquired from the oldest scrolls in Siajotti were no longer enough.

Bija, doing a lot of the nursing, mastered a smattering of Tao-wika also, just enough to get by with.

Livli wanted more than that, and when their patient's fever ebbed he proved an able teacher.

Mananalaysay meant storyteller, *ritwal-pakain* meant rite-nourisher, and *tatlumgpung taon* meant thirty years.

Livli learned that her tutor's name was Malaka-degg, that he'd sought Kaunis-spa – *Hirsamokki*, in his tongue – in hope of healing for his shoulder, and that he was not worried for the brother who'd accompanied him on his journey. The two had become separated during the blizzard, but Kanya-degg was a hunter. He'd be okay.

Malaka-degg seemed to share Livli's interest in fluency. He traded words with her, one Aidinkieli for each Tao-wika.

And his eyes were agate green.

❧ ❧ ❧

Birth-joy was late in Thyaril this year.

The last baby due from Bounty in Jubiante arrived mid-month, and its mother needed recovery time before the fete-day.

Four fathers visited to greet their newly born offspring, along with three brothers who were expecting children. Mahde, Livli's linking-friend, was one of the later.

She met him on the lodge-porch, clasping his hands.

He kissed her cheek.

"You're well?" he questioned anxiously.

She nodded smiling. "And you?"

He looked taken aback. "Of course I'm well."

Celebratory rituals – a noontide calling to ask the Divine Mother's blessing on the children; a feast featuring luxuries such as sturgeon roe, fermented butter pudding, and an omelet of rock dove eggs; and the ceremonial gift giving – delayed any real conversation, but eventually the interval sacred to the new fathers and their babies yielded time for it in the afternoon.

Livli proposed walking while talking. The press of work in the spa had kept her close to home. She wanted to really stretch her legs – and see views other than the familiar ones from Kaunis.

"Let's take the Vrea-way toward Tunkahorn," she suggested.

Mahde's eyes – beautiful blue eyes – widened. "Surely you should rest . . . let's find a sunny glade in the Vyssa-grove. The trees will shelter you from the wind."

She laughed. "I'm not delicate, Mahde. Really. It's good for expecting mothers to be active."

His laugh – still nervous – echoed hers. "I'm as bad as Harral last year, aren't I? We teased him. It was his second, after all. But . . ."

Livli started down the slope toward the valley-rock. Mahde swung in beside her. "How is little Salmo?" he asked.

"Darling," she answered. "He's just learning to walk, and his method is . . . charming. You know how most babies hang on their mother's hands for the balance they don't yet have?"

Mahde wrinkled his forehead.

Hmm. Boy babies were over two before they transferred to the father-lodges. Mahde probably *hadn't* seen young ones learning to walk.

"Well, they do. Most mothers are heartily sick of it after an eight-day – their backs hurt – and it goes on for much longer than that. But Salmo refuses all assistance. He actually cries if you try to hold him and crows when you let him go."

"So what's his method?" Mahde glanced tenderly at her belly, then blushed.

Was he hoping for a son? *I want a daughter.*

"He gets his feet under himself squatting, teeters there until he steadies, then pushes up straight and teeters some more. Then sits down. And does it again and again and again. He hasn't yet actually taken one step, but he will soon. He's getting really steady. And he's adorably cute."

Mahde grinned. "What method do you think our baby will chose?"

Livli shrugged. "Who knows? But I hope she doesn't follow in Nikko's footsteps."

"Davvad's son?"

She nodded. "He's not a puller-upper either, but he's wholly different from Salmo. Nikko springs to his feet like a chipmunk leaping for bluejay eggs, pumps his legs furiously in a run while holding his hands straight up over his head, and then thumps down with a bump when his balance fails."

Mahde laughed – fully relaxed this time – at the picture her words conjured.

"It would be funny," she agreed, "if it weren't also alarming. Nikko's fine in a room or, better, a corridor, but yesterday he was on the porch and his run carried him right over the lip of the steps. Girste nearly broke her own neck tumbling after him."

Mahde's eyes had widened again. "He's alright, isn't he?"

"He's fine. But Girste's hip has the mother of all bruises."

Mahde sighed. "I guess we'll just have to wait and see. But . . . do you truly want a daughter?"

"Don't you?" She had thought he wanted a daughter. He'd *said* he wanted a daughter. Would he be really disappointed if the rockfoil worked? *It has to work.*

"We-ell, I did. During our sweet-moon."

"But not now?"

He looked at her, seemed to sense a hint of her inner strain, and visibly changed his answer. "Yes, I do. Of course I do."

Livli sighed.

She *liked* Mahde. She liked him a lot. They'd been friends since babyhood. She actually had a really early memory of sitting in a patch of sunlight in the Vyssa-grove with him sitting next to her. It was before either of them could walk, she was pretty sure. And they'd been making faces at each other and giggling.

They'd stayed friends even after he went to Tukeva-lodge with his father. They were still friends.

But we don't have that special something that connects Sarvet and Nial.

And Livli found herself impatient with Mahde's flashes of timidity more often than she liked. They didn't occur often . . . but his tendency to avoid conflict was annoying. Why couldn't he just say what he really thought?

"Mahde . . . it's alright if you find yourself wanting a son after all. It's not like we either of us has any say. We get what we get." *Except . . . I hope that's not true. I hope I do have a say . . . with the rockfoil.*

Mahde blushed again. "Yah. The new fathers . . . watching their eagerness grow over the last month in Tukeva-lodge. In Bricember I wasn't sure I was ready to be a father. Which I know was wrong of me. Brother Gealbu who prepares the novices before Other-joy, pounds it in without mercy: if you're not ready to welcome a son, wait to link with a sister. But, now I *am* eager to welcome a son. Which is good, Livli. We might *have* a son. Wretched for him if I weren't eager."

It was true. Livli might be growing a boy within her. And she'd been comfortable with that when she'd started this journey.

Hammarleeding women gave birth to girls and boys. The girls stayed in the mother-lodge forever. The boys went to the father-lodge when they turned two and a half years. It was the way things were done. She'd never guessed she'd feel so differently once she'd conceived her child.

She remembered how casually Sarvet had parted from Jorgan, Livli's youngest brother.

I was there.

Sarvet kissed him on the cheek, put him into Nial's arms, and said, "I love Tukeva-lodge, Jorgan. You'll love it too. And I'll come visit you in a month."

Livli had been holding back tears. *If I cry, Jorgan might cry too. I can't do that to him.* And she'd succeeded. Succeeded too well, because once Nial and Jorgan were gone, the tears were gone too. *I'd have done better to cry then.* But she couldn't. And Sarvet hadn't realized how shaken her daughter was.

We went on. And I buried the memory. I even enjoyed the visit to Tukeva-lodge. It was fun.

But now that her own baby would be born in Jubiante, the memory had surfaced. And she wanted a daughter.

"It *is* good, Mahde," she answered her linking-brother. "Sarvet would say I had sinned, asking you to link when you weren't ready just so I could become a mother."

Mahde's timidity vanished, and he slung an arm over her shoulders. "Don't you dare tell me you didn't enjoy our sweet-moon! You've never laughed so much in your life!"

It was true. The sweet-moon had been fabulous. And Mahde was ready for fatherhood now, even if he hadn't been then. But . . . she hadn't thought things through. She couldn't have.

Why hadn't one of her sisters managed to explain to her that *imagining* being a mother and *being* a mother were so utterly different.

I thought I knew everything I needed to know. I thought I could shape my life myself, not wait on . . . synchronicity. So she'd gone ahead. And one of her mistakes – trading on Mahde's ambivalence – had rectified itself. But the hidden problem . . . was still a problem. *I'll fix it,* she told herself fiercely. *I am fixing it.*

Thoivra was waiting on the Kaunis veranda when Livli and Mahde returned to the lodge.

The matron was a dumpy woman who liked dressing in bright colors. Livli might have spotted her from a distance if she'd been paying attention, but Mahde kept making her laugh, and they'd never looked up while climbing the mountain slope toward home. Thoivra's tunic featured orange and purple and sky blue today. Her face featured pursed lips.

Mahde hastily removed his arm from Livli's shoulders.

"Healing-sister!" admonished Thoivra, ignoring Mahde, "you shouldn't be alone in your situation!"

Livli thought about replying with the obvious – *Mahde's with me* – but decided on discretion. "Did you need my help?"

Thoivra's face soured further.

She'll turn into a preserved quince, if she's not careful.

"Yes, I did, sister. I want to know how long that foreign trespasser is staying in the spa. You're giving the male patients too many weeks. Weeks better spent on sisters." Thoivra's tone on *male* matched her face.

Livli pursed her own lips. Mahde squirmed, but didn't sidle off.

"No sister patient is being neglected, I assure you," Livli asserted.

"Then they're being annoyed!" snapped Thoivra. "The last thing a sister wants when she's sick is to have to deal with a brother."

"Do you have a specific complaint?" Livli probed. *I will keep calm.* "Does one of your acquaintance need something? More privacy? We can switch bednooks."

Thoivra looked outraged. "Isn't it obvious that the mere presence of a male, and a foreign one at that, isn't conducive to healing? I want that interloper gone. And a lot sooner than those Sundin-brothers! Who also lingered over long."

Livli's patience thinned. "Sister. I suggest you confine yourself to your own business. Which the spa is not. But if you truly have a grievance, take it to the mother-healer."

Thoivra's eyes narrowed. "That foreigner is your patient. And I suggest you not force me to seek authority. You won't like the result."

Now the mittens were off.

"No. *You* won't like the result, Thoivra. Gaddja will never permit your meddling."

Thoivra sniffed, spat, "She won't have a choice when our lodge-mother weighs in," and flounced away, not acknowledging Livli's parting words: "Don't count Gaddja weak. She isn't."

Mahde didn't wait until the angry matron was out of earshot. "What a nasty old besom! She can't really order the healers around, can she, Livli?"

"No, but her complaints seem to be getting louder. I'd been hoping whatever bee's buzzing in her balaclava would quiet. As it is . . ." Livli sighed, then shook her head. "Never mind her. She's more shout than spank."

Mahde grinned and slung his arm back over Livli's shoulders.

She checked the rockfoil next morning after the fathers and brothers departed. Its flower spikes were covered in buds, hard little kernels of gray-green. *In an eight-day . . . just an eight-day . . . there will be blooms!* Her step had a bounce as she walked to the bath-hall.

Gaddja met her on the terrace. The day was windy, but fine, and the pines of the Vyssa-grove sheltered the area. They discussed Livli's current batch of patients – who was ready to depart, who could move to more advanced exercises, and who must take a hiatus from treatment due to a set-back. At the end of this listing, Livli stepped toward the spa doors.

Gaddja stopped her with a touch to the back of her hand. Weren't they finished?

"I think you might start Malaka-degg on something gentle today. He's still weak from his lung fever, but in no danger of relapsing."

Livli felt her face light up. "Really?"

Gaddja lifted a quizzical eyebrow. "Indeed, yes. You'll need to assess him, of course. Didn't he have a chronic shoulder complaint? In addition to the injuries he picked up in the avalanche?"

"Yes, frozen shoulder. And I suspect we will need to achieve some success there, before we start on the hip injury. But I'll do the evaluation, before I develop a plan of treatment."

The Reindeer man evinced enthusiasm when he realized Livli intended more than a cursory check. But he calmed his excited words almost before he'd started talking, recalling Livli's limited vocabulary.

She'd been watching how he moved during their language lessons, but now she marked precisely the range of motion that he had with his left limbs. The bruises were fading rapidly, and his shin bone was clearly intact. More serious was a rip in the soft tissue holding the hip together. She'd suspected he might have a labral tear.

She repressed the frown she felt drawing her brows down – no good ever came of discouraging a patient – and went on to examine the shoulder. She had to restrain him from pushing the limits of his arm range.

"Do not," she told him in halting Tao-wika. "Forcing hurts."

He grimaced at this truism.

She tried again. "Forcing hurts *healing*."

"Ah." Now he understood and did what she wanted, moving the arm only so far as he could go without pain.

She probed the shoulder joint itself, then checked along the clavicle in front and the scapula in back. The classic mix of tight spots amidst relaxed ones told her much, but his double disability would make treatment tricky. He shouldn't lean on that arm. *Could* he walk? They'd been bringing a dump bucket to him, rather than allowing him to leave his bed.

She helped him reach his feet, and . . . hmmm. He could walk, but not without a slight dislocation in the hip joint.

Very well, they'd have to use the carry sling. It was good he was a medium-statured man. With his muscles, if he were tall, he'd have been too heavy for four woman. Good also that no patients needed night nursing right now. She summoned all of the nurse-sisters.

When Malaka-degg realized they intended to carry him, he protested, "No, no, no. I walk. Hurts, yes, but I walk." He didn't sound stubborn, just worried.

How can I make him know that we're strong enough?

In the end, she couldn't. But he did respond to her reiterations of "please!"

Bija and Behkka took the handles on one side, Ilina and Janina on the other, and Malaka-degg gingerly sat on the woven fabric of the sling's seat.

It held.

They made the short trip from his closet to the hot spring without incident.

His eyes widened again when he saw Livli removing her robe. Not surprising, really. Many first-time visitors to Kaunis-spa were a little startled when they realized that treatment in the hot-spring would be delivered and received naked. But the heavy wool of outer garments would definitely impede the process, and even the thinner thistle-silk of the inner ones (or the spa robes) would get in the way. The nurse-sisters lowered Malaka-degg onto the small bench beside the spring's steps, and he allowed himself to be disrobed without comment.

Livli slipped into the water. *Oof! but it was hot today!* Or maybe that was just her pregnancy making her overly warm.

She guided her patient in careful moves from bench to paving to underwater ledge. She didn't want him stressing that hip joint in any way for several weeks. She scrutinized his face. He looked alert and interested, his green eyes darting around the space. Was the heat too much for him? No, he was flushed, but not sweating. Was this ledge deep enough? Not quite. She wanted that shoulder fully submerged.

She gestured, and he slid along the ledge to the place where it stepped downward another notch.

Good.

She took his arm and began moving it gently, forward, then out to the side, not toward the back or across the chest. That would come much later. He let her have the limb, not trying to direct it himself.

Very good. She smiled and nodded.

Many patients had trouble with this. Giving over control of one's own body could be disconcerting. Malaka-degg was not a passive man. She'd sensed his authority even in his feverish delirium. But authority rested easily on him, as though he'd worn it for an appreciable length of time. He was easy with sharing control.

She checked the underlying musculature again. *Excellent.* Even further relaxed.

The knotted spots stood out like hailstones in a blanket of new snow. She reached for her knob-stick at the spring's edge. "Tell me if the pressure" – she pressed one of the knobs firmly against his palm – "pressure, is too much." He nodded. She had him shift sideways to give her access to both his back and front, then began a gentle massage of the knots in his flesh. The tightest ones were actually beneath the edge of his scapula, and she had to switch to the smallest knob on her stick. Her work today was not aimed at easing the tightness, but rather at beginning a dialogue with the stuck bits. The problem in these cases was not purely a muscular or skeletal one that massage could fix, but had something to do with how the body communicated with itself.

After a brief interval of simple touch treatment, she set the knob-stick aside and switched to the discipline of the duoja-gift, allowing her eyelids to lower and her awareness to brush her own internal systems.

The rhythm of the touch treatment had relaxed her, too. In her mind's eye she could see the brilliance of her cruces or roots – especially the core ones of fundus, belly, plexus, heart, throat, brow, and crown – and the more subtle glow of the branches connecting them.

Gently she widened the flow of energy through her roots, letting it trickle along her branches and out through her fingertips into Malaka-degg's shoulder knots. He started at the first whisper of tingling, just the slightest twitch, then returned to ease. Livli followed the pattern she'd created using the knob-stick. Touch, touch, touch along the collarbone. Touch, touch, touch up and around the capsule. Touch, touch, touch along the inner edge of the blade bone.

She kept the session short, finishing with a light continuous stroke, then hovering her palm momentarily off her patient's skin. She raised her eyelids to see him gazing at her in bemusement.

"The Reindeer People have not the . . . the" – she had no idea what he would call it – "boon of the healer?"

He reclaimed his poise. "*Paglunas,* yes. But the *manggagamot* use" – he rubbed a hand against the opposite wrist – "not *bibiggay*" – he waved three fingers in the air.

Ah. His people did have . . . something . . . but he'd not experienced it. Why hadn't his healer tried this *bibiggay*? She nodded, then shook her head. They'd explore this another time. It was time to leave the water.

Getting Malaka-degg out of the hot spring was straightforward. The four nurse-sisters descended into the water with the carry sling, slipped it under his buttocks, and simply climbed up the steps with him. Livli fetched his robe and her own before they moved to his closet.

Once settled there, she let him know to expect another session after the noon dinner.

He nodded, but gestured to the tray-table beside the massage bench. "Join me? Trade words?"

She hesitated. The idea held definite appeal . . . but she'd planned to hurry through her meal and review her notes from Siajotti. She wanted to be ready when the aegis-foil bloomed. "Supper?" she countered.

He looked slightly rueful, not at her answer exactly; perhaps at his own lack of hostly wherewithal.

"I'll give instructions in the kitchens," she told him. "And . . . thank you. It's a good notion."

For one thing, his treatment would progress more smoothly, especially as his abilities advanced, with complete communication. For another, she'd learn more Tao-wika, faster, if they conversed. *And I want to learn more. I doubt Sarvet knows Tao-wika.* Livli's birth-mother had gone south, not north, during her wanderyar.

Livli worked with three more patients that morning, then checked the rockfoil plants on her way to the refecting-hall. Were the buds a little less gray, a little more reddish? Maybe.

I need make sure the glass goblet, the glass pitcher, the pottery crock, and the crystallized honey are all that I need.

Her plan to hurry through her meal lasted no longer than the time it took her to find a seat at the long table beside the front windows.

The earlier breezes had stilled, and the day was warm. The kitchen-sisters had removed most of the hide coverings, and the view across the sunlit Vrea-vale was beguiling. Lowland grasses glowed bright spring green, and the wild pears were in bloom.

Niyena, another healing-sister in Kaunis-spa, gestured for Livli to join her, strengthening Livli's inclination to linger.

I've been so preoccupied, we've spoken only in passing, she realized in surprise. But it wasn't guilt that motivated her. She really liked Niyena. They'd apprenticed together under Gaddja, as well as sharing the linking-rite and sweet-moon last Bricember.

Have I been worried she's jealous that I'm with child and she is not? Surely not. This healing-sister wasn't the jealous sort. Nor one to hold grudges. Niyena smiled, her smooth red hair gleaming in the sunlight, clearly glad for her friend's company in an unhurried moment. Livli moved closer and sat.

"Glorious, isn't it?" Niyena declared, waving one hand at the open windows.

Livli found herself grinning. She offered a sideways, sitting hug. It was *good* to see Niyena and have a chance to catch up.

Over the salad of fresh greens, goat cheese, and smoked chevon, they talked shop. Niyena focused on acutely ill or injured patients – rather than chronic ones – and also worked with the wilding-sisters to weave together the disciplines of herbalism and duoja-gift treatments. She always had some new tidbit of knowledge to share.

"Mother Sunna thinks that the fragrant nut oil from southern Giralliya might prevent common colds! Wouldn't it be incredible if we could lessen winter illness?"

"Only if you like helping the sisters in the spinning-hall!" answered Livli. "Even if we doubled our output of woolens, we'd not be able to trade for enough *kokos-oliu* for everybody."

Niyena wrinkled her nose, chuckling. "You would have to point that out! I hate colds." Livli tilted her head. Who could disagree?

Their talk drifted after they gathered crisps and poured themselves mugs of kerin-tea – Livli's pregnancy and health: good; Niyena's social turmoil: over; threats from her sweet-sister retracted; plans for the summer: enticing, with Livli's baby to arrive and Niyena to visit Oikessa-lodge by the sea!

On their walk back to the bath-hall, Livli urged her friend to a detour. The day was fine; it deserved their appreciation. And . . . she wanted to ask Niyena about a snippet of gossip she'd heard a few weeks back.

The path along the porches of the spa cabins wound uphill through the Vyssa-grove, eventually emerging from the pines on the grassy slopes of the alpine meadows. Livli waved to the distant herd-sister watching the goats there and perched on a convenient rock. She hadn't wanted to disturb the peace from their woodland stroll, but she'd better speak, if she were going to speak. Niyena settled beside her, stating: "Something's worrying you."

Livli began obliquely. "Have you heard some of the murmuring? Thoivra and her cronies?"

"Just talk," scoffed Niyena. "There's always somebody thinking we should either 'return to the golden age' or else 'leap forward into our golden future.' Thoivra's a ninny anyway."

"Mmm." Livli shifted. *Should've visited the dump-buckets before I left the lodge.* No help for that now.

She continued: "But I've seen Sister Ulvve with them lately. She seemed in sympathy with their complaints. She's always tended toward . . . a traditional viewpoint."

"Oh." Niyena's offhand breeziness deflated. "Hmm. That's . . .

concerning." Sister Ulvve attended on the Kaunis lodge-mother and was deep in Seagga's counsel.

"I thought so. You know they've been suggesting that the brothers of Rakas-lodge found a brother-spa to treat men. That we welcome only women here at Kaunis."

Niyena snorted. "That won't work. What would they have us do when someone like Malaka-degg shows up on our terrace? Turn him away?"

"Maybe. This 'return to simplicity and tradition' idea seems to be gathering strength. Sarvet says that when she was a girl, the division between brother-lodges and sister-lodges was much wider. She and Nial saw one another only three or four times a year before their linking! And no sister had ever, *ever*, visited Tukeva lodge."

"That's crazy!" exclaimed Niyena. "Just as crazy as turning injured men away from Kaunis-spa to die en route to Rakas. And Rakas doesn't have a healing spring!"

"Thoivra says they could just use the lake."

"The lake! As though any water counts as healing water."

Livli sat silent a moment.

"And you saw Ulvve listening to this drivel? Seriously listening?" probed Niyena.

Livli sighed. "No. They weren't talking specifics right then, just generalities: sisters are less feminine than they used to be; sisters and brothers are better apart; less contact breeds mystery, the heart of our worship."

"Ugh."

"Ugh," agreed Livli.

"Does Mother Gaddja know?"

"I haven't asked, but she's not your remote eyes-on-the-sky type. I'd be surprised if she didn't."

"Make sure."

"Yes. But, Niyena, I think *we* should do something. Not leave it all to our elders. They're the ones most likely to favor a return to those 'good old days' when brothers were brothers, sisters were sisters, and the wild sheep all grew denser wool."

Niyena cocked an eyebrow. "Like your birth-mother and hers?"

A snort escaped Livli. "Well, no. But you know they're . . . unusual."

"Ha! Unusual, huh? Rebels, both."

"Paiam says she was the most traditional sister in Kaunis during Sarvet's childhood."

"I bet." Niyena shook her head. "Not! But I don't think the old ones are the ones to worry about. They lived under the old ways and . . . they like the new ones better. Most of them," she added. "It's sisters like Thoivra, the matrons, vaguely dissatisfied with life and seeking . . . something to fill that gap. They're the ones who will push this."

"And Mother Seagga? Will she hear them? I never pegged her as linked to the old ways."

"No, but she's absolutely knitted to hearing the 'voices of the lodge.' If enough sisters speak loud enough . . ." Niyena sighed. "I wish your birth-mother hadn't declined the appointment. She knows how to listen without ceding authority. Why did she? Decline it?"

"Sarvet?"

Niyena nodded.

"She likes exploring, not governing. There's a reason she was the first sister to take a wanderyar."

"She's not doing much wandering as Holy Caller."

"She says she's got two frontiers to explore: the mind and spirit of the women under her aegis, and all of the past as recorded in Siajotti's scrolls."

"Huh." Niyena frowned. "Listen, you should talk to Mimmi, Oaja, and Risten. I'll try Suoina, Vohkku, and Rahkel. At supper. And we can see where we are after evening rounds."

"Umm."

"Livli! It's the spa at risk!"

"That's not what I meant. I'm eating supper with Malaka-degg."

"Postpone it till the morrow," suggested Niyena.

"I need to get up to speed in Tao-wika. Quickly," Livli insisted. And flushed. "His progress depends upon it."

Niyena leaned her chin on one hand. "Like him, do you?"

Livli straightened and said with dignity, "I don't think that's appropriate, healing-sister. I'm rising to the challenge of treating someone with linguistic limitations."

Niyena gave over her teasing. "Yah, alright. But you will speak with Mother Gaddja? To be sure? Or should I?"

"I'll do it. I see her more often, ever since you started concentrating on wilding lore. And I'll talk with my friends over the next few days." Livli paused. "I am . . . not worried . . . but this isn't something to ignore. That's why . . ."

"You brought it up." Niyena stood. "Come on. We're late for afternoon rounds."

"And I need the dump-buckets or I'll burst."

"Use a tree, for Sias' sake!"

"Niyena! Ugh!"

"I think being pregnant should give you *some* concessions."

"It does. That's why Gaddja sends me off to put my feet up every afternoon at tea time. Using a tree is *not* a concession I want." She followed her friend along the path back into the pine trees.

Supper with Malaka-degg that evening proved more interesting than she'd thought possible, given their limited ability to talk to one another. *He must be a natural linguist,* she mused, *and I . . . am learning faster than I thought I could.*

Their conversation was a garbled mix of Aidinkieli and Tao-wika, but they managed to communicate clearly for all that.

"So, what does a rite-nourisher do?" she asked, leaning forward and spearing a morsel of herbed cheese with her skewer.

"You have 'holy caller' to nurture souls of your sisters?" he responded.

"Yes, my birth-mother is the Caller of Kaunis-lodge."

"That what I do for Minmahal-tribe."

She learned that the rites of the Reindeer People included *panahon-himala,* a wind-magic similar to her own healing duoja-gift. Malaka-degg used it in the ceremonies he conducted to directly bring the cruxes and branches into the worship experience. That was very different from the Hammarleeding way, which featured the duoja-gift in its programs, but used only words and singing to induce awe. Malaka-degg was not merely a religious leader, but a shaman-priest with magic at his fingertips. Did he follow spiritual laws to ensure the well-being of his tribe-folk, just as she obeyed a healing oath to do no harm to her patients?

She shivered, noticing that her left hand had moved to shield her belly. *Am I safe?*

He reached to touch her shoulder. "I make a vow to . . . heal? . . . only *help* . . . the eyes and the . . . the reaches. Only in the *kamatayan-ritwal* do I close the eyes. Other *ritwal,* I . . . help and heal."

That sounded even more alarming. He *closed* the cruxes? But she felt easier. His culture had rules, just as hers did, to protect its members.

"What is *kamatayan-ritwal*?" Obviously a ceremony of some sort, but she wanted to know more.

"When someone die . . . gates of eyes open. Demon can escape unless eye is closed. I shut."

Ah, that made sense. Hammarleedings smoothed the branches of their dead before burial, not the cruxes. Malaka-degg's people must sooth the cruxes – *eyes* – not the . . . what did he call the branches . . . *reaches*, that was it.

He talked about the last time he'd performed this particular custom, a few months before he'd departed to seek healing for his shoulder. "My helpmeet . . . she ill for long."

Dear Sias! He meant his linking-sister. Livli reached for *his* shoulder. "I am so sorry."

"Niya." He shook his head. "The long illness, her pain, that bad. The dying . . . Wind-goddess take away all pain, bless the last days. Sweet."

"But . . . you miss her. Surely."

"Yes, always."

He paused, reminding her of Sarvet with Sister Brionne, when Brionne's mother died. *I can't believe* he *wants to comfort* me. *This is his loss.* But he was a spiritual counselor before a bereaved linking-brother, apparently.

"Livli, her *life* good and happy. That . . . important."

Yes, but it was hard to contemplate death, when she herself was approaching birth. *Let my baby be well. Let my birth be . . . protected.*

Malaka-degg changed the subject. "When baby born, I *open* the eyes. Better, yes?"

She smiled. "Tell me about your celebrations to welcome a child into the world."

He did.

The birth-festivals of the Reindeer People were raucous and merry. The *tambulero* beat her wide, flat drum while the *kalansingors* shook their rattles. Wine was drunk, red and white ribbons twirled, kisses exchanged.

I wish I could do that when my daughter is born.

Hammarleeding birth-fetes were . . . not solemn – joy was predominant – but less frivolous.

The next few days were busy. Mother Gaddja did know about Thoivra and her cohorts, but her savvy was of little use. "Not to worry, Livli. Sisters are sisters in any year. This will blow over."

"But you're talking with our lodge-mates? I think Thoivra has the voice to make trouble."

"I doubt it's necessary. Most of Kaunis is busy with ordinary life. They leave the spa to us healers."

"They'll care fast enough, if Thoivra points to our brotherly patients as sources of corruption!"

Gaddja laughed. And laughed. "Oh, that's too ridiculous," she sighed, wiping her cheeks.

Since Livli couldn't bring the Mother-healer to take the threat seriously, she tackled the conversations with her childhood friends with greater alacrity than she'd felt under Niyena's urging. She'd grown apart from Risten and Mimmi and Oaja during her apprenticeship, but some affection between them would always remain.

Mimmi was easily found.

This was a busy season for the kitchen gardens, and the green-sister enjoyed getting her hands dirty. Livli detoured from a routine check on her aegis-foil plants, trolling through rows of radishes and neeps and knob celery. Mimmi, emerging from the tool shed with a trug, saw Livli first and pounced on her eagerly.

"I'd been wondering how you were! Where've you been? Did you visit Siajotti again? Did the corner of the skirret bed work for your seeds? Are you finished with the queasy insides yet?"

She plunked her trug down at her feet and beamed.

Livli leaned forward to receive the embrace Mimmi clearly wanted to offer. *I should seek her out . . . not more often, but more regularly. She's not clever, but no one has a warmer heart.*

"I'm very well. And, yes, the nausea is over with, thank Sias!"

Mimmi grinned. "And your seeds? Aegis rock-foil, right? They should be blooming tomorrow or the next day, if this warmth continues."

"Oh, I hope so!" She'd not meant to let vehemence into her utterance, but Mimmi seemed not to notice.

"Have you been sipping purslane tea? I've heard it strengthens the baby's blood. Wild leek conserve, too. Oh, and beet kvass." Mimmi captured Livli's hand and squeezed. "Can't be too careful!"

"Thanks, Sister Marja has me under her eye, and I'm doing everything right.

"Good. That's good." Mimmi sighed. "Oh, Livli! I just can't wait to hold your daughter! You have to let me watch her for you sometimes!"

"I'll be glad to. You know you're wonderful with children. But Mimmi" – she had to stem the gusts of her friend's enthusiasm, or they'd spend her entire break time discussing pregnancy and babies – "what do you think of Sister Thoivra's notion that Kaunis-spa should not heal brothers? Do you think that's right? Or fair?"

Mimmi's brow wrinkled. "I . . . does it matter? There are enough sisters to fill the spa, surely. You wouldn't lose your place, would you, Livli?"

Trust Mimmi to worry for her friends first.

"That's sweet of you, but no that's not what I'm concerned about. The waters of our hot spring help sick and injured folk heal. I don't feel that anyone who can get here – sister or brother – should be deprived of their benefit."

"Oh!" Mimmi didn't like that notion either. "I see. No, that's not kind."

"I think that Sister Thoivra may work to make that happen."

Mimmi's face grew downcast. "Oh, Livli, is there anything we can do?"

"Why, I hope so. That's why I'm talking with you about it. If enough of us speak out against Thoivra, the lodge-mother will listen."

"Speak out . . . but, Sister Thoivra is . . . older, wiser. I don't like to go against her."

"It may not come to that. I hope it won't. If Thoivra can't get many to join her murmurings, Mother Seagga will just quash it. Do you think you might speak of treating brother patients as the compassionate thing to do when you're just among your friends? Privately?"

Mimmi's face cleared. "Oh, yes! I can do that. And" – uncharacteristically, she firmed her chin – "I will! You can count on me, Livli."

Well. That went better than I thought it would.

The conversation with Oaja was less promising.

Livli saw her the next afternoon plucking goatsweed in the lower meadows. The wilding-sister was intent on her work, separating roots and courm into one pouch, leaves and stem into another. She didn't look up even when Livli stopped right next to her.

"Oaja?"

"Mmm?" Her gaze still directed downward, she pulled the flaps to her pouches closed, then bent to pick another bunch of goatsweed.

"Oaja."

Now she glanced up. "Oh . . . Livli . . ." She sounded almost as though she were saying, "Oh . . . I wonder if I should try the salt-herb in the upper meadows . . ."

Oaja had always been the dreamy sort. Livli had thought her mysterious, glamorous even, when they were younger. At the moment . . . well, Oaja still exerted an exotic fascination. Her eyes wandered across Livli's face. "Do you feel it?" she asked.

"Feel what?"

"The is-ness of the day, the promise of all? There's a fullness to the sky."

"Umm . . . it *is* lovely: warm sun, cool breeze."

"No, *that's* not it." Oaja's gaze sharpened. "Mere weather," she dismissed. "I mean the way the middle is full, and the distance equally so. The wilding-greens should hold perfection on a day like this."

Livli hadn't a notion what Oaja meant. *Maybe this is why I'm a healer, not a gathering-sister.* But Oaja undoubtedly perceived something. She wasn't just speaking mystically to be interesting. The wilding-mother claimed that Oaja's finds were always fresher, more potent than those of anyone else. And Oaja could locate the rarest of plants when no one else could. She possessed a gift.

"I'm glad," offered Livli.

"I wish you could feel it. The richness of it is . . ." Oaja sighed.

"Maybe I do feel it, just not here amidst things with shoots and leaves. Maybe I feel it in the hot spring when a patient moves a paralyzed limb or takes weight on a palsied foot."

Oaja tilted her head, considering. "Yes . . . I think that is so." She smiled. "I should have known to expect you, Livli. The very mountain is singing of you. How could you do else than walk its slopes here."

Great Sias! Today seemed much like yesterday to her. If it were special . . . should she somehow reap its benefit? And how?

"If I performed the blessing rite this evening, would it do more for me than if I left it till tomorrow?" she asked.

Oaja's eyes turned soft again. "Oh, tomorrow holds even more promise. Wait till then."

"I will." And she would. Not for a blessing rite, but for the aegis-foil. The first petals had emerged that morning. The flowers would be fully open on the morrow.

"Worry leads to action, I know," mused Oaja, "and action is good. Would that you might arrive there with less worry."

"I'm not a big worrier," insisted Livli. *How does she know? I've hardly said anything intelligible.* "But I am worried by Sister Thoivra's wish to expel the brothers from Kaunis-spa."

"Oh . . . Thoivra merits no worry. I meant . . ." – she didn't finish her thought.

Livli shook her head. Oaja's discernment was uncanny, but her communication was more cryptic than Livli preferred. *Was* Oaja talking about Livli's baby? Or something else? *I'm not going to be side-tracked. Not this time.*

"Thoivra may merit no worry, but I think she does merit action. Have you heard her go on? About the purity of the sister-lodge and the health nurtured by purity?"

"You've heard her."

"Obviously. Have you?"

"Perhaps."

"And?"

"Her aura taints my vision. I avoid her." Oaja resumed work on the goatsweed, cutting the stems at their base, sorting the plant parts. "Livli, one's own calling is enough. Walk through today's steps. Your own."

"I think my day's steps include this: talking with you about

Thoivra. Mother Seagga won't ignore Thoivra. She attends to the voices of *all* the sisters. It's important that I – and you – raise ours."

Oaja finished her sorting. She looked up, meeting Livli's eyes squarely. "Very well. I'm listening."

"Thoivra intends the Tukeva-brothers to return to the old ways of visiting Kaunis-lodge, but thrice per year and never welcoming sisters to their lodge at all. She also wants Kaunis-spa to admit only sisters. Neither foreigners (with their impure ways) nor brothers. I think those of us who don't agree with her should do our own murmuring, about how the children benefit from seeing both birth-mother and sweet-father as they grow."

Oaja was listening, but her eyes were distant, void of sympathy.

"Oaja, can't you see? What if my baby's a boy? And I never see him after he goes to the father-lodge?" She hadn't meant to say so much. But it was the truth. Not the only truth, but the heart-truth that scared her most.

Oaja's face turned suddenly sad. "I'm not a murmurer. You mustn't expect it of me."

No, she wasn't. But wouldn't she do anything to help?

"When the cusp is here, I will speak."

"I'd rather avoid a crisis."

"But fever burns out contagion, does it not?"

Livli nodded.

"So."

And that . . . was that. Oaja urged her friend to trust in the goodness that came from walking one's own journey and sent her on her way.

I'd hoped for something more definitive, but I suppose I should have known better. You'd think Oaja was ninety or more, if not for the way she dances in the Ponce-ring at herd-luring. The image of Oaja spinning and laughing – arms flung overhead, curly strawberry hair flaring wide – captured Livli's memory. Oaja was young, alright, but young unlike any other sister in the Fiordhammars. *I'd wager my teeth on it.*

That afternoon's treatment of Malaka-degg brought Oaja's words back to her.

She focused her duoja-gift on his hip joint for the first time – including the duoja-currents of the hot spring with her own energies – and felt the finest extensions of his branches take up the flow, growing fuller and more elastic.

There was richness in the middle, where the branches hummed with life, and in the "distance" where the remote twigs curled and spiraled.

Ah! Livli's breath huffed out. The energetic connection in the labrum had bridged the gap. Good! There was a scaffolding now on which healing would proceed. She withdrew her duoja-projection gently.

Malaka-degg's eyes were lidded, allowing him to focus on the inner experience of receiving Duoja. Although he would likely call it "laving the sight." His people were not ignorant or unskilled. If their migration path crossed a healing spring, he might never have sought Kaunis-spa. But a frozen shoulder needed more than just massage and exercise and duoja-gift. Or *paglunas*, as he called it.

It was good he was here.

And if Thoivra had her will, he wouldn't be. Livli's lips tightened.

I'll talk to Risten . . . not on the morrow; there wouldn't be time. The next day . . . same. I'll talk to her as soon as I can.

Malaka-degg opened his eyes. "Thanks to you. And to the Lady." That was the Deathwind Woman placated by his tribe. He touched his brow crux and bowed his head. "Would she bless Kanya-degg well." That was his brother, still lost.

"You fear for him?" she probed.

"No, not yet. Kanya-degg be strong and canny. I no fear until I go back and he be not there. But I . . . miss?" – she nodded – "miss he."

Yes, just as she missed Jorgan. Assuredly her sweet-brother was well on his wanderyar. She just wished he were coming to this year's herd-luring. *And . . . I doubt I'd be so sanguine if the last time I'd seen him was in a blizzard!* Kanya-degg must be older and more experienced than Jorgan.

"Is Degg a surname among your people? That you share it with your brother?"

Malaka-degg smiled. "No, no. Mean 'man with *paglunas.*' I share with *salamangero* and drummers – not woman ones – and all Minmahal-men who have *paglunas.*"

"Not the women?"

"They *liga.*"

"So the shaman-healer who visited Kaunis-spa last winter year was Paglunai-liga."

"Ah! Paghet-liga. Yes. She tell her journey. She why I be here."

Of course. It all fit together now. The Minmahal shaman-healer would have known that Kaunis-spa, with its hot spring, was the place to send a man with Malaka-degg's shoulder ailment.

"Do your people have short names? Sometimes I'm called Liv. Short for Livli. Would your brother ever call you Mal? Or Malaka? Meaning no offense," she added hurriedly.

Malaka-degg took no offense, but he shook his head. "Minmahal-folk go long, not short." He grinned. "Sometime I be *Masya*-malaka-degg. Or *Paka*-malaka-degg."

She was sure her face reflected her dismay when he laughed.

"But I be here in Kaunis-spa, not home on *pamateng* circuit. You call" – he pointed at his chest – "Malaka or Mal. I be fine."

She didn't think she would, somehow. *I've gotten used to Malaka-degg.* And now that she knew it was actually short among the Minmahal . . . well, spending time on his name felt right.

She woke the next morning as soon as the first gray light started seeping in through the cracks of her bednook's shutters. There were yet six eight-days until Long-light in Joiesse, but the sun rose early once spring was well started in the Fiordhammars.

She got up and dressed quietly, careful with the cabinet doors under her nook despite her rising excitement.

This is it! The aegis-foil was in full bloom!

She'd checked it late last night in the lingering dusk, and all the buds were open. She wanted to dance and shout . . . but not to wake any of the dreaming sisters in their nooks along the corridor. So she was deliberate in her movements and soft in her footfalls to the dump-buckets.

None of the kitchen-sisters were at work on breakfast yet, but the canisters of crispy pinyons on the sideboard in the refecting-hall would keep her stomach from rumbling. She wasn't usually hungry immediately anyway, even under the necessities of pregnancy.

The sun was already clearing the tops of the far peaks, tinting the sky pale gold, when Livli crossed the front porch of the lodge. The night had been warm, so no dew glistened on the turf or the plants in the gardens. *Good.* The rockfoil petals needed to be dry before she layered them in honey.

She draped her sack of supplies over a shoulder and whisked down the steps.

Kneeling among the *khrin* at one end of the herb garden, she studied her plants. The aegis-leaves were large and triangular with two deep lobes at the base. *I won't need more than four or five at most. And they'll be easy to strain out at the end of the day.*

Mimmi would be happy. The rockfoil would thrive, never missing the few leaves Livli required. The green-sister should be able to harvest the rhizomes at the fall-evener. The aegis-flowers were composite – but with florets on the large side for composites – and deep pink in color. Picking the petals wouldn't be too time consuming.

Livli pulled out the goblet and the pitcher from her sack, set them on the ground, and pulled three aegis-leaves from their stems.

She held the foliage to her nose and sniffed – sort of . . . dusty, hard to describe – then placed them in the pitcher. Yes, three were more than enough.

Next she set to work on the flowers, separating the petals from the sepals and stamens, discarding the latter, and collecting the former in the goblet. *I didn't need many leaves, but I think I'll need all of the flowers.* And she did, although the goblet was not big enough to hold them all. She ended with a heap on a fourth plucked leaf in addition.

Was there time enough to continue?

She measured the height of the sun in the sky. She could hear voices in the lodge-hall, and a few byre-sisters had already started clearing out the byre. They'd need it in a few days for the herd-luring. But it was still early. Aside from Janina, who had the duty to check patients this morning, no one would be arriving at the spa for a while.

Livli bent to her rite.

First a wodge of honey smoothed into the bottom of the pottery crock, then a pause while she released her duoja-energy. Her hips dropped, sitting less tensely on her heels; she lowered her chin a smidgeon, allowing her crown to lift. The realignment rippled all the way down through her cruxes. She sighed as strength rose from her fundus.

I should have done that sooner.

It still surprised her how small misalignments bred fatigue. Within her relaxed straightness, the duoja welled upward along her branches, passing through her belly crux (wider than usual under the influence of her pregnancy) and on through plexus and heart and throat and brow. When it filled her crown, she opened the way through her fingertips, scooped aegis-petals from the goblet, and sprinkled them along with a spritz of duoja over the surface of the honey.

Strange prickles tickled her fingers as the petals settled.

Yes! It was working!

She filled the crock, layer by layer.

My baby is a girl. A daughter. A sister. Yes.

She licked her fingers, sticky from all the honey, gritty with its crystals, when the crock was full. She tied a leather covering over its mouth, then placed the vessel in the sunny crevice between two glacier boulders framing this end of the garden. The honeyed petals needed to stay warm.

I must remember to bring them into my bednook each night.

But she wasn't done.

She stowed the honey pot and dipper in her sack, also the empty goblet, added the leaf now bare of petals to the pitcher, and carried it to the spring-house.

The rush of cold water through its plank interior kept the air cool. She knelt at the edge of the platform, trailing her hands in the current flowing out of the spring, out under the arch in the lower wall to dance down the mountain slope as the Kasta-beck. So odd that this source was chill; its sister in the spa, so sultry.

She took the ladle from its hook and filled her pitcher, again directing duoja-energy along with water into the container.

There was a nice, flat spot on the upper boulder of the pair cradling the honey-petals, perfect for making sun-tea. She covered the pitcher to keep the brew clean and left, sack once more over her shoulder.

Do I feel different?

Her fingers were sore. Had the rite worked?

I think so. I hope so. I guess so.

She'd intended it to bring her certainty, but instead her anxiety felt stronger.

I'm doing what I can. That will have to be enough.

Her worry for her baby lessened as she went through her day. A message from Cuuji's mother arrived, reporting that Cuuji matched her age-mates in physical ability and thanking Livli for the little girl's healing. Hegon, returning for therapy on his hand, had brought that news, along with a rumor that the Sundin brothers' frost leopard now haunted the meadows above Iloiset and Rakas.

Livli frowned, but Hegon exhibited distinct unconcern.

"No worries, Livli," he assured her. "The hunters will get it soon."

Hegon's first session in the hot spring showed his tendons to be more shortened than Livli liked, but there was a decent chance he'd regain partial grip and range of motion despite it. At least the duoja-work on Malaka-degg's hip had anchored well while he slept and was proliferating. He might be able to forego the carry-sling and walk from closet to hot spring on the morrow.

Livli checked her sun-tea before supper.

The light would linger after the meal, but the warmth of the day was already fading. The liquid in the pitcher was pale green. She fished the aegis-leaves out, limp and browned on their edges, and discarded them on the compost heap.

Should I taste it? It's supposed to be chilled.

She bent over the vessel inhaling. Still that dusty scent, but with a hint of . . . spice?

Better stick with the exact sequence followed by the queen of the folk tale.

Livli recovered the tea and carried the pitcher to the spring-house. Would the cook-sisters appropriate it, if she placed it with the other chilled foods in the spillway? *I'll put it at the back, behind the urn of cream, and hope.*

The crock of honey-petal conserve was easier to store. She simply took it up to her bednook and placed it on the shelf just inside the nook's shutters. The crock's pottery felt hot against her palms and weighty for its modest size.

After supper, Livli sought her birth-mother.

She'd been avoiding Sarvet ever since her own return from Siajotti.

She'll ask me about my heart-deep preparations for being a mother, and she won't be satisfied with superficial answers. I'm not ready to talk about it. But I should be able to put her off this evening by mining her thoughts for ways to deal with Thoivra. *I hope.*

But Sarvet was not among those gathered in her sitting room. It was located on the eastern side of the lodge, dim even on these light-filled spring evenings in the shadow of the flanking pines. Little Julija danced in the lamp glow with littler Salmo to the resonant hum of a bowed lyra.

The player, wizened old Paiam, listened to the children's mother, consulting about . . . a goat. Of course. Haidde's appointed position was cheesemaker – and she was a good one – but she retained a keen interest in the animals providing her with milk. She'd been a goat-sister as a girl, and Livli suspected Haidde wished she might still accompany the herd up to the highest meadows.

Girste, Davvad's linking-sister, was the only other adult present. She leaned back in her armchair, face tired, and nursed Nikko.

"How's he doing?" Livli asked her, gesturing at the toddler.

"I hope the tooth will crown tonight. He's been fussy all day, not enough sleep last night, doesn't want to do anything but nurse. Haidde had her hands full during the dinner hour."

"You were in the kitchen then?"

Livli was surprised. Haidde watching Nikko was nothing unusual, but Girste was the whey-cook, not one of the dinner-cooks. And the making of gundru, kraut, kvass, and other fermented foods wasn't tied to meal schedules.

"Erityi has a sick stomach, so I filled in for her."

No wonder she looked tired.

"Let me gift the little one with duoja."

Girste smiled. "That's kind of you, but no. You've worked hard all day, too. He'll be better on the morrow."

"I can't hold my own baby yet. I'd like to hold yours."

"Ah. In that case . . ." Girste disengaged Nikko with expert unconcern. He whimpered, face tight, as she held him against her shoulder and patted his back. "*Viyai, viyai.* Aunt 'Liya shall make it better. There now." His burp came up, and she handed him to Livli.

"Nikko, I'm going to make your mouth feel better."

He looked piteously at her. "Ma-ma-ma! Nu-nu-nu!"

"Yes, you'll go back to your mama to nurse." She didn't waste any more time talking. The teething measure was simple, really. She cradled Nikko on her lap, placed her hands on either side of his jaw and let her duoja-energy flow. The smallest trickle was best, easily accomplished, even relaxing.

Nikko's eyes – blue like those of his mother – widened. His whole body softened, and he started to smile. "Liy-liy-liy," he chanted. "Ni-ni-ni!"

She poked his tummy, provoking giggles, then bent and kissed him. *What a precious sweetie! Oh, I want a boy just like him!* Except she didn't. She wouldn't get to keep a boy. How could Girste bear the thought of parting with Nikko in a year?

Girste looked merely relieved. And phlegmatic. She took Nikko back into her arms and started him nursing on the other side. "Thank you, Livli. He and I both should get more sleep tonight." In fact, the little one was asleep within moments.

Haidde was finishing her consultation with Paiam. The cheese-sister got to her feet, addressing Girste. "You had a question about yesterday's whey?"

Girste rose as well. "Yes, it was yellower than I've ever seen it."

Haidde collected Julija and Salmo, let them kiss Paiam good night, and drifted out through the sitting room doorway with her moon-sister. "The kultainen-blade is rampant this spring. That's why. I'm glad of it – " Haidde's voice ceased as the door closed behind her.

Paiam was easing the strings of her lyra, putting the instrument in its case, stowing the bow in its bag. "Sarvet's making the gathering rounds this evening."

"I wanted to know what she made of Thoivra's clique. She does know of it, doesn't she?" Livli changed her chair for the one Haidde had vacated. "You've heard her talking, haven't you?"

"Oh, yes." Paiam took Livli's hand in her own, patting the palm twice. "Worries you, does it."

"Her idea of a Kaunis-lodge free of brothers does not please me."

Paiam grimaced. "When your birth-mother was Jorgan's age, I'd have agreed with Thoivra. Not now, of course. I never guessed back then how different and how much better things could be with the men-folk present." She paused, leaning back. "I used to dread the herd-luring, can you believe it."

"But why?" Livli had heard mention of this before, but never what lay behind it. Paiam was the lodge herd-lure, and had been for decades. How could she ever have disliked it?

"The wild sheep were so free, so fierce, almost . . divine in their mastery of the rock faces. I *feel* them in the duoja-trance. I *am* them."

Livli waited, gazing at her *maghra's* face. Paiam's skin was tan and wrinkled, but her cheekbones retained their grace as always. Her eyes were almost black in the dim lamp light, their normal shimmer of gray and green and gold hidden.

"I feel the change when I reach with the duoja-crook to bring them home. They lose their wildness. I lose *my* wildness."

Livli shivered, not sure she wanted to learn these craft secrets. *I see why she didn't like it. Why does she . . revel? . . . in it now?*

Paiam smiled. "After your mother left for her wanderyar, I saw . . . that all things have their season. There's a time to be wild. And a time to be gentle."

Livli felt her brow wrinkling.

"Losing wildness can be about losing something. Or it can be about gaining something. Receiving tranquility and connection and quietude."

"I see that for the spring shearing, but" – Livli scrubbed her other hand across her brow – "in the fall, we kill them. Some of them."

Paiam patted Livli's palm again. "And there's a time to receive death. You know this."

"But I don't like it."

"Of course not."

"You do?"

"Not like, exactly. But I trust the goodness of the Divine Mother's creation. Death is a part of it. I don't understand it; not from this side. But I am . . . coming to trust it."

Livli shook her head. Paiam's words added up to something, and Paiam clearly knew what she meant, but Livli didn't.

"Shall I tell Sarvet you're looking for her?" Paiam released Livli's hand with a final pat.

Did she want that? *No, I want to talk to Sarvet, but I want to approach her. If she comes to me . . . I might . . . not be ready. Might say . . . other things. I want to talk about Thoivra.*

"No. I'll catch her when I catch her."

"Want to tell me about it?"

Livli looked up, startled. Paiam wasn't referring to Thoivra. *She must guess I'm hiding something.* "Not . . . yet."

"Your choice, sweet-heart." Paiam smiled. "Restful dreams."

Livli left before her *maghra's* invitation persuaded her to break her silence. She took a spoon with her to bed.

Using the utensil next morning to ingest the petal-conserve felt fraught beyond its simplicity.

She awoke tense. *Will it work? Will I know if it's working? When will I know that it's working?*

The conserve had cooled since its sun-bath yesterday. She untied its leather covering, dug out a wodge of sticky petals with her spoon, and placed it between her lips.

Spicy sweetness burst against her tongue. As she chewed and swallowed, a cascade of stinging prickles danced across the back of her mouth and down her throat, fading swiftly.

Oh, my! That certainly felt like it worked. Why do I feel *more* anxious? *I should feel less!*

Again the routine of her healing work soothed her worries.

She coached Malaka-degg in the careful moves she wanted him to use for his first walk to the hot spring, and he made the passage without hazard. If every patient were this . . . not compliant – most hurt folk were cooperative – intelligent? Malaka-degg was intelligent, but that wasn't the quality she was thinking of. Wise? Discerning? She couldn't find the right word, but if all her patients were thus, they'd recover in half the time.

She treated both hip and shoulder with duoja, then turned her open perception on his shin. The flesh bruise had faded long since, but she wanted to check the bone bruise. *Ah, yes.* It could do with a touch of the gift. She had him raise his leg closer to the water's surface and directed a delicate wash of energy into the injury.

There.

That should move the rebuilding process along.

She could see a real difference when he walked back to the massage closet: more even weight distribution and a less tentative footfall on the left.

Could he venture outside?

Not without close supervision, and she wouldn't consider it if the herd-lure weren't on the morrow. *Surely he's tired of seeing only the spa-hall week after week.* He was so patient, it was hard to tell. *But I won't be dancing in the Ponce-ring this year.* I could sit with him on the veranda of the branching-hall. If Bekkha helps me get him there, it should be safe.

When Livli entered the refecting-hall at noon, she saw that the brothers of Tukeva-lodge had arrived and were eating their dinners in company with the Kaunis-sisters. Amazing how the male voices deepened the sounds of the meal-time babble.

Mimmi snagged her sleeve as Livli surveyed the crowded tables looking for a free spot.

"Sit with us, Livli, do. I've been telling Naddja and Kearti about how important the hot springs are for healing. And how Sister Thoivra wants to deprive some folk of that help." The green-sister scooted over, making room for Livli to sit. "But they have questions for you."

She'd been hoping to see Nial, but this was too good an opportunity to pass up. Like many sisters, apparently, Naddja and Kearti both thought the chief benefit of the spa-spring was its heat, that the skills of the healers were the greater necessity, and surely a hot bath might be had anywhere there was a tile stove with which to boil water.

Flattering, but not quite right.

Livli explained that the spring was duoja-gifted. "It's the combination of duoja-waters and their currents with the skills of the healers that sometimes produces miracles. Sister Jaska would be blind, if she lived in Iloiset-lodge instead of here. Unless she traveled to Kaunis, of course."

"O-oh!" This was clearly new information for Mimmi's friends.

"So Karral might have lost his leg? If he'd not been brought here?"

Livli remembered Karral. He was Naddja's linking-brother, and he'd been crushed by a falling tree. "Karral might have lost the leg. More likely he would have died." That was blunt, but also the truth.

"Oh!"

She spent the rest of the meal correcting further myths about injury and healing. It was surprising how many there were.

We need to do something about this. This amount of ignorance is . . . dangerous.

Sisters took linking-classes before Other-joy, and ramble-classes before a wanderyar (if they chose a wanderyar). There should be a class about health.

I'm going to talk with Mother Gaddja about it.

Livli walked down toward the father-camp after dinner, but Nial found *her* before she passed the smoke-house.

"Livli!"

He started to scoop her up in his characteristic off-your-feet embrace, but checked himself, delivering a mild squeeze to her shoulders instead. "Sarvet sent word to me that you're to have a baby in Jubiante. Well, I can see you are!"

Yes, her belly showed quite a convincing roundness.

"It's wonderful! I'll be a *mapah* all over again!"

She leaned into his chest, suddenly teary.

Why didn't I think of telling him before this?

She came of a line of unconventional sisters. Why had she been following the conventional saw that birth wasn't a concern for brothers?

"What is it, Liya-li?" He kissed her brow and led her to the bench overlooking the Vrea-vale. "Tell me."

She would. She would tell it straight out, without excuses or embellishments.

"*Mapah*, I'm afraid my baby will be a boy."

He took her hands in his and gave them a little shake.

"And what's so wrong with that? Mahde's eager for a son, and I'll enjoy having another child of Sarvet's line at home in Tukeva."

"But he won't be home in Kaunis with me!" Her voice broke. "That's what's wrong with it!" Now she was crying, openly sobbing.

"Ssh, ssh. There now." He folded her in against his side, stroking her hair.

Receiving his comfort and concern felt good. Maybe she'd just needed a good cry.

Her sobs slowed. She pulled a kerchief from her waist pouch, dried her eyes, blew her nose, and looked up. Nial was looking at her, sadness in his smile.

"You're so like your birth-mother, sweet-heart."

Like Sarvet? Who'd parted so easily from Gaiju and Jorgan? Surely not!

"She took on something fierce when it was time for Davvad to come to me in Tukeva. I think she'd have kept him despite all, if it hadn't been for my father-longing. But" – Nial grinned – "she loved me too, and couldn't bear to deprive me."

Livli hiked her jaw back up from where it had dropped. "But, but . . ."

"She was even worse with Harral. Claimed I had a son, so it was only fair she keep the second one. If you'd been a boy, I think she would have kept a son for herself."

"Lodge-mother would never have let her," gasped Livli.

"It was Johtaia back then, not your current careful Seagga. But even if it had been Seagga . . . who do you think would have won that conflict?"

Sarvet. Oh, definitely Sarvet.

But I'm not Sarvet.

"Uh huh." Nial nodded. "Luckily you were a girl-child. But Sarvet herded her own way, as the saying goes, biding in Tukeva nearly as much as she did in Kaunis-home. Her sons know her, no question." He stroked Livli's hair again, and his gaze grew keen. "Couldn't you do that too? Visit often enough that it was more dwelling than guesting?"

Livli shook her head no, said, "Yah. I could. But . . ."

"It's not the same. I know." He took her hands with his free one. "But perhaps it will be enough, if you do birth a boy. I'll pray Sias for a girl . . . but if it's a boy . . . you've never taken a wanderyar. Perhaps this is the time for it."

"Mapah!" She couldn't believe he was suggesting she travel with a baby. Didn't he remember how much work they were?

"Your birth-mother threatened to take a second one when she was pregnant with you!"

"Well, she was mad then! No one takes a boy at birth. That's thirty months later." Her voice sound acerbic in her own ears. "A mother needs her sisters at birthing . . . and a safe place. What *was* she thinking?!"

"I doubt she *was* thinking. You know her fierceness."

Yes, Livli knew Sarvet's . . . everything. Fierceness, independence, determination, and . . . creative resource.

I wish I had more of that. But Sarvet's way . . . isn't my way. What is *my way?*

Maybe she needed to resign herself.

Or maybe . . . her baby would be a girl. *I'm doing all I can to make it so.*

Livli sighed, pressing her brow into Nial's shoulder. "They say carrying high means a girl. And I'm carrying high."

"So you are, so you are." He hesitated, then continued. "Livli, I know it seems worrisome now, but everything will be all right. You'll see it's so, when the time comes. Try to trust for now, sweet-heart."

She felt herself relaxing almost against her will. Nial had always been able to make her feel better, even when – as now – she disagreed with him.

"I've got to get back to the spa." Actually, she had some moments more, but she wanted to leave while she was feeling good. Also to check her sun-tea. Had it escaped notice by the cook-sisters?

Nial kept hold of her hands. "Liking the healing work still?"

She settled back, irritation mixing with the brightening that mention of her work brought. How could Nial not know? This was exactly the problem she saw with visiting her son at Tukeva. *She* wouldn't know either when he discovered *his* heart's joy.

"I love it!" she answered. "I feel . . . like the sun itself is holding me up when I let duoja flow through me. Like the Mother's love is in me and around me and through me. Like my patient's need is a gift and a privilege that is mine to fill."

She found herself telling him about Malaka-degg, his patience, his foreign perspective, his gentleness.

"I'll have to meet this paragon," murmured Nial.

Livli blushed. "He is special. And I'll introduce you before the herd-luring on the morrow, if you come to the veranda of the branching-hall. We'll be watching from there." Although she needed to invite the shaman-priest first. But she couldn't imagine him saying no.

And he didn't.

"Might I observe with demon-eye also? No just outer eye?" He brushed his eyelids, dripping spring water from his hand.

"Of course."

Why haven't I thought to let my own duoja-sight be active in our rituals? But she hadn't. *I'll join him in it tomorrow. I wonder . . . what will I see?*

"That's a wonderful idea."

"You no try before?" His eyes were shrewd.

Her voice sounded distant. "It had not occurred to me."

"You check with . . . Paiam? Is okay for sure?"

"I doubt that's necessary. Hammarleeding law contains no prohibitions."

"Then . . . ask . . . advice. Caution? For better . . . chances?"

She felt chagrinned. *I'm still acting like a child, sneaking instead of confident.* Malaka-degg was right. They'd likely have a better experience using suggestions from her *maghra*.

"I will," she assured him.

But she couldn't catch Paiam non-busy; and her conversation that evening with Risten, her old friend and the luring-sister learning from Paiam, didn't go as planned.

When Livli approached Risten after closing postures on the branching-hall veranda, Risten got in the first words: "I've heard you want brothers to live at Kaunis-lodge and work as healers in Kaunis-spa." Her lips straightened. "I can't understand your thinking, and I don't agree with you."

For the second time that day, Livli felt her jaw dropping. "Who said that?" she blurted.

"Sister Thoivra. I think you should give her views a listen, Livli. She's got some good points."

"She does?"

The last of the other sisters were moving down the veranda stairs, most engaged in conversations of their own, a few glancing back curiously at the shaping conflict.

Livli blinked, trying to regain her mental balance. "Risten, I never said . . . what Thoivra reports me as saying. I've never even thought it. Although . . . it's an interesting idea. Maybe I *should* think it."

Risten tossed her shiny blue-black hair, narrowing her dark eyes. "You would. After all the constant visiting at Tukeva when you were a child, it's no wonder your outlook is warped."

"Risten . . . can we start this over? Tell me the parts of Thoivra's stance that appeal to you. I'd like to know." She felt a little dizzy, but her healer's training – stay calm in emergencies – was beginning to assert itself.

Risten relaxed too, seating herself on the veranda's top step. Livli sank down beside her.

"You know that brothers used to visit their sisters but thrice a year: for Long-dark in Bricember, Other-joy in Falnary, and Mother's Bounty in Jube."

Livli nodded.

"Then that started to change . . . oh, when our birth-mothers were girls. Kaunis-lodge welcomed the Tukeva-brothers at Death-joy. Then Lodge-day. Oikessa-lodge was visited by Patava-lodgers on Giving-day. It all started to break down, until the only fete-day that remained pure was First-light."

Livli opened her lips to object, then closed them again. *I need to listen first. She's obviously worked up about this. I'll not convince her of anything until she's calmer.*

"Now the brothers walk in and out of Kaunis-home as though they lived here. And the sisters visit Tukeva so frequently, it will soon be the same there." A sob escaped Risten. "Livli, don't you see? All our mystery, all our glory, all the wonder of cherishing our differences is fading. I don't want the brothers to become just like sisters: ordinary and familiar and known!"

Umm. She could see Risten's point. Sort of. Her own linking-brother Mahde had seemed more glamorous when she hadn't known him so well. But . . . Mahde's tendency to retreat under pressure would still be true, whether Livli knew about it or not.

I'd rather know. In fact, I wish I'd known sooner. I might have made some different choices.

But how could she explain that to Risten.

"You're talking about linking-brothers, aren't you? Or do you mean all the brothers?"

Risten gulped, scrubbed at her eyes, then straightened her shoulders.

"It matters the most among the linking-brothers, yes. But . . . I liked it better when I was little, and all of the brothers seemed . . . big and bold and . . . oh, magical!" Her gaze became a momentary glare. "And don't tell me that's because I was little!"

"But . . . I believe it was. I mean, think. When we were little girls, so much of everything seemed magical. All the world was new to us."

Risten sighed. "Yes."

"Remember our first taste of hoolinberries? So sweet with a hint of mint, a flash of warmth under the minty coolness. *That* was magic. So was our first hike to the high pastures, our first witnessing at Other-joy."

"I suppose you're right. But I still want my first linking to be . . . miracle."

"I think it can be, Risten."

"Well, I don't!" Risten flashed. "How could it be, when the only brothers likely are bony Issat with his everlasting talk of bird life, Lavrras and his non-stop laugh, gloomy Voitu, or – oh, Livli, you know how it is!"

Yes, Livli did know. It was partly why she'd chosen Mahde, who was a decent sort all told, just not . . . as confidant as she'd prefer.

"I think that . . . you just haven't met the right brother yet."

"Given I've met every brother in Tukeva, how am I supposed to meet this mythical right brother?" Risten looked angry.

"Maybe Hammarleeding lodges need more mixing, not less. What if the brothers of Kessel-lodge or Mirski sometimes came to Kaunis?"

"Then they'd soon seem just as ordinary as Voitu and Lavrras and Issat."

"I don't think so. I think that when you find the right one, he's ordinary *and* extraordinary, familiar *and* utterly strange, mundane *and* miracle. That the mix is dizzying, transcendent."

"You can't possibly feel that way about Mahde." Risten's voice was skeptical. Then she blushed. "Or do you?"

"I don't." Livli made her reply crisp. No need to embarrass then both with overt emotion on this. "I'll probably chose someone else next time."

"Oh."

They sat silent for a time. A herd of wild ponies moved into the Vrea-vale far below. The sun inched down in the sky on the western horizon.

"I think Thoivra has the right idea. At least it's something we *can* do. Asking the brothers of Kessel or Mirski – it'll never happen, that's what."

"Things *can* change, Risten."

"For the worse!"

"And for better," Livli insisted. "Especially if we keep trying."

Risten gave a short laugh. "Your birth-mother certainly made things change. For the better for *her*. But most sisters aren't like Sarvet. *I'm* not like Sarvet."

"You're like yourself, Risten. But I believe you can make things change too. For the better for *you*."

"Huh."

"Thoivra's change wouldn't be for the better for me, and I don't believe it would be better for you either."

"Well, I do!"

"Just because you see Issat and the others less often won't change who they are. And you know them now. They won't magically become strangers."

"Oh, I don't know. They aren't really grown yet. Maybe if I don't see them at all for three years . . . they will be different. Stronger. Taller. Older."

Risten had a point there. The younger brothers were still growing into themselves. But Risten wouldn't be getting any three-year hiatus, even if Thoivra had her way. The largest visiting gap in the old ways was a mere five months.

"Maybe you need a wanderyar."

"Ha!"

"You could stay away three years if you wanted. Or more."

"I didn't want a wanderyar when I was sixteen, and I don't want one now."

"Why didn't you want one?"

Risten's face turned wistful. "I'd miss the herd-luring."

Ah. That was what Livli had wanted to talk about. "Tell me about it. The herd-luring. What's it like?"

"It's wonderful! Magical! You couldn't possibly understand. You're not a herd-lurer!"

Maybe that was why Risten found the Tukeva-brothers too mundane. Her wielding of the duoja-crook was so blissful it made ordinary life flat. Except Livli felt equal bliss in duoja-healing. *And I don't find life flat.* Maybe Risten really did need a wanderyar, if only she could be induced to take one.

"But I am a healer. And I use the duoja-gift. Maybe I would understand."

"I can hardly find the words," Risten protested. "At first it's so . . . tentative . . . ephemeral. Then there's the moment of contact, almost a jolt: vibrant and wild and scary. Then the fury, the fight, the passion. And the sweetness, the surrender." Risten's cheeks were flushed. "It's like sunrise or a star shower or a rainbow. Only better."

No, that didn't tell Livli much. She could relate: duoja-healing could be all those things, but there wasn't much in Risten's description to help her and Malaka-degg.

"What if I opened my duoja-sight? On the morrow?"

Risten's eyes widened. "You have duoja-sight?"

Didn't she know? Just how much ignorance was there among the sisters of Kaunis-lodge? *How can I organize classes to teach these things, when I don't know how much my sisters don't know?* It seemed an insoluble loop; except . . . *I don't have to teach everything.* Less ignorance was surely better than mountain ranges of it.

"Duoja-sight is how I see where to direct duoja-energy for healing."

"Then try it. On the morrow."

"It won't be dangerous?"

Risten's mouth flicked up in a wry smile. "I'd suggest you pull back once the shearers start fleecing the sheep. That can feel unpleasant to a duoja-witness. But it's not harmful. I'll tell Paiam you want to observe. She'll be flattered that her *gahchi* is interested."

Livli felt herself blushing. Had Paiam been hoping for Livli's curiosity all this time? The memory of her *maghra's* accepting grin flashed in her mind's eye. No, Paiam's happiness had never rested on the decisions of others, not in Livli's experience of her.

So. Livli had the information she'd promised Malaka-degg that she'd seek, but this conversation with Risten need not be finished. Should she attempt more persuasion on the issue of the brothers' role in Kaunis-home? Or let it rest?

"Livli?"

"Yes?"

"I'll consider what you said. About brothers. And magic. Maybe Thoivra isn't right."

"Thanks."

Let it rest then. I'd forgotten that Risten needs to think things over. She wasn't one to change her mind in an instant. But she did change her mind, given new information.

There's hope. Risten might speak against Thoivra, when all was said and done.

Livli sat a while longer, watching Risten walk down the slope below the branching-hall to enter the byre, enjoying the golden peace of this late spring eventide. Long-light was coming, but now in Ponce the days were still lengthening.

I could sit here forever.

But she mustn't. There was her ritual tea to drink. And she needed her sleep.

The way the sun lingered above the far range was deceiving. Easy to think bedtime was a ways off, when it had arrived. She rested her chin on one hand, leaning the elbow against her knee.

I'll follow Risten down the slope in a moment. Just a moment.

And there, in that moment, she felt it. A feathery thrill, the faintest of ripples, gentler than a tingle . . . magic.

My baby! He's kicking! Oh!

Would it come again?

And it did, twice more.

Livli waited some while longer, but all was quiescent in her belly. *He – no, she – must have gone back to sleep.*

Smiling, Livli rose to her feet – so much easier when positioned at the top of a flight of stairs – and walked over to the spring-hall. Her sun-tea stood at the back of the items in the spillway, seemingly undisturbed. She uncovered the pitcher and poured a splash into one of the dippers. *This is it!*

She took a deep breath, let it go, and opened her duoja-gift.

As the energy rose through her roots and branches, she took in a mouthful of tea. Barky, slightly sweet, slightly salt, and clean. How odd. Then the duoja reached her throat root, and sparkles burst on her tongue. She swallowed, poured the rest of her tea into her mouth, and swallowed again.

Yiy! It was surely doing something!

She hung the dipper back on its hook, recovered the pitcher of tea, and replaced it in the spillway.

She was late repairing to her bednook.

The fading gold of the delayed dusk beguiled prudence, and she loitered out of doors, wandering through the Vyssa-grove, perching on the valley-rock, and paying a last visit to her rockfoil plants. They were bloomless now, but already recovering from her raid on their foliage. She couldn't see where she'd torn the leaves for her tea; no wilting was visible. *I should tell Mimmi I'm done with them.* The green-sister would want to coax them toward producing full, juicy rhizomes.

Sitting on the edge of her mattress, legs dangling in the corridor, Livli fingered the shoulder-length ropes of her hair. *I'd planned on oiling it – and my scalp – tonight.* She probed at the skin between the clumps of her wooly tresses. Dry, definitely dry. And the hair roots were growing out. She needed to do some work with the latch-hook tool to re-weave the base of each lock, but that would have to wait. She was yawning hard enough that even the stroking on of pinyon oil would stretch her ability to stay awake.

She pulled her feet up onto the mattress to sit cross-legged and reached her oil-jar down from its shelf. The salve inside felt silky and soothing on her fingers, quickly growing more liquid as she smoothed it into her crown and down behind her ears to her nape. Her hair –

from root to tip – took up a generous portion; clearly she was a bit late in this application.

She wiped her hands over her heels, knees, and elbows to free the palms of oil, re-stoppered the oil-jar, then slipped her hair-bag over her tresses and tied its drawstrings. She was asleep almost before she closed her nook's shutters and lay down.

Despite her late night, Livli woke early. Light from the clerestory windows above the sleep-corridor was already seeping through the cracks around her nook's shutter doors, and she was eager to discover what could be seen of herd-luring through duoja-sight.

Perhaps it will be . . . magical.

She swallowed a mouthful of petal conserve, bracing against its violent prickle on her tongue; dressed; snatched a fried chevon pastry in the refecting-hall; and sought the spa.

Malaka-degg was also up betimes, fully dressed in the Hammarleeding garb the nursing-sisters had found for him: green thistle-silk smock and braies covered by the thin sweater-tunic for warm weather.

Livli checked his gait as he left his closet and walked toward the front doors: steady, even, and slow. Good. She wasn't being irresponsible to sanction this outing. But . . . she insisted on one concession to his invalid status: the crutches she'd adjusted in readiness for his first real walk. The path from the hot spring to the branching-hall was smooth, but its gentle slope would be more challenging than flat floors and terraces.

Malaka-degg accepted the crutches with a twinkle. Had he guessed she was half expecting youthful masculine resistance?

I keep forgetting he's not a young Helmer. Why do I forget? His air of mature authority impressed me the moment of he arrived.

Malaka-degg placed the padded tops against his ribcage and grasped the hand grips. "I take no chance, eh?" He smiled, waiting while she held open the rightmost panel of the double doors, and then took prudent, crutch-supported steps outside.

So, he's used crutches before and requires no instruction. Somehow that didn't surprise her. *I wonder if he's experienced just about everything.* He'd been link-bonded. Did he have children?

She followed him across the spa terrace and along the Vyssa-grove trail.

The tops of the pines swayed in a light morning breeze, brushing broom stroke shadows on the needle-carpeted ground and sweeping Malaka-degg's blond hair from darkness to brightness and back.

Oh! That's why.

His hair was wooly, like her own, like Mahde's, in spite of its paleness, and he wore it in the same chin-length rolled locks favored by Livli's linking-brother. She'd been so distracted by Malaka-degg's golden skin and hair, that she'd not noticed how like his hairstyle . . . and firm lips and tidy nose . . . and close-knit joints and controlled gestures . . . were to Mahde's.

He's like Mahde will be in ten years. If Mahde could get over his fear of conflict. *Huh. No wonder he feels like a friend.*

The branching-hall veranda was only one step off the ground at the back of the building, so her patient didn't have to tackle the full flight of stairs at the front. But he'd have an excellent view of the proceedings there.

Livli dragged out two chairs (generally used for posture support, not for sitting) from the branching-hall's supply onto the veranda. She supervised Malaka-degg in his sitting, then went for one of the large bolsters to place beneath his feet.

"You also?" He waved toward her legs as she plopped herself more carelessly into her seat. He had a point. As she planned to open her duoja-sense, extra support might be welcome. She ferried another bolster outside, then settled herself and looked around.

The brothers of Tukeva-lodge were already arranged in a large circle on the slope between the branching-hall and the lodge. A few talked among themselves in low murmurs; three or four warmed up their voices, humming and chanting, "om, lom, rom;" and the rest sat quietly in meditation. The contrast between the power of their gathered maleness and the serenity of their quietude felt . . . magical, indeed.

I would miss this, if Thoivra had her way.

The first of the Kaunis-sisters trickled across the lodge's back deck, down its three steps, and into the circle of the brothers. Then a larger clump of women rounded the corner of the byre, Paiam and Risten in their midst. It would be a while before the action started, but things were underway.

She saw Nial open his eyes and stand. He'd been one of the meditators. Her father stretched, looked around, then strolled over to the branching-hall steps. As he climbed up to Livli and Malaka-degg, his gaze was on the Reindeer man. "*Aking mga mata ay may kaligtasan,*" he intoned, stopping a few steps below the top so that his daughter and her patient need not crane their necks.

"*Aking mga mata ay may kaligtasan, salamat,*" replied Malaka-degg. "You speak the Tao-wika?"

Nial shook his head no. "All my wanderyars took me among your people, and I learned a little. I don't have my linking-sister's gift of tongues, alas. Or yours, from what my daughter has told me." He glanced warmly at Livli, then back to Malaka-degg. "*Ay malugod sa amin sa mga bundok, ritwal-pakain.*"

My eyes have safety, Livli translated belatedly. And: be welcome among us in these mountains, shaman-priest. *I'd forgotten Nial took more than one wanderyar.* They'd all been before she was born, even the two later in his adulthood. *I should ask him for Tao-wika vocabulary while he's here at Kaunis.*

Blinking, Livli dragged her attention back to the two men. She'd made a poor job at introductions, but this pair hadn't really needed them. Nial was easy with strangers under any circumstances – *no wonder he took multiple wanderyars; I bet he'll take another before all is said and done* – and she'd seen ample evidence of Malaka-degg's adaptability.

Nial was asking after members of Tumatakbo-clan, the tribe he'd traveled with and made friends among. "What of Gumaga's dye experiments? Did she succeed in creating purple beads as she wished?" And: "Is the Halaman grazing area still under contention?"

Livli looked away toward the gathering sisters on the slope. Mother Seagga had emerged from the lodge with Thoivra and some other conservatives. Seagga wore a strained smile. Was Thoivra agitating to expel the brothers even now? Evidently. The lodge-mother shook her head gently, patted Thoivra's arm, and moved away.

But where was Sarvet?

Livli searched among the growing crowd for her birth-mother. This was Paiam's show, but a Holy Caller must lead the hallowing summons that preceded the herd-luring.

Ah! There she was. Last onto the deck and standing tall, Sarvet wore the ceremonial vestments proper to the fete: creamy suede robe with tassels of unspun sheep's wool hanging from its shoulder yoke. Her feet were bare like those of all the celebrants, honoring the warming of the earth and the blessedness of direct contact between skin and soil. Her smile, contrasting with Seagga's earlier one, was genuine, bright, energized. She lifted her arms, gazing jubilantly out toward her flock.

Muttered conversations faded. Brothers who'd drifted while greeting old friends returned to their circle. Sisters lingering by the byre or the spring-house entered the ring.

Nial, suddenly aware that he needed to take his proper place, broke off his inquiries regarding a group of young *scolf* players and took his leave. "Livli, if you'll linger here after the luring, I'd like to rejoin you."

She nodded.

"*Mga makatarungang hangin at magandang kapalaran na maging iyo,*" he declared to Malaka-degg – fair winds and good fortune be yours – and then bounded lightly down the steps.

Sarvet lowered her hands, then raised them again. The voices of the Kaunis-sisters rang out: "Iyiyo-o-o, Sias! We are yours!"

Sarvet's hands moved again, and the brothers' lower call rose and fell: "Iyiyo-o-o, Sias! We are yours!"

Then the Holy Caller's invocation: "Iyiyo, Sias, Divine Mother, our hearts are yours. Rest upon our reverence. Bless and hallow us. May your wild glory infuse us."

Livli glanced aside at Malaka-degg. What did he make of this? She suspected his Deathwoman rites were very different. He looked interested, absorbed in the spectacle below.

The familiar – to her – words honoring ferocity and freedom came next, and then the brothers began their rumbling chant: "Iyiyo-o-o, keaya keaya keaya, iyiyo-o-o." And sharper, in counterpoint, the sisters' song: "Descend and give, wild and free, leap and cede, brute and soul."

Some of the women were swaying. Their dance would build through the morning even while their hymn approached silence.

Paiam and Risten stood at the exact middle of the clustered sisters, still, eyes lidded. Livli turned to look at her companion and saw that his eyes were also closed. Was he opening his brow root or, as the Minmahal called it, his brow *mata*?

One way to find out.

She let her feet relax into the bolster beneath their soles, pressed her sitting bones down onto the chair, lifted her crown slightly. Ah! She'd been marginally slumped. The straighter posture felt good.

Her eyelids fell as she allowed her duoja-energy to rise and directed her attention outward, encompassing Malaka-degg – yes, his wind-sight was active – sweeping down across her gathered sisters. Oh!

In the ground under the sisters' balancing feet she could "see" whorls of something – sound made visible? – beginning to swirl toward Paiam. Was this the duoja-crook that her *maghra* spoke of? As the swaying transitioned into stepping, the coiling energies enlarged and quickened. She saw Paiam drawing them in through the phalangeal root at each toe and through both second condyloids. Then it rose along her leg branches and passed through each torso root on its journey upward. *Interesting.* Healers started the energy collection at the fundus root and directed it out the hand phalanges. It appeared herd-lurers pulled duoja through the feet and projected it out the crown.

The men's chant boomed steadily – *iyiyo-o-o, keaya keaya keaya, iyiyo-o-o* – its intensity deepening as the women's dance quickened.

Paiam's duoja fountained above the celebrants, mounting higher and ever higher, swirling toward the puffs of cumulous overhead. Then a gust of – wind? no, it was wind and yet not-wind – caught the duoja-energy the way a linking-brother embraced his linking-sister and swept it toward the high peaks.

Oh! Livli felt a shock, a thrill, a wild rhythm invade and buffet all her roots and branches. The feral sheep! They were *there*, they were *here*, they were . . . *her*. Joyous freedom burst at her throat root; she was singing: *I am, I am born anew! I am, I am springing!*

This, *this*, was the duoja-crook! She felt the wind against her fleeces, the pointy rocks under her cloven hooves, the dizzying spaces stretching away from her. She leapt, she climbed, she nibbled, she scented, she surveyed. She was bounding from cliff to cliff. She lost all sense of time, thought, understanding. Up and up, ever higher. She stood tingling.

And then the swirling duoja penetrated. Like the lake growing behind a blockage, like rain seeping into garden loam, like the water filling a sacred rill, quietude permeated her being. She was numinous, resplendent, glowing within divine peace. *I am, I am born anew! I am, I am being!* She was holy, she was sublime, she was all.

Then down and down, surrendering, giving, grace in descent. She leapt down, climbed down, picked her way from cliff to cliff, trotted through the high meadows, traversed the low pastures. She was . . . here.

Paiam's low murmurs to Risten, audible throughout, pierced her exaltation. "Follow it – higher – north now – connect! Tether – pull – and pull – steady. Pull out." Livli abruptly returned to her own body, chilled and stiff from its long abandonment.

How long had she been absent? Her sojourn had seemed timeless, but . . . she checked the sun: cresting toward noon. *I've been gone all morning.*

The sisters' dance, still frenzied as the first small flock of snow *ovis* approached, reflected the fatigue of tried endurance. Their flourished arms flailed, their spins tipped off-balance, and their stamped feet rose low. Yet their determination held. They understood – better than Livli ever had – that Paiam's power stemmed from their efforts.

Four brothers detached themselves from the chanting circle along with three sisters. They were the shearers, and they snagged the nearing sheep, guiding them around the Hammar-lodgers to the byre and inside.

Paiam, Livli observed, remained deep in her trance, conducting several other summoned flocks in their journey down the mountain to Kaunis.

The shearers were fast. Almost as soon as a flock of sheep entered the byre, a trickle of shorn ones exited the far door. The gaps between arrivals were long, the flurry of shearing, brief.

All told, Paiam brought ten flocks out of the Fiordhammars, although she gave the tethering and guiding of three to Risten. There would be spinning and weaving and sewing aplenty for the wool-sisters. And a bounty in the trading season, when Merella, Iloiset, and Rakas lodges came to collect their share.

Livli led Malaka-degg inside to the branching-hall dump-buckets, aware that her own visit there had been uncomfortably postponed. She fetched water from the spring-house, and a snack of dried cloudberries from her pocket. The fete-day was a long one.

When Paiam released her trance, when the last sheep bounded away from the byre, the sun was low in the west and it was past the evening meal.

Sarvet pronounced the closing invocation: "May our ferocity be innocent in your gifting, may our quietude be sweet in your care, may our warmth be blessed in your love."

The hungry celebrants surged toward the lodge, but Livli – equally ravenous – waited. She could see Nial making his way toward the branching-hall, moving against the tide of tired brothers and sisters. *I should have ordered double for Malaka-degg. Or triple.* She wished she and her father could join her patient for his meal in the spa. Maybe she could put off this chat with Nial until she'd eaten. Her belly rumbled.

"*Ritwal-pakain*, Livli, I begged a favor of Janina. She promised to bring a tray for us to the spa foyer. Will you join me there for supper?"

"Thank you!" Livli exclaimed. Food and chat could be combined, and both would arrive sooner than if she repaired to the refecting-hall.

Janina had set up a folding table in the foyer. Nial dragged chairs from various corners up to it, and Livli placed a lit oil-lamp in its center to supplement the wall sconces. The meal was simple – chilled sour-fruit soup, hot bone broth, cheese, pinyon cakes, and dried rockberry leather – but the portions, large.

Livli concentrated on eating, while the men conversed in an inventive blend of Tao-wika and Aidinkieli.

Nial mentioned that Tukeva lost two goat kids to a frost leopard in the lodge's high pastures – the Sundin brothers' leopard? – but passed quickly from news and gossip to items more interesting to a visitor. He described curling matches held between brother-lodges in winter, then segued to avalanches by way of a curling sheet buried in snowslip during the last-stone hammer.

Malaka-degg contributed a tale of *scolf* scored and finished amidst a blizzard. Then he recounted the mythology of the Death-wind Woman, his words conjuring visions of snow and chill and silvery blueness.

She dwells at the source of all storms, in cold so deep it cracks rock. North-bears straying across her bounds turn to granular ice dispersed by gales. Ordinary small breezes invading her precincts transform, either into roaring tumults that scour flesh from bones or into a stillness so profound it cannot feed the lungs. She is death without renewal, loss without emptiness, pain without cessation. Yet in her wake, there is change.

Livli shivered as Malaka-degg fell silent. The lamp and sconce flames flickered, the air – heated by the adjacent healing spring – reminded her that all warmth had not fled.

"Yet you worship her," Livli objected.

"Almost," Malaka-degg answered.

Livli felt her brow crease.

"They respect her, appease her, sometimes use her," interjected Nial. "Am I right, *Ritwal-pakain*? Or heretical?"

"Right." Malaka-degg tilted his head. "She power, and power bring danger. But also choice. Right knowledge, right skill, and power bring life."

"We Hammarleedings say that she who seeks power seeks evil."

Malaka-degg smiled. "Power" – he gestured, rounding his arms and stretching their circle wide – "make mistake bigger, wrong aim come quicker. But power not wrong, not mistake."

As Livli sighed, the foyer doors swung open on her birth-mother. Sarvet had removed her ceremonial robe. She wore the ordinary knee-shift and trews of thistle-silk with a light-knitted tunic over them, all in her favorite black-figured red. She stood still a moment, enjoyment relaxing her lips as she contemplated her daughter and her linking-brother.

Then Nial swooped to his feet and stepped forward to engulf her. Livli heard her mother laugh. Her father pressed his cheek to Sarvet's, then released her. "I've hardly seen you to utter greeting," he declared. He scavenged another chair and seated his linking-sister at the table.

"No, nothing," she answered Livli's offer of tea. "I'll float away, if I swallow another mouthful."

"Malaka-degg, this my birth-mother, Sarvet Paiam-spring. Sarvet, Malaka-degg guests in Kaunis-spa to heal his injuries. He's a *ritwal-pakain* among Minmahal-clan."

"*Pagbati.*"

"Good e'en!" Sarvet picked up a pinyon cake to nibble. "I vow I need a wanderyar just to get some peace." She shook her head in deprecation. "As *ritwal-pakain*, do you find the counselor's role has its ebbs and flows, Malaka-degg?"

Malaka-degg looked amused. "The one who wish to do a thing, make a change, need counsel, good. The one wish *me* to do a thing, harder."

Sarvet laughed again. "Precisely. A troubled sister seeking a formula to make the outer world change to make her happy has some growing to do."

"Sometimes the outside world does need to change!" Livli had not intended to give voice to her thought.

"Of course." Sarvet surveyed her, kindly, but with a question behind her eyes. "As a Holy Caller, I focus on the inner world. Seeking spiritual tools and skills when you need political ones . . . wastes everyone's time. As does trying to make the world change when really an inner change is called for." She reached forward to pat the back of Livli's hand. "Is there a worldly change *you'd* like to see at the moment?"

"Yes!" This didn't seem like the best time, but it might be the only time she'd get for a while. Her daily routine didn't mesh well with Sarvet's. "Or, rather, no. There's a change I *don't* want to go forward. Thoivra's change."

Both Nial and Malaka-degg looked puzzled.

Livli turned toward the Reindeer man. "You know that Hammarleeding sisters live always with other sisters. And brothers with brothers."

He nodded.

"But the brother-lodges visit their linking sister-lodges for fete-days."

"This day. Herd-lure day."

"Yes. And the others: Long-light and Lodge-day. Mother's Bounty and Fall Evener. We have – oh, nine? ten?" Livli glanced at Sarvet.

"Eleven fete-days, Malaka-degg," Sarvet finished for her. "When I was a very little girl, the brothers visited only for three of them. Four when I was older. Thoivra wants the return of those day."

"Is that what she was fussing about this morning? Right in the crook-circle, too." Nial sounded disapproving. "Seagga put her off pretty quickly, I thought."

"Seagga's no ascetic," agreed Sarvet. "But she'll listen fast enough once Thoivra rounds up a chorus. That's your concern, Livli, isn't it."

"Yah. Niyena says she's going even further. Saying that Kaunis-lodge should be the sisterly version of Jakkiat-lodge." The Jakkiat brothers had cast off their sister-lodge and celebrated fete-days in brotherly solitude, avoiding women altogether.

Sarvet snorted. "That won't happen."

"Are *you* gathering a chorus to speak sense? Gaddja considers the whole thing so ridiculous that she's not doing anything. But if sensible sisters do nothing, then the daft ones gain more influence than they should." Livli could hear the tension in her own voice. She'd meant to sound calm and well-reasoned. Hard to do when she felt strongly.

"I'm not ignoring it, Livli." Sarvet's hand moved from atop Livli's to below, clasping it. "I visit our Tukeva-lodge nearly as often as the brothers visit here in Kaunis. I'm hardly one to urge greater separation between men and women."

"What about greater unity?" Livli's other hand went to her mouth. *I didn't mean to say that.*

"Like Rakas and Iloiset?" Sarvet looked not the least bit shocked. She directed another explanation to Malaka-degg. His eyes were relaxed in his lively face. Evidently he was following their discussion with little trouble. "Rakas is a brother-lodge, Iloiset a sister-lodge, but they occupy the same slope. The brothers and sisters see one another every day."

Malaka-degg nodded. "Like Minmahal-clan."

"More than Iloiset and Rakas," Livli insisted. "Like Minmahal-clan, indeed. In the same lodge-hall." *I'd never have to leave my sons, if they lived here in Kaunis.* Except . . . her baby was a girl. She was making sure of it.

"What are you afraid of, Livli?" Sarvet's voice grew gentle.

Livli burst into tears.

"Nothing. It's nothing," she gasped. "I'm just tired."

Sarvet reached toward her daughter's cheek, catching a salt droplet on her fingers. Nial's touch went to her shoulder. "Bearing melancholy?" he asked.

"No," she choked. Then, "Maybe."

Malaka-degg pushed his chair back. The crutches leaning against it fell, but he caught them before they clattered on the floor. "I go. Mother, father, daughter talk. Is good, yes?"

"No. Please stay." Somehow she wanted him to stay. He felt . . . safer? yes, safer . . . than her parents. "You're a friend."

His lips wricked in skepticism. "Sure?"

"Yah, I'm sure. Please." The interchange steadied her. Was she going to speak her worry? Probably. Keeping it a secret for another four months was likely not possible anyway. And now was as good a time as any for sharing it. "I'm scared my baby will be a boy." Her voice started out even, but grew wobbly on that last word. "That I'll have to give him up to Mahde in Tukeva, once he turns two." She gulped, stifling a rising sob.

Malaka-degg had relaxed with her invitation to remain. Now he stiffened, startled. "Eyes of mother and eyes of child still lace together. Parting young, wounds the *mata*!" Confined to the spa-hall, he must not have realized that all the children dwelling in Kaunis were girl-children.

"It does hurt," admitted Sarvet, "but boy-children need their fathers. And the hurt heals. I should know. I've parted with four myself."

Malaka-degg bowed his head in respect. "Hammarleeding women tough!"

Livli's strangled sob puffed out as a laugh.

"This has been bothering you since First-light? Oh, sweet-heart!" Sarvet squeezed her hand. "I wish you'd told me!"

"You couldn't have done anything."

"Perhaps, not, but . . ."

Livli sniffed. "Keeping it secret didn't help either."

"You tell me. Did it?"

"No." Livli sighed. "Except, it did."

Nial let his hand on her shoulder slide away. Sarvet lifted her brows.

"You know I'd have been teased, if it got out. Who could resist? Planning on dressing him as a sister when he walks, Livli? Naming him Aila instead of Ailu, Livli? Ugh!"

Now Sarvet sighed.

Nial chimed in: "We'll keep it between ourselves, naturally."

Livli, directing a stern stare at him, realized her mother was doing the same. "You knew about this," Sarvet accused. Unspoken: you stayed silent, too?

"She told me yesterday."

"Oh." Conflict avoided.

Sarvet gripped Livli's hand again. "It's long past dreaming time. Can you spare some moments in the morning? When we're rested?" She meant: was Livli willing to talk about it with her then?

"It's fleece-washing," she objected.

"Much more demanding on the washers than on the Holy Caller. I hardly say anything."

Livli knew that. Why was she dragging her heels? "You'll tell me why I should feel differently."

Sarvet smiled ruefully. "I wish I could. But, no. I was thinking you've had this pent inside for five months. Let it out a little? I'll just listen. I promise."

"Yah, alright."

Sarvet nodded, rose to her feet, and began loading the remains of the meal onto its serving tray, waiting on Hibma's desk. Nial folded their table. Livli just sat, rather limp from her long day and the burst of emotion at its close.

"To your nook with you," urged Sarvet.

"I have to see Malaka-degg safely to his closet," she reminded.

"Surely the nurse-sisters could do that."

Livli just looked, exasperated.

Her birth-mother got the message. "Yah, alright. You'll no more shirk your duties than I will mine. But" – her lips tensed – "no lingering."

Livli smiled, old enough to recognize the lure of motherly advice. "Sweet dreams, Sarvet."

Sarvet grinned, Nial paused to hug Livli's shoulders, and then both her elders departed.

Malaka-degg was rising, in the careful approved fashion. He arranged his crutches beneath his arms, took his first step toward bed. Livli put away his chair – Nial had replaced the others – and accompanied her patient to his closet. She helped him resume his sleeping gown, made certain the nurse-bell was within his reach, and bade him dream well. His hand pushed the blanket aside to encircle her forearm.

"Livli."

"Yah?"

"When baby born, I open eyes. Yes? You like?"

"Oh! Yes! I *would* like that." Why did she feel so relieved? Almost as though his ritual might allow her to keep even a boy. Which was crazy.

"And, later, if he be boy, I do *paghuhugas ng mata*." Forgiveness?

Her voice was fierce: "He won't be a boy. I've taken care of that." Although she hadn't shared that secret.

"*Paghuhugas ng mata* – how you say? – laving the eye – heals heart. I hope you not need." But she might. He was right, even though she didn't want to admit it. And *he*, unlike anyone else, truly felt for her. His people didn't separate mothers from their sons.

"Thank you, Malaka-degg. I'll remember."

His hand firmed on her arm. "Dream deep, Livli."

"Dream deep, Malaka-degg."

She detoured by the spring-house on her way to the lodge and her bednook. The sun-tea still occupied the back of the spillway; its flavor was yet the odd mix of bark, sweet, and salt; the swallowing provoked the same stinging sparkles in the back of her throat.

Moments later in her bednook, when her head touched the pillow, heavy sleep swept her under.

The next morning found her plumped on her knees, elbow deep in soapy water, side by side with other sisters, scouring sheep fleeces at the long outdoor trough. The harsh lye cleanser needed for removing the grease from the wool was leaching oils from her hands, and her palms were already wrinkled from the constant immersion. *Thank Sias the hot spring was gentler.* But her mind was not on physical annoyances. She was thinking of her talk with Sarvet.

Her birth-mother had snagged Livli the instant she emerged from her bednook – petal-conserve swallowed, dressed, and not much else. "*Namah*, I need the buckets!"

Sarvet had the grace to blush, but she stuck close, shadowing her daughter along the corridor and accompanying her to breakfast.

"Do you think I'll leap away to the high meadows like a goat, if you take your eyes off me?" Livli protested.

Sarvet smiled. "Isn't that what you've been doing for the last few months?"

Well, yes. But she wasn't hiding from her mother now. And wouldn't. Or . . . she wouldn't mean to. It was just so tempting to slip away to . . . the spa or the low pastures or the valley rock. *Sarvet has reason to cling like a cocklebur.*

But once they settled in her caller's parlor, Sarvet really did just listen. Livli talked. And talked. About her mistake in choosing Mahde, about her love for her coming child, about her fear of losing a son to Tukeva, about her longing for a more inclusive community.

"Thank you for telling me, sweet-heart."

"Do you see . . . what I see?"

"Hammarleeding ways are restrictive and insular. The range of tolerated difference is narrow. Support for big dreams or different dreams is missing."

"Why did you come back from your wanderyar? When you'd won a larger life in Imsterfeldt all your own? How could you bear to give it up?"

Sarvet rested her chin on her hand. "Sometimes the most joyous melody is played on the fewest strings. Limits breed strength and beauty. And Hammarleeding limits felt right for me."

"Well they don't feel right for me!"

"Maybe they aren't."

"But what should I do?"

Sarvet took both Livli's hands. "I see three choices for you, but do you really want *me* to speak them?"

"I can leave the Fiordhammars," Livli started. Her birth-mother nodded. "I can influence the Kaunis-sisters to change. Or I can accept things the way they are."

"Or some combination of those last two," added Sarvet.

"I'm not going to solve it today, am I?"

"The most important questions often have answers that evolve, if we keep trying to find them."

"Thanks, *namah*." Livli leaned in for an embrace, and felt comforted in her mother's arms. *Why did I think she'd be critical?* The answer came: *because sometimes she is.* But not this time . . . this time she'd been more Holy Caller than birth-mother. No wonder most of the lodge-sisters sought her wisdom. *I'll talk to her again, I will.*

The fleece-washer next to Livli jostled her way to her feet. "Ooof! My back's going to go, if I don't take a break!"

As she moved away, someone else took her place, plunking down with a grumble: "Girls! Will they do their share? No. Will they help? No. Can they be pleasant? No. Grrrmph!"

Livli choked back a laugh. Juudet's daughters were reaching the age when sisters butted authority, and Ristlinna and Sivne exhibited restiveness to a high degree. But Juudet deserved sympathy, not derision. *Considering how I was at thirteen, my daughter will be just as bad.*

"Ristlinna? Or is it Sivne who's misbehaving?" she asked her neighbor.

Juudet scrubbed furiously at the fleece passed to her by Livli before answering, "If it's not one, then it's the other, and these days it's always both!"

She handed her fleece down to the next sister kneeling at the trough and accepted the one Livli had been working on.

"I asked Sivne to fetch me a skein of the butter-yellow yarn. The altar cloth I've been working needed but twenty *Fresange* knots to be finished."

Juudet stopped swishing her fleece to touch Livli's arm. "I had the broidery frame re-positioned and tightened, my needle in my fingers, and then discovered the tail end of the butter-yellow skein too short." She shook her head and turned back to washing.

"Does she scamper across the hall and get it? No. We have the eye roll and the indignant protest: 'But, *Namah*, it's Ristlinna's turn – I helped you all yesterday!' And then Ristlinna arrives just in time to hear Sivne and get in her own reason why she shouldn't help either. Next thing I know, they're screeching insults at one another and pulling hair!"

"What did you do?"

Juudet's frustration ebbed, and her smile turned wise. "Ignored them, of course. Those tantrums are bids for attention. Best not to reward ill behavior."

"And then?"

"Sivne fetched the yarn and sewed ten knots. Then Ristlinna sewed ten and put the yarn away."

Now Livli did chuckle. "Short-lived rebellion. Good for you."

Juudet sighed. "If that were all. I remember when they started this kvetching and disputing. Last year I was horrified, but it's all in a day's nurture now."

Livli lifted her gaze from her fleece to look around. Paiam was feeding the dry fleeces in at one end of the trough, while Gaddja pressed water from the wet ones at the other. Neither Sivne nor Ristlinna were present at the washing channel. What about the rinsing trough? No, not there either. Waiting their turn? Livli didn't see them anywhere. She turned back to Juudet, whose lips pressed together in an unhappy line.

"Oh, what happened?" Livli blurted.

"I'd promised to help Erityi serve the berry ferment. It foams so, if you try to pour it swiftly." Juudet fell silent, focused once more on washing, although more gently than before. Good thing, or the fleeces would be unusable from her rough handling.

Livli waited. Sivne and Ristlinna must have said something truly awful.

Juudet resumed her tale. "I asked the girls to carry the altar cloth to the calling-hall and give Sarvet any help she needed there." A head shake.

"They refused?" Livli guessed.

"I wish they had."

What?

"Your birth-mother's a brave and resourceful woman, but I wish she'd set a better example. Stay closer to Kaunis, keep *you* closer to home, speak more of chastity in her homilies."

Livli didn't know what to say, the attack was so unexpected.

"Ristlinna came back from the calling-hall giggling and planning her wanderyar. I thought I'd talked her out of such foolishness. And now Sivne has put her name on the list for the ramble-class along with her elder sister. I won't have it!"

Juudet almost punched her fleece along to the next sister, whose jaw had dropped, ears open despite her downcast eyes. *I'll bet each sister up and down the whole trough is listening in.*

Best to skirt the criticism of Sarvet. "Why are you so set against a wanderyar for your daughters?"

Juudet's eyes went flat. "They might not come back."

"But that's what the ramble-classes are for. To make it safer. In all the years since our first wanderyar, *Sarvet's* wanderyar" – she couldn't quite refrain from that defensive jab, however oblique – "we've not lost a single rambler! It's a better record than any of the brother-lodges!"

Juudet sniffed. "Brothers! Reckless. Of course, they forfeit their lives. Or bring troll-disease home."

"Ristlinna and Sivne will be fine. I know they will."

"Yes. Because they're staying home where they belong!"

"You would keep them from their wish?"

"Livli . . ." Juudet's voice warmed. "Kaunis lost a sister just two years ago. Vivva Olga-spring didn't return."

Oh. Juudet was worried about a different kind of loss: Ristlinna and Sivne choosing to live elsewhere. And there was some foundation for her concern. Not often, but every once in a while, a Hammarleeding rambler decided lowlander culture suited him or her better.

"Don't you want your daughters to live their heart-deep desires?"

"I think I know life's essentials better by far than they do. The romance, the fantasy, of a journey to exotic locales beguiles them.

They'll drift from the essence of our Hammarleeding way without ever realizing the sacrifice that trade entails."

Livli glanced up along the length of the trough. Was her *maghra* hearing this? Juudet's voice was not lowered. But Paiam's expression remained serene. The twins, Ulla and Ulletta, across from her showed less discretion, all agog to see what Livli would say next. Was Juudet one of Thoivra's clique? If she could convince Juudet, would some of these others come round?

"Most ramblers choose home. Even Sarvet chose home. Why not make Kaunis-lodge so welcome and warm that even lowlanders wish to settle *here*?"

"Lodge-mother Johtaia saw to that in her day, but not in a good way," scoffed Juudet. "Brothers dancing in and out continuously. I bet they like our welcome. Now Seagga permits lowlanders in the spa, month after month. Girls approaching their link-fete might like that sort of bait, but it dilutes the Hammarleeding-duoja just as badly as wanderyars."

"Nothing living stays the same forever," argued Livli.

"Living *traditions* lend us poise and equilibrium. Wild grabs at novelty and tolerance for leniency mutate into disaster. Livli, I know you want to defend your birth-mother, but think a little. Ponder the beauty of our way of life, the wonder of our calling-rites, the harmony of our community. Surely you don't want to risk these."

I'm not persuading her. She's trying to persuade me.

Livli thought about last Giving-day, bleak and chill, when a blizzard kept the brothers lodge-bound in Tukeva. She recalled (again) her farewell to Jorgan, when he crested the midpoint between his second and third year of life. She mused on the discord between mother and daughters recounted by Juudet herself.

I don't see the same things she sees.

"I believe Hammarleeding beauty, wonder, and harmony can grow and change while we sisters grow and change. I believe in heart-deep wishes. I believe in supporting big dreams and big dreamers. Even when it means old gifts are lost. I believe in welcoming new gifts." Her eyes felt moist. "I believe in Ristlinna and Sivne. In Sarvet. In my baby. I believe in letting go," she whispered.

"Well, I don't. Excuse me."

Juudet rose and stepped away to the rinsing trough where Thoivra worked.

Livli gulped.

That didn't go well.

She looked at Paiam again. Was that sympathy in her face? Her *maghra's* left eyelid shivered and her head tilted slightly. Livli twisted to peer over her own shoulder. And there was Sarvet, robed as yesterday, but wearing the green-wool turban signifying the completion of shearing. Her lips smiled gently. Was that pride in her gaze?

"Sisters, let those waiting have their chance. Water must cross the hands of all who desire warmth in winter." Sarvet's words were rote, yet Livli knew she meant them just for her. *Let all have their chance. Warmth belongs to us all.*

Why had she doubted her birth-mother all through Janary and Falnary and Nerich?

Because she gave up four sons to Tukeva.

Yes, she did. But it was a narrowly focused judgment. Perhaps a more balanced assessment was called for. Livli rose to give her place to Niyena.

Her friend murmured: "Good speech! You didn't convince Juudet, but I'll bet you inclined some of the others toward reason."

Livli felt suddenly stronger. *I don't have to enlist supporters all in one go.* Bit by bit would do just fine. *I can win this contest.*

Late that evening, after supper, she lingered in the spring-house, cloaked by dusk, sipping her sun-tea, reflecting on the day.

Marja, the birth-sister, had curtailed Livli's further participation at the troughs. So she'd fetched Malaka-degg to the veranda again – this time for a shorter interval than for the luring-fete – to watch the fleeces grow snow-white after washing, rinsing, and dripping dry. Or dryer.

Juudet had utilized the entire afternoon to display her allegiance to Thoivra, hanging on the conservative sister's every word, face sober whenever she glimpsed Livli sitting beside the Reindeer shaman. But Ulla and Ulletta had attached themselves to Mimmi and Niyena, and a few of the twins' friends hovered at the fringes of their progressive group.

I should plan who I'll talk with next. If I'm going to persuade most of Kaunis sister by sister, it will take a while.

Why did her thoughts keep sliding to Paiam's parting words?

"Livli, you're gifted with the water-duoja, but you might consider training in wind-duoja, and voice-duoja too."

It was an unusual phrasing: water-duoja. She thought of her gift as healing-duoja, but Paiam had tied duoja to the elements: liquid, air, sound. There was some sense to those categories. Herd-luring clearly used wind-duoja, as she'd learned only yesterday. Livli's healing gift was intimately tied to the hot spring, but she handled the water instinctively.

The disciplines of the healer's craft were designed to be practiced in dry conditions. She knew of no other Hammar-lodge featuring a thermal bath.

And what did Paiam mean by voice-duoja? Livli's debate with Juudet?

A faint prickle of intuition, echoing the stronger sun-tea's prickle fading on her tongue, stirred far back in her awareness. There was something – mysterious and occult – waiting to be discovered. *I must think about the different duojas more.* And she would. But right now she needed bed.

An entire eight-day passed before she returned to her desire to investigate elemental duoja.

Five demanding new patients arrived at the spa, and none of the existing cases were ready to wrap up. Livli found it hard to squeeze in the afternoon rest prescribed by Marja, let alone begin an unusual research project.

She finished her sun-tea at week's end and debated the wisdom of continuing to ingest the petal-conserve. *Should I have made a larger batch of tea? Should I make another?* But the queen in the folk tale had taken only seven doses of the remedy. *I think I'd better stop.* She did, wondering what to do with the leftover conserve.

An impulse to consult Malaka-degg assailed her. *He's no herbalist. Why would I want his opinion?* She did want it. His advice about the herd-luring had been spot on.

Her treatments for Malaka-degg's hip thus far had been incremental, designed to build scaffolds for his healing tissues. Her focus on his shoulder was more obscure, still intent on restoring communication between islanded portions of flesh. The shaman was doing well. It was time to push toward more ambitious therapies.

She was glad crutches were unnecessary for the trip from closet to spring. She'd noticed Malaka-degg's shoulder binding more the day after the herd-luring. Crutches stabilized his hip, but stressed his upper body.

Malaka-degg gestured along his left side as he walked prudently through the spa-hall. "Stronger now. Exercises? Yes?"

Livli slipped his robe off and hung it on the hook next to hers. She checked the hot spring with her toes. It still seemed hotter than usual. Gaddja assured her it was not. And Marja reminded her that pregnancy always made a woman feel warmer. Still . . . the light sweat breaking on Livli's brow felt premature. Usually she was well immersed before her skin grew dewy.

She steadied Malaka-degg down the spring steps.

"I'll start you on water exercises today, but your shoulder needs more healing before land ones will be safe."

"Ah. Yah." His voice was resigned. "Shoulder. It all start with shoulder."

Had he forgotten that it was the shoulder malady that had brought him to Kaunis? That the hip injury was acquired on the way?

"The water exercises for your hip will come this afternoon, and once I teach them to you, Bija can monitor you while you do them. This morning . . . this morning" – could he sense the excitement rising in her – "I'll harness the full power of the water-duoja to address your shoulder."

She was grinning.

"Now, Malaka-degg, now you'll see what Kaunis can really do!"

"What you can do." His eyes met hers, gleaming subtly. Yes, he discerned her excitement, participated in it. "I watch? With the *mata*?"

Of course he would want to see as fully as possible. She'd not worked healing-duoja on a sister healer before, but this might be similar to that. A shaman-priest held abilities like to her own. It would be interesting to learn what a talented recipient of the duoja-gift perceived.

"Please do."

First she took up the knob-stick in a reprise of the remedy he was familiar with: touch, touch, touch at each tight and painful spot. Then a trickle of her personal duoja through the area. The third therapy would be . . . something new.

"Malaka-degg, the next may be very sharp. Very strong. Be steady through it."

He nodded and closed his eyes, the better to open his *mata*, she suspected.

Livli let her own lids fall shut. Her duoja-energy hummed along her branches, coiled in her roots.

She was ready.

The duoja in the hot spring . . . looked subtly different. Was this an effect of pregnancy also? She studied the currents pulsing through the water: curling in sinuous streamers, spinning into diminutive vortices and then out again through surging flows.

No, it wasn't difference she was noting; it was similarity, a similarity she could not have noticed before last week's herd-luring. *I've felt the healing currents as power.* Now she was seeing them as direction, just as she'd seen Paiam's luring-crook as curving bolts of wind passing through the air. *This is important*, she told herself, *pay attention.*

She let her duoja furl out through her fingertips, strong in its impetus, engaging with the water-duoja, interweaving like braided fluid ice. She took her time with it, more time than in the past.

This new perception gives me greater precision! Oh!

Her merging grew finer, finer still, metamorphosed into spun transparency. Where did the water-duoja leave off and her own begin? Her fingers were water, her branches were water, the vast elegant lace of duoja that was her . . . was water. She was water, water-spirit, supple, gliding, puissant.

She felt Malaka-degg intent beside her. Following her deep into her transformation, anchoring her with his awareness. Would he falter when she turned her power to him?

She reached with her translucent self, reached into his flesh, pierced the first knot, stabbing through its isolation, stitching through its shoreline, felt him flinch . . . but not falter. *Ah!* She moved on, strong and sure, diving from knot to knot, threading through, here and here and here . . . and then . . . the lode of pressure sunk profoundly in his flesh. *There!* Once through it, she melted, softened, relaxed, ebbed out of him.

Then the water ebbed from her, and she was Livli again, fleshly Livli. She opened her eyes, almost surprised to discover herself sitting shoulder deep on the ledge in the hot spring.

Malaka-degg's eyes were dark. "Kaunis-spa among the great ones," he adjudged. "Amihan-anak, Kamatayan-anak, Malamig-halimaw." *Those were names he spoke.*

"Are you . . . alright?" Silly question. Clearly he was unharmed, if not untouched. "That was more potent than ever I've known it."

"You merge more . . . more . . ." – he swept one hand from his crown downward in a comprehensive indication – "all."

"Yes." She was still gasping. "I could . . . perceive more . . . more delicately."

"From the herd-luring?"

"How do you know?" How *did* he know?

"Herd-luring *duoja* like to Minmahal sight-wind. Water-*duoja* . . . new, but . . . not new."

She glanced a little wildly around the spa-hall. None of the other healers or patients happened to be present. Usually the hot spring had more votaries. She couldn't question them about what they'd seen. "Malaka-degg, we must, we have to learn more."

"Minmahal-magics and Kaunis-duoja together birth . . . who knows?"

"Yes. Yes, that's it."

"Livli . . ."

She reached out tentatively, touched a fingertip to his shoulder. Indeed, he had truly taken no harm. He smiled at her.

"Livli, we learn. We see. We look." His hand touched hers. "Find peace, yes?"

"Yes." It was safe to let this frisson of terror go, foolish to cling to it. There was space and time in which to learn more. And her partner was eminently capable.

Across several eight-days, Livli and Malaka-degg experimented. With practice, her perception grew more finely grained. Finely grained perception yielded more thorough meshing between her duoja and the water's. Thorough meshing generated more power. More power meant she required stronger anchoring. Nearly a month later, at the beginning of Joiesse, Livli's awareness of Malaka-degg wavered, inundated by the potent duoja-resonance juddering through her branches.

The next instant she was drowning, slammed down to the bottom of the hot spring, scalding water filling her mouth and nose, limbs askew and thrashing. She felt two strong hands make contact under her arms, and then she was hauled to the surface, coughing. Malaka-degg drew her to the pool's edge, away from the hottest currents, steadying her while she fought for breath.

Her ribs ached and her throat burned when she finally stopped choking.

Malaka-degg's concerned face swam before her stinging eyes. "You alright?"

She nodded.

"I slip?"

"No," she reassured him. "It was me. I lost sight of you in my mind's eye."

"Need tether to tie mental anchor to physical anchor."

"Yah. That's a good idea, but how?"

"Minmahal use sacred cord. Send sight-wind along cord before touching demon-wind."

They tried it.

Malaka-degg helped her braid the sacred cord using a mixture of dark green thistle-silk and her own head hair. And then they explored different ways of tying it. Almost any connection between him and her worked, but winding loops through the fingers of his right hand and then through those of her left produced a rock-solid linkage. Livli never lost sight of him again, no matter how wild the duoja-maelstrom grew.

The flutter of her baby moving grew more frequent, thrilling through her belly many times each day. It strengthened, too, becoming gentle taps and then outright kicks. The first startled outcry from her – "Oh!" – right in the middle of supper. Livli was glad he'd – no , she'd – not started kicking during the first experiments with water-duoja. Now her concentration withstood the diversion without faltering.

Malaka-degg's frozen shoulder was free by Long-light. She and he both envisioned attending the ceremonies of the fete-day together. What might they see, what might they learn, observing these rites with open duoja-sight?

Thoivra put an end to that plan.

Her influence among the conservative sisters and upon the Kaunis Lodge-mother was growing, and she pursued a covert campaign to exclude Tukeva-lodge from the festivities.

"Just this once," she pleaded publicly, at the finish of her clandestine lobbying, "let's experience the ways of our past. The dream of the abiding sun, the marvel of the evanescent night, the delicacy of our feminine essence. Long-light was the last of our sacred liturgies to be shared with the brothers. Can we not reclaim it for sisters alone, just this once?"

None of Thoivra's opponents had expected this move, and none were prepared to refute her eloquence. Mother Seagga declared Long-light a sister-only celebration, just this once, and all males were excluded from it. Including patients at the spa.

"But Malaka-degg was looking forward to participating in the sun-change veneration as well as the dark-vigil," Livli protested in a private visit to Seagga's sitting room. "He benefitted immensely from the herd-luring. Please, can we not welcome him to this fete as well?"

"Surely his injuries preclude it," asserted Seagga. She was playing for time, Livli knew. *Why can't she be more assertive? I wouldn't mind if she said, "No!" to me, if she'd also say it to ridiculous requests made by the Thoivra's of the lodge.* But Seagga was ever a conciliator, never a champion.

"His injuries are healed," Livli told the lodge-mother.

"Then why is he still here? You should close the case and send him home."

Livli felt a chill bloom in her stomach. There was an unpleasant idea: send him home. But although his shoulder and his hip were *whole*, they were not *sound*.

"Oh, mended flesh is necessary, but not sufficient," she assured Seagga. "Now the real work begins, restoring full *function* to his limbs. That takes months of specially designed exercises which change as function returns, until *full* function is achieved. It would be grossly irresponsible to close his case." That was why she felt cold, wasn't it. A healer's just concern for her patient. Not because . . . Malaka-degg was her friend?

But, he is my friend! she realized. *What's wrong with that?*

"Hmm." Seagga pursed her lips. "I suppose you know what you're doing."

Livli didn't answer that. Seagga was just dithering.

"But I've promised Thoivra. And the others," Seagga added. She'd never admit to being swayed by one voice alone. That would involve standing firm on her own. "Besides, it would be so unfair to the Tukeva-brothers, if your patient participated and they did not."

Livli gave it up as a lost cause, but she refused to attend the worship services out of solidarity with Malaka-degg. Sarvet smiled at Livli's decision, but her friends Niyena and Mimmi were distressed. "How can you?" fussed the latter. "Just two months before your baby will be born! The veneration would be so good for her."

If it's a she, Livli's inner voice piped irrepressibly. And: *she is a girl*, she answered her inner skeptic.

Mimmi protested again in Labresse when Livli set off to visit her *napah*, Ivvar, at Rakas-lodge.

"It's an entire day's trek to Rakas. Surely you shouldn't! What if something happens? And that frost leopard's still roaming free. Livli, you're vulnerable. Please stay home!"

"I want to see Ivvar. He'd planned to come for Long-light, even though Iloiset is his sister-lodge. And we both know what happened to Long-light."

Mimmi sagged. "Yah. Oh, Livli, is Thoivra winning?"

"No. She's really just starting her crusade. This skirmish went her way, but I don't believe subsequent ones will. The sensible sisters – the majority – are still realizing they need to respond. That Thoivra won't just go away."

"Right." Mimmi smiled. "But couldn't Ivvar come here? Since he *didn't* come in Joiesse?"

"He wanted to."

"Then . . . why . . . ?"

"I love it at Rakas. The view of the lake from its veranda soothes my eyes. Boating across to the herb-lea, the canoe rocking gently, soothes my soul. And sitting in Ivvar's parlor, talking with my *napah*, makes me happy."

Mimmi blew her breath out in frustration. "I wish you weren't hiking alone."

"I'm not. Where did you fetch that notion? Hegon's going with me, and we're going to take two days for it. Truly, Mimmi, you needn't worry. I'm following Marja's advice in every detail. And . . . it'll be a long while after my baby's born before I can visit Rakas again."

"Hegon?"

"You remember Hegon, the brother with the mangled fingers?"

"Oh! Yah, how is he? Can he use his hand now?"

"Completely. The new technique I'm exploring with Malaka-degg worked wonders for Hegon. When I sent him home after his initial treatments to heal, I knew I could get him most of the way there. But then I watched the herd-luring with duoja-sight, and . . . well, he's fully restored."

"That's marvelous! I'm so glad you and Mal are making discoveries."

"Malaka-degg," Livli corrected her.

"Malaka-degg." Mimmi sighed in satisfaction. "Imagine if no brothers were allowed. Hegon would be crippled."

"Exactly. But we're not going to let that happen."

"You're not."

"I need your help, Mimmi."

"And I'm helping. But I'm not good at planning and challenge. You know I'm not, Livli."

"I think you under-estimate yourself, but, yah, I'm pushing this resistance to Thoivra. That's what you mean, Isn't it?"

Mimmi nodded. "Although . . ." – she looked suddenly speculative – "I have been thinking . . . and planning . . . and, and *strategizing* about who to talk to next. And what to say."

"Ha! You see?"

"Yah, I do see." Mimmi paused, a surprised expression in her eyes. "Thanks, Livli."

The walk to Rakas-lodge was uneventful, pleasant. Livli found Hegon a comfortable traveling companion, silent in the presence of spectacular grandeur, conversational during more mundane intervals, eager to handle *all* the work of setting up camp, and unhurried in his pace. Spreading the hike across two days meant it felt more a spontaneous stroll than a directed expedition. Livli was unfatigued upon arrival at Rakas-lodge's porch where her gray-headed *napah* awaited her.

"Livli! Well!" Ivvar unfolded his long, knobby frame from the wooden slant-back chair. *Yiy! He was tall.* Her birth-mother was slim, but Livli's *napah* was where she got her height. Ivvar wrapped gentle arms around Livli's shoulders. "Good to see you, *gahchi ghi.*"

A remnant of tightness so hidden she hadn't even known it was there dissolved. *I was right to come here.* "Napah," she murmured.

"There. There, now. You mustn't get teary the moment you set eyes on me."

She pulled her head out of his shoulder to smile at him. "I'm not. It's just so good to see you."

Later, over the noontide dinner served in Ivvar's parlor, she told him more. And confessed her scheme with the aegis-foil. "Oh, Ivvar, was I foolish to try to make my baby be a girl?"

"No. No, not at all. Only a victim accepts her fate without issue.

The rest of us try for what we want."

"But what if the rockfoil hurts him? Or her?"

Ivvar looked amused. "You checked that. All those research trips to Siajotti, no?" He shook his head. "And here Paiam and I were thinking you shared Sarvet's scholarly bent.

Livli blushed.

"The scrolls *are* interesting. There's some really strange stuff in the Mathema section. But I like the healing lore best. And really" – she straightened – "I think all healers should visit Siajotti once a year. Learning basic theory and practice from your teacher is necessary, but the most obscure disorders don't come around often enough that every teacher knows their treatment. And the sister-lodges have copies of only a small selection of healing-scrolls." She slumped. "Napah, I keep dreaming up more projects! I can't possibly do them all!"

"And what is the latest project? Besides this idea you have for extending the learning of healers?" Ivvar always wanted to know. *And if brothers and sisters shared lodges, he could know right away.* Except . . . she supposed that *Ivvar* wouldn't. He and Paiam had parted ways long, long ago. But most *napahs* could know. They'd be living in the same place as their grandchildren.

She told him about her plan to create health classes similar to linking classes and ramble-classes. His enthusiasm, never really in doubt, encouraged her to share her experiences mixing water-duoja with healing-duoja.

He leaned back in his chair, sipping after-dinner tea, and looking at her bemusedly. "Livli, never change. Never stop."

What did he mean?

"You're doing important work, just by being you, just by tackling the challenges important to you. Keep on, and don't let anyone or anything stop you. Go around, or over, or under. Or persuade the barrier to change, become permeable." He grinned. "You're like your birth-mother: incendiary. And it's beautiful."

She got up and stepped around the table to lean into his embrace.

"Not sure I'll be doing anything much for a while." She brushed the protruding arch of her very round belly. "New mothers don't."

Unknowingly, he echoed her words to Mimmi. "You're under-estimating yourself, sweet-heart. The first few months, no. But just wait and see when you've got your balance."

"Not sure I will catch my balance, Napah."

He raised an eyebrow.

"I think I'm carrying a boy," she blurted. "In spite of the research and the rockfoil."

"Then that will be your next project." *How did he stay so calm in the face of upheaval?*

"But it's an impossible project!"

He stroked her back, then stood and led her over to a settee.

"Livli."

"Yah?"

"You remember Duoja's guidance? Seek acceptance only for the impossible. Seek courage for the possible. Seek wisdom to discern the difference."

Yah, she remembered it. Surely every Hammarleeding did. *So?*

"There's nothing in there about the probable."

Now he had her attention.

"So much that is probable or improbable depends on our choices and our actions and chance-met travelers in our life's journey. The impossible rarely becomes possible, but the improbable does it all the time."

He fell silent.

Then: "Let go, Livli. Let go, but be of good heart."

Oh! I was right to come here. Only here, in the space that Ivvar alone of her family seemed able to create and hold, did she release her sense of her limits. *I could do anything. I could be anything. I could do everything. I need only choose.*

"I'll do what I need to do," she said.

"Yes!" Ivvar gripped her hand. "And it *will* be enough. You'll do what needs doing, and you'll trust that *you* are enough."

"I *am* enough," she realized aloud. "I always was."

"Always."

"Even if my baby is a boy." She rested her head back against the wall. "Thank you, Napah."

He released her hand, touched her cheek. "You'll keep this one."

She knew he didn't mean her son, although she felt hopeful of that issue. He meant her sense of confidence. This was not a temporary gift. Even were circumstances to become dire, somewhere under her desperation, this indomitable seed of certainty would remain, waiting for her to draw upon it.

"Thank you, Napah," she repeated.

And her baby was a boy.

It was late in Jubiante when her pains began. She'd walked to the valley-rock and stood upon its utmost jutting tip, surveying the hazy vista below, grasses rippling in a gentle breeze, hares scattering when a peregrine stooped, wild ponies drifting into the meadow across the land-saddle to the east.

She felt happy. She was ready for her child's arrival, her patients in the spa were progressing well, and her work with Malaka-degg continued to be . . . fascinating.

Then her belly cramped.

Oof! Ow! Why did I think it would be like a bad monthly? She hunched forward, cradling her middle until the pang subsided. Where would she find Marja at this time of day, late afternoon? Probably in the potters' cot. The birth-sister was currently following only a few pregnancies and usually finished her rounds by the noon dinner. Shaping stoneware was her other love, and she gravitated to clay in her spare moments.

Treading the slope up from the lodge, Livli encountered Niyena, who sent little Aira to fetch Marja. Then her friend followed Livli into the Vyssa-grove. She protested when Livli swung onto the trail fork bypassing the spa-hall.

"Aren't we going in?"

Livli's belly was cramping again, and her answer held only irritation. "Why are you chasing me? It's just my baby coming."

Niyena looked surprised, but her voice was matter-of-fact. "You might need help."

"Well, I don't. I just want to pace. It helps."

Niyena said nothing in reply, but stayed on Livli's tail, footfalls soft. Then Livli's belly cramped again, and she stopped paying attention to her companion.

Marja met them on their return to the spa-hall. "Ah, you're moving, good. That always gets a labor going nicely. Keep on."

Livli did keep on.

Different people escorted her: Marja for a while, then Paiam, and then Niyena again. When her legs began to quake, she followed Marja indoors to one of the patient rooms where the bednook conveniently had two open sides. The relief of lying down lasted until the next contraction, which was much worse.

"I need to walk!" she gasped, struggling up. But her legs wouldn't hold her. She felt sudden liquid drenching her thighs, dribbling over her knees. Her birth-liquors had released. "Oh," she groaned.

"Livli, you need the hot spring," came Sarvet's voice.

Oh! Mother was here. Now it would be better.

Except it wasn't. She didn't know how they got her to the water. They didn't use the carry sling, but she couldn't walk any longer. Somehow she was sitting on a generous ledge in the pool with warm currents massaging her tired, aching belly. That did help. She could stay looser, and looser meant less pain. She gripped Sarvet's hands, surfing the waves of pressure. *I can do this, I* can *do this.*

And she did, until the pain grew abruptly sharper, more internal, stretching something deep inside that wasn't meant to be stretched.

Ah! Livli's eyes still saw, but the images in her mind made no impression. Her ears heard, but her mother's words – comforting? – made no sense.

Please, make it stop, please make it stop. Stop!

Someone was crying.

And then Malaka-degg was there. The same anchoring presence he'd been when she mingled healing-duoja with water-duoja. *Oh!* She reached for him, with her physical hands and her duoja-sense both. Reached and was caught. *Thank Sias!*

The terrible tearing sensation inside her went on, but now she could bear it. Malaka-degg held her, steadied her, contained her. She could find a center now. She clenched his hands and held on. Pain, and pain, and more pain, and suddenly – she was through!

Her eyes flew open.

He was smiling, gently, and there.

She smiled back, whispered, "Thank you."

"Brave-root," he murmured. "Hardest part complete."

As she nodded, Marja's voice reminded her: "You'll have a brief respite now, Livli. Catch your breath, and let me check you. Learn how your opening is progressing."

After that it felt easy.

It wasn't easy; it was hard work. But the pain was past, and Malaka-degg stayed with her, directing air-duoja down through the spring's waters to caress her laboring belly and ease her. She bore down on her toil, birthing her baby: head, one shoulder, the other. He emerged in a slippery rush into Malaka-degg's cradling palms. The shaman raised him swiftly to the surface for his first breath. *Oh!*

He was beautiful. Beautiful.

Black fuzz across his crown, dark eyes, alert and watchful. Livli drew him to her breast. *Ow!* His mouth on her nipple was a hard pinch. Someone laughed, low and joyful. Sarvet helped Livli re-adjust her son's clamped lips. *My son!* That was better; much better. *He's perfect!*

She settled back to nurse.

The celebration of Rede's birth, an eight-day later, was all Livli wanted it to be.

There were no *tambulero* drummers or *kalansingor* rattles in Kaunis-lodge, but Paiam played the traditional Reindeer melody – the *malalim na kaligayahan* – vividly translating its merry feeling on her bowed lyra. Malaka-degg taught the *kagalakan*-dance to all the young sisters approaching linking age, and they pranced through its circling figures with glee, hands held high, trailing red and white ribbons, ankles ringed by small bells.

Mother Seagga released several jugs of *kirsikka* wine for the event, so the Minmahal practice of kissing both cheeks in congratulation of the new mother was adopted with enthusiasm rather than embarrassment. Livli had never felt so appreciated in all her life. Hammarleedings tended to be more restrained in expressions of approval.

Then Malaka-degg opened Rede's *mata*.

Gathering air-duoja with intricate and precise gestures of his fingers, he secured awakening energy at the baby's toes and condyloids, then brushed it along the branches – reaches – through fundus, belly, plexus, heart, throat, brow, and crown. He made a second sweep from the finger *mata*, again moving the energy upward.

Rede grimaced in his sleep, but did not open his eyes. Livli stroked his fuzzy head. *So precious; so very precious.* His baby weight felt right on her lap, in her arms.

Malaka-degg knelt, signaling her to lift her feet enough to admit his palms beneath them. "Now *ina*." Now the mother. *Oh!* Livli hadn't realized her roots would be anointed as well.

Malaka-degg's hands were smooth, warm, strong. The passing air-duoja felt light, almost feathery, shivery, yet soothing. As it sprang from her crown, it carried all difficulty away. Contentment and serenity flooded in.

Livli smiled at Malaka-degg smiling at her.

"Blessed be," she murmured.

He kissed her cheeks.

She'd expected to revel in the Minmahal rites, and she did. Her deep content in Rede's first-calling – the Hammarleeding tradition – in the Kaunis chapel next morning took her by surprise.

His dedication to the goddess and the formal speaking of his name – Rede tem-Livli Mahde-spring – three times made his presence real and firm. *I won't be losing you, little son. Ever. You are here to stay.* The misgiving she'd felt during her pregnancy seemed irrelevant.

Somehow, she would find a way.

The customary closing hymn – *Love Resplendent, Mother Glad* – sounded sweet and fresh. *I am Hammarleeding,* she realized. *In my bones, in my heritage, in my ancestry. This is who I am. This is where I bide. This is haven . . . hallow . . . heart-spring.*

She was happy.

Facing Mahde after the worship service was less exalting. He'd arrived at dawn along with Bavvi, the other new Tukeva-father, to attend the first-calling and to meet his child. He was nervous, excited, and very unsure.

Rede, supported gingerly in Mahde's arms, let out a small cry.

"Is he hungry? Is he cold? Is he wet?" dithered his father.

"You need to hold him more firmly," Livli explained.

"Oh, I see." But Mahde grew even more fidgety and apprehensive. Rede's fitful yowls turned to settled wails. Mahde tried a jerky rocking motion, unsuccessfully, and finally Livli had to take the baby back and put him to her breast to calm him.

Mahde did better as an onlooker, his chest swelling with pride, his eyes shining in wonderment.

"He's so little, Livli," he whispered. "So perfect. So marvelous. So . . . so magnificent."

At least Mahde *appreciated* Rede, even if he hadn't the faintest bit of sense in looking after him. Livli was relieved when he went home to Tukeva, although his parting words irritated her: "I can't wait to see him grow!"

"Let's savor him fully now," she responded tartly, "before we look toward his future."

Malaka-degg, on the other hand, knew just what to do.

His handling of the baby was confident, his demeanor calm, and his growing affection for Rede evident. Livli began spending evenings in the spa. Malaka-degg would walk back and forth across the foyer, comforting Rede during this fussy time and giving Livli a much-needed break.

She loved waking in the mornings with her baby snuggled against her side. She loved nursing him, so sweet, so content, once she taught him to stop clamping down so hard! (A firm "no!" and take him off the breast the instant he pinched. Then put him back on to try again.) Bathing him and massaging his precious limbs was bliss itself. Even changing his nappy was agreeable – baby excreta was wholly different from anyone else's, and not noisome. Basically she liked doing everything an infant required.

Except . . . she was so *tired* by the time she reached supper.

And Rede was colicky then, crying and squirming no matter what she tried. He needed the most when she had the least. Malaka-degg was a boon. The shaman was good with Rede, propping the baby up against his chest and pacing, or draping him over a forearm while rubbing the little one's small back. His suggestion that the hot spring might ease Rede's discomfort proved truly inspired. There was a shallow spot at the edge of the pool, a scooped out dish, where Livli had sometimes soaked her feet. The water was cooler there, just right for a baby. And Rede actually smiled his first real smile – of relief – there.

The first few eight-days Livli couldn't imagine returning to her work. Rede seemed to absorb her entire attention, even though he napped three times each day. She was still getting used to the shoulder sling in which she carried him and still convinced that the slightest jolt, the faintest sound, would wake him.

Besides . . . she liked to watch him sleep, gazing at his placid baby face, his faintly puckered eyelids, his cute little chin. He enraptured her.

Fortunately, her patients were all well into their recovery arcs, doing exercises set by her before Rede's birth, thriving under the generic help of the nurse-sisters. Even Malaka-degg had reached the strength-building stage, taking some of his drills to dry land.

Livli concentrated on birth-motherhood without distraction. Until, one day, she realized she was bored. The tasks of motherhood had become routine, and while Rede slept – she let him be.

She needed something else to do.

Gaddja smiled when Livli (toting a sleeping Rede, of course) turned up at the spa the next morning with questions on the progress of Evva and Tresta. "I thought you'd be ready for work soon. But don't over do. Just mornings for now. Hear?"

Livli nodded.

"Evva's ready to go home to Oikessa, but I thought you'd like to see how well she's healed before she left."

"That's wonderful." Livli had been worried about this patient in particular. The scar tissue across her neck was so dense and tight. Evidently it had yielded to the rare *kokos-oliu* – the oil Niyena wished they could use for common cold – and grown sufficiently pliable to give Evva full turning range for her head. Livli *did* want to see.

"Tresta . . . well . . ." Gaddja's tone said much, but what had gone wrong? The last Livli had seen, Tresta's internal infection was clearing rapidly. Finding the right herbal combination had taken some time and several experiments, and Tresta had endured considerable pain while this transpired. Livli knew the sister would require special loosening movements to correct the internal weakness and tightness resulting from the infection, and she'd prescribed them.

"Tresta's become melancholic, and isn't responding to either sympathy or challenge."

That happened sometimes. A patient's wound or injury would heal, her sickness would pass, but the mind and heart still lingered in its shadow. Talking helped some. Time and long mountain treks helped others. One sister, tragically, had drowned herself in Lake Iloiset after returning home.

"Is she dangerously sad?" Livli probed.

Gaddja hesitated, opened her lips, closed them. "I'm worried."

That was bad then. Livli really didn't want a reprise of the Iloiset-sister's decline.

"You've tried pine needle brushing?" It was sufficiently unusual, without being rough, that the sheer novelty brought some sufferers back from the dark place they'd surrendered to.

"We've tried everything. Each one of us. I even asked your birth-mother and then your *maghra* to come. But I'm wondering . . . I'm hoping –"

"– that the experiments Malaka-degg and I have been pursuing –" Livli chimed in.

" – might work," finished Gaddja.

"I have some ideas." Livli nodded. Firmly.

"Let me bring you to her. I think . . . you're the one person who hasn't tried with her."

"I need to consult with Malaka-degg."

"Malaka-degg? I thought . . ."

Gaddja must be more worn down by this than she'd indicated. Surely she realized – "Mother-healer, the air-duoja is something Malaka-degg is teaching to me. He has no healing gift or skill, but his wind-mastery for ceremony is assured. And the wind-and-water magic is a practice we do together."

"Oh. Thoivra won't like that." Gaddja's voice was flat.

"What does Thoivra have to do with anything?"

Gaddja hesitated again. "I haven't wanted to disturb you with it, but you were right. Thoivra is more than a disgruntled matron. She has a set purpose, it seems: cleanse Kaunis-lodge of all masculine presence. And she's making progress."

Livli's belly, slowly regaining its pre-pregnancy tone, abruptly clenched. With some effort, she kept her voice neutral. "Oh?"

"After Rede was born . . . Thoivra organized a protest – a work-fast she called it – in which all her supporters sat outside Mother Seagga's parlor, refusing to move or do their tasks until the lodge-mother promised that never again would a foreigner be permitted to be present at a Hammarleeding birth celebration or to demonstrate his culture's rituals."

"And she promised." Livli knew she had promised. When had Seagga ever shown she had backbone?

"She promised," Gaddja confirmed. "And if Malaka-degg uses wind-duoja on Evva . . . it's forbidden now."

"Are you going to be bound by that?"

Gaddja sighed. "I'd hoped you could wield it solo."

"I can't. It is . . . powerful, you know. Dangerous."

"Oh!" Apparently Gaddja hadn't known.

"Do we abandon Tresta to darkness?"

Gaddja straightened. "No. No!" Her words grew brisk. "We'll go forward with healing. You and *Malaka-degg* will go forward. And I'll back you. At need. But, Livli" – she lowered her voice – "let's be discreet, eh?"

That was practical, certainly, but it didn't feel right. "Must we?"

Gaddja gave her an exasperated glance. "I won't lie about it, if that's what's worrying you. But I'd rather not borrow trouble. It will have to come out in the end, but, Livli, if we have some spectacular successes to brandish, that will help our cause: full treatment to every sick or injured person who comes here, male or female, foreign or familiar. I *am* a healer first," Gaddja insisted.

Good! Gaddja was motivated at last. And Livli had to acknowledge that her impulse toward full disclosure was . . . actually constrained by healer discretion. As well as . . . politically naive.

They discussed logistics.

Livli and Malaka-degg had performed their wind-water duoja unselfconsciously before Rede's birth. Now they would need to be mindful of who else was present in the hot spring.

Rede woke during the conversation, but all he wanted was nursing – easily provided.

Then Gaddja took Livli to see Evva. The sister's scar had faded ever so slightly, and she proudly demonstrated her ability to turn her head fully over each shoulder.

"We will send you home with a crock of *kokos-oliu*, and you must return to Kaunis for more when it runs out."

Evva beamed. "Oh, I will! I'm so excited about what it's done so far! I'm free of actual pain now, but I bet even the discomfort will ebb with more of the *oliu*."

"I think so, too," Livli agreed.

So strange that Evva – who had been through so much, suffered much, and still faced challenge in her healing – was radiant, while Tresta (who was entirely physically healed) succumbed to melancholy. *There are probably events or . . . deep essence . . . we don't know that complicates Tresta's recovery.* Livli didn't judge her, but she wished she understood more.

She peeked through Tresta's doorway briefly before noon dinner, but didn't enter. The woman sat unresponsive, gazing at a wall hanging without seeing it, tears in her eyes. Livli wished she could begin at once, but . . .

"Yes, she needs help, Livli," Mother Gaddja admonished, "but –"

"– but healers are sisters, not goddesses," Livli echoed.

"Off to the refecting-hall with you." The mother-healer shooed her away.

She did get food, but she ate it with Malaka-degg. He questioned her about Tresta's history and current demeanor, nodding as Livli described her patient's apathy and disengagement.

"Young one from Timog-tribe brought to Minmahal-tribe three, four circuits ago. Root *mata* – blurred? – no, *fouled* by demon, and belly reach severed. *Paglunas* not flow, pool between root *mata* and belly *mata*. Bad. She be like Tresta."

"Did you heal her?"

" Paghet-liga be Minmahal-healer. I am *ritwal-pakain*, but sometime counsel from *ritwal-pakain* bring heart-strength. And sometime . . . counsel with air-*paglunas* do much more. Young Timog-child . . . counsel no use to baby, but I try air-*paglunas* and child improve."

"She was a baby?" Livli glanced down at Rede, busily engaged in nursing.

"Not Rede young. Nikko young. Salmo young." Both of whom – at two and a half – were now living in the moon-huts with their birth-mothers and their sweet-fathers, nearing the time of their transfer to Tukeva. *Ugh!*

"Too young," adjudged Livli.

Malaka-degg nodded. "Too young. But she live and . . . time . . . she thrive."

"Oh, that's good, then." Livli felt more relief than seemed warranted.

This is that sense of vulnerability I've seen before in other new birth-mothers with young babies. Huh.

She'd thought that she would feel strong and capable; that her sense of power would fuel her care and protection of Rede. Instead, her awareness of his fragility was heightened, and her mothering sprang from a sense of her own weakness. A much more disconcerting, uncomfortable feeling.

"Will you help me? With Tresta?" she asked.

Their combined wind-water duoja brought results for Tresta faster than air-*paglunas* had delivered relief to the Timog-child of Malaka-degg's account. The fog within Tresta's fundus root – or root *mata*, in Reindeer parlance – was subtle. Clearly Malaka-degg's people had an expertise lacking among the Hammarleedings. Livli could see the root miasma now that she knew to look for it. And the wind-water duoja dispersed it rapidly.

The severance between fundus and belly was less subtle – Livli would have seen it upon close examination – its significance, more so.

The break manifested the way a hairline fracture might in a bone, weakening the duoja-branch and contributing to the fog that collected in the root *mata*. Over the eight-day while Livli and Malaka-degg worked to mesh the lower end of the duoja-branch to the upper, Tresta's root *mata* kept refilling with foulness. Her ability to eat and dress and respond varied with the clarity of her *mata*.

Livli hated the days when Tresta was almost comatose. Would they mend her duoja-break in time? It was *so* tiny, its influence, immense. And weaving the duoja-tendrils to recreate connection, the three of them seated in the hot spring, was fiercely hard.

On the ninth day of their labors, they did it. Livli felt her spun duoja-tendrils mesh with Tresta's. A zinging flash of joy and pain combined, coursed throughout Tresta's branches and fountained from her crown, her palms, her soles, then bounced as an echo through Livli's duoja-pattern. *Oh! It was intense!*

"Oh!" gasped Tresta, speaking Livli's thought. "*That* was what was wrong! Oh!"

"What?" pounced Livli. There was something in this whole experience that she was missing. Something . . . important. Could Tresta give words to the essence of the mystery?

"It changed," whispered Tresta. "It all changed! And I'm different. I'm better. Oh, thank you!"

Three days later, Tresta went home, ready to practice the exercise regimen prescribed for her and as radiant as Evva before her. But Livli was puzzled. Their success was marvelous, of course. But . . .

"I'm going to Siajotti," she finally announced to Malaka-degg.

"What you thinking?"

"I need to know more about what we're doing, and I think some of the Mathema scrolls at Siajotti relate to it. They held diagrams . . . that made no sense then, but now – Malaka-degg!" She leaned forward to grasp his hands. "Those drawings traced out exactly the pattern I perceive when I spin the water-duoja together with your air-duoja! And . . . there's something we're missing. I feel it!"

He was nodding, pulling at his lip with one finger. "Yah. I feel too. But Livli, is Ionaber." His pronunciation of the Hammarleeding word for the first month of autumn was awkward, but it highlighted his growing mastery of her native tongue. Language was less and less a barrier to their communication. "Snowfall yester-eve. Rede young. Frost leopards prowl? Is safe?"

"We need to know what those scrolls depict," she insisted.

He smiled, levity at her impetuosity twinkling in his eyes, but said nothing. Wiser than her birth-mother when Sarvet wanted to rein Livli in. How did he know that resistance made her more stubborn?

"Yah. Alright." She acquiesced, and then remembered: the Tukeva-brothers would be in Kaunis for Giving-day. Thoivra had tried to exclude them (again), but not succeeded this time. Livli could hike with the brothers when they returned home. Likely Nial would even leave his lodge-clan mid-route to accompany her along the spur to Siajotti. She need not make the trip alone. And Rede would be another month older when the end of Noulember rolled around.

"I go with?" suggested Malaka-degg.

His injuries *were* fully healed. But the strength in his left side still lacked robustness. A half day's hike would benefit him. Two days of hiking would not.

"It's too far," she explained regretfully. "For your hip. I wish you could come with me." And she did. What if Mahde tried to companion her instead of Nial? *I have some say in that,* she reminded herself. *I don't need Malaka-degg to keep Mahde at bay. I will simply tell him no.*

Ibba welcomed Livli back with a warm hug on Siajotti's front porch.

"Livli! So this is the little one." The scroll-sister turned back the fold of blanket protecting Rede's face. "Oh, what a cutie! What did you name her?"

Awaiting Livli's answer, Ibba nodded to Nial. He stood a little back from them, smiling slightly. He must have as many good memories of Siajotti as did Livli herself. But this moment would not be among them. This was awkward. Decidedly awkward. Ibba knew exactly why Livli had sought and unearthed *The Lindworm and the Queen* last Thyaril.

"Um. His name is Rede."

Dismay flitted across Ibba's features, but briefly. She had admirable social control. And judgment. "Ah, a boy, then. Your linking-brother's the lucky one. Rede looks intelligent."

He was awake and gazing alertly into Ibba's close-bent face.

His mouth stretched into a grin. "Ah ooh gah!" He was well into a sociable phase.

Livli exerted herself to match Ibba's patch on the situation. "Yes, Mahde's already counting the days until Rede comes to him. But I intend to enjoy every one before that time myself."

"He looks like a bundle of joy," agreed Ibba, ushering Livli and Nial toward the lodge door and opening it wide. "I often wonder why the good goddess gave me love of scrolls to match love of children. In the Fiordhammars, a sister has to choose, and I chose lore above offspring. But, oh, I do love a baby! Will he let me hold him?"

Later, when Nial had departed to continue on his way home, and Livli started her hunt through Mathema for the scroll she'd glimpsed eight months ago, Ibba's adoration of infants proved handy. Rede would have been content to nap in the sling, but he was beginning to reach and grab for things that caught his interest when awake.

Damage to Siajotti's scrolls . . . would merely follow the precedent set by me at age five, but . . . how mortifying! Sarvet's line, the marauders!

Livli found the freedom from Rede's weight pleasant. Equally so, temporary freedom from responsibility.

Entering the scroll-hall produced unexpected mental dissonance. She was so different from who she'd been eight months ago. Yet the chamber was the same as always: heavily carved wooden cabinets raised above the floor on short legs, two broad tables surrounded by armchairs, and a vast expanse of window glass laced with small circles of bronze. Even the view matched that of her last visit, a dusting of snow giving the late autumn vista the guise of winter.

I'm a mother now. And no longer strictly a duoja-healer. A water-healer? A wind-healer? I'll find out.

She stepped across the threshold and walked decisively to the Mathema cabinet.

Locating the scroll with that strange, half-remembered spiraling diagram was not nearly as hard as unearthing *The Lindworm and the Queen* had been. It occupied a pigeonhole halfway down the array and on the right edge. Its title was *Physika for an Admixture of Aeros and Potentia*. That said it all right there, but she read the text.

The language was one of the more obscure dialects found amongst Siajotti's documents, the ancient Ennaidja, appearing only on the oldest vellums. (One of the scrolls in Sagas claimed the scholar hero of old, Botolv Stone-slayer, brought a cache of lost knowledge out of the south and that the Ennaidja scripts were his legacy.) Hauling her focus away from the lure of pure scholarship – *I have a practical purpose for being here* – she settled in a chair to peruse the *Physika*.

The first paragraphs outlined the theory of a vibrational foundation for the essence of air (Ennaidja's *aeros*) and set forth complex equations describing its physical properties.

Livli skimmed these.

There was a reason this scroll was filed in Mathema, and she was not a *mathematikos*.

Next came an overview of *potentia*, which she also skimmed, albeit for the opposite reason. *Potentia* was the forebear of duoja, and she didn't need explanations for something she did every day.

Although the incomprehensible equations for it tickled her attention for a moment. Would she understand her own discipline better, if she could follow the mathematical descriptions a long-dead sage devised for it?

Then, there at the beginning of the next section was the diagram she remembered, labeled below each of its three parts: *Aeros Solus, Potentia Solus, Aeros et Potentia Admixtus*. Air alone, duoja alone, air and duoja mixed.

The spirals with long tails in "air alone" reminded her of mares' tails in the sky warning of a coming storm, although the following text asserted that the air pattern was visible due only to the presence of water vapor.

The softly curving arcs of "duoja alone" were identical to the energy that rose through her branches when she performed duoja-healing.

And the corkscrew spirals of "air and duoja combined" were similar to the spun coils she saw in her mind's eye when she and Malaka-degg experimented with combining air-duoja with water-duoja.

Why were the helices in the diagram so tidy? Hers were ragged and uneven. Was it just because she was a novice?

I think I'm doing something wrong.

The very end of the scroll explained where she'd gone astray.

"*Aeropotentia* is the most common and easily learned of the *magika*, but there are two other forms. *Aquapotentia* requires more strength from the *magikos*, while *sonopotentia* requires more subtlety. Ancient rumor tells of a third form, *caldaripotentia*, but no modern, credible *magikos* takes this seriously.

Odd to read of "modern" notions that were now a thousand years old.

"The very idea of harnessing a volcano's power is ludicrous. The differential between the vitality of the *magikos* and that of the mountain is insurmountable. Ancient rumor also makes mention of *aspirare* and *eccomare* as modalities, that is, *aeros* combined with *aqua* and *sonus* combined with *aqua*, and these are more plausible possibilities. The late Nikolo of Barrodarin spoke of one of his students as an *aspiramas* and recorded this caution: should one hold the gift of touching both wind and water, then achieve mastery of each alone, before attempting their combination.

"*Aquapotentia* requires firm but fluid handling, rather akin to the power in the lungs developed by players of the ophicleide" – a brass instrument that produced tones low enough to rival an alpenhorn, Livli believed – "while *aeropotentia* demands rigid, fine-grained pressure, more resembling the tight lips of a flautist."

Ah! That's it! I'm aspirakas who works with air and water, like Nikolo's student.

And she'd thought that because she was comfortable with water-duoja, it would be wisest to use that as a foundation for what she was learning: the air-duoja.

Evidently not.

Physika continued: "It is possible to create parallel channels for each simultaneously, but the challenge is an extremely advanced one. Euphrateles of ancient Deironos wrote of an adept who burst into flame when attempting her first admixture of *aeros* with *sonus*. This is the only mention of *eccoaerae* in the ancient record, which is why it is not included by serious scholars as one of the combinatorial disciplines."

So *that* was why she'd been slammed to the bottom of the hot spring the time she faltered. *I wonder if the ancients knew about the anchoring technique that Malaka-degg and I are using?*

It didn't really matter.

Nor would she abandon the combining of water and air, even temporarily. *I think I'm past the dangerous bit. But I can practice air alone, and get better faster!*

She stretched, raising her hands high and arching her back. How long had she been bending over this scroll? Too long? Should she break to nurse Rede? She could feel milk in her breasts, but they weren't engorged.

And I want to check one other thing.

She retuned *Physika* to the Mathema cabinet, and then went rummaging in the Gathering Lore section. *The Lindworm and the Queen* came easily to hand, now that it was filed correctly, but what was the scroll sharing its pigeonhole?

Livli drew it out.

Batty Baugheid.

What was this?

She read the first words: "There once was a sister who could not speak, nor could she spin or sew. She danced in the forest by day, like the wild fauve, and roamed the high meadows by night. When she visited her lodge-home, she never met her birth-mother's gaze. It was feared that Baugheid would never be a mother herself, or else a bad one, so the Holy Caller undertook a ritual to ensure that although the sister felt no ties to other sisters, she would know her baby as her own."

Duoja's demons! It was the rockfoil ritual!

Hands shaking, she set *Batty Baugheid* on the nearer table and weighted the curling parchment, then hurriedly unrolled *The Lindworm and the Queen* beside it to compare paragraphs. Was it the same?

Yes. Nearly word for word.

She leaned back, staring at the dark carved ceiling and feeling limp. *That wisewoman gave the ritual to the queen not so that she could choose a girl-child. She gave it to ensure the queen would love even a boy-child! Is that why I love Rede so much?*

Her stomach roiled.

Footsteps approached in the corridor leading to the scroll-hall, and she sat up.

"Goo gah *gah*! Gah *gah*!" Rede's demands, however unclear, were loud. Ibba appeared with him in the doorway.

"I think he's hungry," she declared, smiling. Then she saw Livli's face. Her own fell. She frowned at the scrolls. "I'm sure it's not true. Sure sure."

Livli shook her head dumbly.

"Gah *gah*! *Gah*!" reiterated Rede.

Ibba moved from her involuntary halt, and Livli pushed back from the library table, loosening her sweater-tunic, to receive her son. He burrowed his head into her ribs and took the breast eagerly as soon as she offered it.

"I thought you were looking in Mathema today," protested Ibba. "I'm so sorry. I wanted to tell you. Not leave you to find out alone." She gestured toward *Batty*.

"You knew?" Shock muted Livli's voice, but her stomach was settling. Nursing calmed her as efficiently as it did Rede.

Ibba answered Livli's unspoken "why didn't you tell me?"

"*Batty* lived in Oikessa for the past decade. We didn't even know it was missing, until their Holy Caller brought it home to Siajotti this Sanember. I told her it wasn't ours, but she assured me it didn't belong to Oikessa either. They'd found it in an unused bednook during Evener cleaning, and it's not listed on their records. Sister Hilka here discovered it on one of *our* old lists of missing scrolls."

Ibba touched Livli's cheek. "But I don't think *Batty's* right. Really I don't."

"It must be. That's why the old woman –"

"No." Ibba's voice was firm. "There's a reason both *Lindworm* and *Batty* are stored in Folktales, not in Being-truth, not in Healing Arts."

Livli looked down at Rede. His face was intent, but placid, thoroughly engrossed with the important business of swallowing nourishment. Her heart turned over.

He's so darling, so precious, so much . . . mine. Could such feeling come from the aegis-foil?

"And there's another obvious reason why the wisewoman gave the queen that ritual," Ibba continued.

"Because worry doesn't help a pregnancy," Livli stated slowly. "And a *maghra* would know that once the baby was born, it wouldn't matter. Its mother would love it. Unless she was Batty Baugheid."

Ibba nodded.

Rede let go the nipple and grinned at Livli, reaching for her mouth with an errant hand. She captured it, pressed a kiss to his knuckles, and then sat him up on her lap.

"Aahp!" His burp was loud, but not messy.

She switched him to the other breast, thoughtful.

Ibba still looked worried. "You'll not brood on this, Livli," she urged.

Livli brought herself back from pondering the first moment after Rede's birth, when she'd set eyes on him and felt an instantaneous connection.

"No, it's alright, Ibba. I'm sure you're correct. I just wonder . . ." She didn't finish her thought. No need for Ibba to know that she planned to use duoja-sight to investigate the petal-conserve forgotten on her bednook's shelf. *I don't care if it did produce that first connection,* she decided. *My love for Rede is all mine now.*

She came home to trouble.

Gaddja met her at the valley-rock, detaining her there to give warning of what awaited at Kaunis-lodge.

Thoivra had seized on Livli's absence to petition that Malaka-degg be declared fully healed and discharged from the spa, no longer eligible for continued residence there.

"Livli, he's not my patient, and I haven't been following his case. You seemed to have him well in hand." Gaddja's lips straightened. "I'll admit I thought Thoivra a tempest in a teapot when all this started, but she seems to have a talent for finding people's weak spots. And using those vulnerabilities to gain adherents to her cause."

Livli refrained from saying, "I told you so." She'd rather have been wrong.

"*Is* Malaka-degg ready for discharge?" demanded Gaddja.

"No." Livli felt calm and cool. Some part of her wanted to get hot and impassioned, but . . . somehow she'd grown beyond that kind of response to challenge.

I'm not reacting; I'm . . . winning, she realized.

Gaddja looked puzzled. "I thought you'd miss him, if Thoivra succeeds," she said.

"I would. I'm learning air-duoja from him. And I need him to help me while I figure how to blend air-duoja with water-duoja most effectively. But he's going nowhere. It will take another half year before both arm and leg are back to full strength. And he'll need specially designed, graduated exercises prescribed throughout."

"Just professional concerns." Was Gaddja disappointed?

Livli couldn't help smiling. "Malaka-degg is my friend, Mother-healer, but Mahde was my friend too. And I made a mistake there. I expect you know that."

Gaddja nodded. "And I'm just an interfering old matchmaker," she concluded.

"No. You care about me. But, Gaddja, think! Even if Malaka-degg is the right linking-partner for me – and I think it's too soon to be thinking that way – he is destined to return to Minmahal-tribe. You've heard him talking of his flock. As shaman-priest, he's dedicated to their well-being. He *will* return to them once he's healed. Would you have me left heartsore then?"

"If he loved you enough –"

Livli snorted. "What you are, Gaddja, is romantic! Malaka-degg would no more abandon his people than I would abandon my patients. Have done with this notion of yours."

Gaddja sighed. "No doubt you're correct." She stood in silence a moment, gazing out across the tan grasses of the autumnal valley below. The light snow from the previous day had melted. "So, you're confidant about getting a reprieve on his discharge?"

"I'd appreciate your authority backing me up. Will you come with me to Seagga?"

At Gaddja's nod, Livli resumed climbing the slope toward the lodge. They went straight to the lodge-mother's parlor. Seagga herself opened her door at Livli's knock.

"Gaddja! Livli! You're back!" Seagga sounded flustered.

Livli shrugged out of her rucksack, then her coat – letting them fall to the floor – and checked Rede. Still napping. She spoke her point: "I understand Thoivra's requesting the discharge of one of my patients. He's not ready, so I won't be discharging him."

Seagga flushed. "Please. Gaddja, Livli, do sit. No need to rush these things. Let's talk it over a little."

Gaddja objected, her tone smooth: "Mother Seagga, it's perfectly straight forward. The man requires more therapy for his healing injuries. Livli, and I as the Mother-healer, will decide when any patient has completed the course of his or her treatment. Not Thoivra."

"But it's not just Thoivra!" Seagga was unexpectedly valiant. "I share her concern. The man's been seen doing pull-ups on pine boughs and jogging uphill in the low pastures. Of course, he's healed. He obviously requires neither the hot spring nor your supervision."

Patience, Livli told herself. *Pushing her is one way to make Seagga dig in her heels.* She sat. Gaddja sat.

"Seagga," began Livli. The lodge-mother frowned. "*Mother* Seagga. The pull-ups and the hill running are part of Malaka-degg's current therapy regimen. His exercises will get more vigorous yet as he improves. He was a strong man. He'll be strong again at his discharge."

Seagga sank into an armchair across from them. "Your standards are high."

Gaddja pre-empted Livli. "Naturally. We send our patients home fully well, entirely restored. We *are* healers, Seagga."

The lodge-mother sniffed. "So you've never sent someone home with exercises to finish healing there? I doubt it!"

Livli opened her lips for rebuttal, but Seagga overrode her. "In any case, you'll have to make an exception this time. The man's disrupting all of Kaunis, flaunting himself before impressionable young linking-sisters, and I won't have it."

Livli giggled. She couldn't help it. The idea of Malaka-degg "flaunting himself" was ludicrous.

Seagga glared.

Gaddja spoke, drawing the lodge-mother's attention. "I'm sorry you feel that way, but Kaunis-spa is my purview, not yours. Malaka-degg will remain until Livli pronounces him ready to leave."

"The spa answers to you," said Mother Seagga, "but the lodge is mine!"

"Yes?" Gaddja was polite.

"And I'll have that Reindeer man out of Kaunis, if I must dismiss you to do it. Sister Pihja would be an excellent mother-healer. I've often thought her talents overlooked."

Livli knew a sensation of shock at these words, but Gaddja merely leaned back, one eyebrow raised. "Yes?"

"I'll do it, Gaddja Algen-spring."

"I don't think you will. Kaunis-spa is renowned from Kylma-lodge to Oitava. Would you jeopardize that?"

"Kaunis will achieve new glory under Pihja."

"I don't think so. And even were that true, glory without Livli and Niyena seems unlikely. A spa needs healers to retain its reputation."

Ah! Gaddja was brilliant. Two could play at Thoivra's game. And a "work-fast" of healers would have impact. *If we could bring ourselves to do it.* Livli tried to imagine herself sitting idle when a sister fell sick.

Seagga straightened. *Sensing weakness?* "And you *are* healers," she repeated Gaddja's emphasis.

Gaddja replied, undaunted, "Indeed. We can practice our calling at Iloiset, if need be."

Now Seagga looked shocked. "You wouldn't!"

"I'm not giving on this, Seagga. Know that!"

"But Iloiset has no sacred spring!"

Gaddja's expression grew pitying. "*Kaunis* had no sacred spring forty years ago. It's a gift."

"You really would, wouldn't you?" Seagga deflated.

Gaddja nodded. "I took an oath to Duoja herself, and I will not practice healing to suit your political convenience, Seagga."

"Alright, alright." Now Seagga was pettish. "Have it your way, then. But" – the lodge-mother's lowered eyes grew abruptly keen – "the next time your doings land square within my reach, you'll not receive leniency from me."

Gaddja's lips twitched, repressing a smile. "I can accept that."

Especially since it's not true, thought Livli. If Gaddja were sufficiently stern, Seagga would bend. That's what *this* ruckus was all about. Thoivra had been strident, and Seagga wilted. But Malaka-degg was safe for now.

Festive preparations for Long-dark occupied the next few eight-days.

Livli delighted in this time of year. Fragrant aromas drifted from the kitchens as the cooks concocted special treats. Garlands of pine and wool adorned chair rails, bannisters, and lintels, the greenery and bright ribands enhancing the dark polish of the paneling. An air of expectant joy pervaded Kaunis.

Thoivra was particularly active, devising orbs of braided wool to hang in the garlands and from the ceiling rafters, and urging the young novitiates to pray the devotions of Saint Bastiane often in readiness for their linking.

Good. She's too busy to make trouble.

Livli confined her own arrangements to creating a knitted marmot, aglow with red pompoms on its paws, for her son to receive in the dawning after the Long-dark vigil. That, and she took her jar of petal-conserve to Malaka-degg.

She had to confess why she'd made the conserve, of course, and was relieved to discern that mild twinkle in his eye. *He always smiles when I push the limits, never frowns. Even when I'm unwise.* She loved that about him.

"Where be Rede?" he asked.

"Mimmi's been wanting to watch him for me ever since he was born. This seemed like a good time."

Malaka-degg looked amused again. "You plan to try new . . . witness."

"I found a scroll at Siajotti that calls the effect of the aegis-petals into question. And . . . I'd like to know what they really do."

"Ah. You taste, I watch." He was nodding.

"Well, I'll watch, too. But I want you to anchor me like when we do our water-wind practice."

"Safe?" he asked, questioning not the duoja – they'd done that enough to know the risks – but the effect of the remedy on her body.

Livli flushed. "I asked Niyena." Was she spreading her secret with too little concern? "She said that since I'm not pregnant, it probably won't have any effect at all."

Malaka-degg started for the hot spring. She checked him. "I know we've always been in the water before, but I don't want to use water-duoja, or even air-duoja, for this. I'll just open my duoja-sight. Do you think you can do the anchoring on dry land?"

"Like when I partner Paghet-liga for Timog-child. Yes."

She settled herself cross-legged in front of him on his table-bed.

We should switch him to a nook. His hip is strong enough that he won't hurt it scooting in and out.

Malaka-degg adjusted his pillows for better support, tried his legs in a variety of positions before deciding cross-legged was best for him too, and then laid his arms along hers, resting his fingers gently atop her hands.

"Breathe," he whispered.

Livli allowed her eyes to close, felt her breathing fall into rhythm with his. The sparkle that was duoja shimmered into being in her mind's perception, glinting within her roots, gliding along her branches, flaring to delineate Malaka-degg's pattern as well. She groped blindly for the spoon of conserve she'd placed in a saucer on his bedside table.

There it was.

She turned her duoja-sight on it: faint sparkles marked each petal within the honey.

Interesting.

She placed it in her mouth. Spicy. Sweet. And prickly tingles in her throat.

She swallowed and watched as the petal-duoja spiraled out from her heart root through her branches, down into the curling twiglets and threads, deep into her being, matching a pattern already there. *Oh!*

"Malaka-degg!"

"Ssh," he murmured. "I see. I see."

They waited there, in that moment: breathing, taking it in.

The spoon fell from her fingers, slipped over the edge of the mattress, clattered on the floor.

Livli ignored it, focusing on the coiling travel of the petal-duoja. At the last, the trailing sparks grew too delicate to see.

Livli sighed and relaxed, leaning back into Malaka-degg's embrace. He felt warm and solid. His fingertips lingered along her arms, traced her shoulder. One hand cupped her cheek, urged her head to turn.

He shifted, she shifted.

His lips were warm, live, gentle. She opened hers to receive his kiss. His mouth tasted of . . . him. Clean, faintly sweet, faintly salt. She wanted more.

He drew back, humorous affection in his gaze. "Too soon?" he asked.

She shook her head no, wordless, wanting him. *What did he see in her face?*

Whatever it was beckoned him, and he bent to her lips again, taking her in a deeper kiss, sliding her spa robe from her, loosening its belt.

She turned, reached for his shoulders, disrobing him with urgency in her touch. She felt his hand trace her breast, circle the nipple, then pass downward and behind, lifting her to straddle him. *Oh!* He was ready, as ready as she. Vaguely, she thought, *this will never work.* But she didn't care. His hands on her hips were guiding her home, her hands on him achieving the same. *Oh! This is sweet, so sweet.*

⚜ ⚜ ⚜

*A*fter, she lay beside him, supported in his loose embrace.

"Livli?" His questioning tone called her back to thinking.

"Umm?" She didn't want to think, to reason. Lazing in the pleasure of his proximity was enough.

"Long-dark has linking-rite, yes?"

She sighed and sat up, pushing her hair behind her shoulders. She'd let it get longer than she preferred. "Yah. Long-dark linking yields babies for Mother's Bounty."

"Minmahal do demon-binding, but we not there. Will you . . . link with me?"

She laughed. "We just did."

His smile was too relaxed to be a grin. "Hammarleeding rite," he persisted.

She felt her own smile fade. "Oh . . . I wish . . . but, Malaka-degg, Mother Seagga has written a new warrant in the lodge-book. Outlanders are banned from our rituals now."

"Just us? Alone?" he said.

"I . . . I'm not sure how, really. I suppose I could ask Sarvet, see if she'd do a private rite for us, except . . ."

His lips – beautiful lips – compressed. "Except no private place."

"Yah. Maybe in summer. We could find an out-of-the-way spot in the valley."

He reached for her hand, brushed it with a kiss. *"Ginang"* – milady – "this summer you *magpakasal"* – take vow with – "me? Yes?"

She felt oddly relieved. Did she not love him? After that?

It's not a thrilly feeling, she mused. *Just trust, all the way down. There is no place in him I do not trust.* And yet . . . even if she could have a linking-rite this Long-dark with the other postulants, she didn't feel ready. Would she be ready by summer?

"Yes," she answered him.

He looked happy. "Good. I wait," he declared. "But, Livli, you see deepest spirals? Petal-*paglunas*? Same! Same as Livli-*paglunas*!"

"Yes! I did see. It mirrored the pattern that holds my love for Rede. I think it really might enhance a mother's bond to her child. Not sure it could create it" – she was more and more certain her love for her son was her own – "but . . . I wonder if it might help mothers with certain complications. I'm going to tell Niyena what we saw. She had questions and ideas almost as soon as I finished telling her our plans for testing the conserve."

She was smiling again.

Malaka-degg reached for her, and she went into his arms, willing.

This time their linking was leisurely, lingering. *I am already bound to this man*, Livli realized. *I just didn't know what love felt like when matched with equal trust.*

Malaka-degg's touch reached intimate places. She might have rushed toward completion when her longing grew unbearable, but her partner stayed her, teasing her toward delight. She teetered on the brink, laughing, amazed. Then ecstasy spiraled through her, intense through its delay.

⚜ ⚜ ⚜

One side of the spa-hall featured a sleep-corridor with bednooks along its inner wall. The passage ended at the far corner in a private closet, also with bednook, intended for a healer at times when vulnerable patients required expert care through the night.

Livli moved Malaka-degg into this chamber that afternoon. It would be a more private location than the massage closet off the passage between the foyer and the hot spring. And the bednook mattresses were softer than the padding on a massage table!

Mimmi was not eager to give Rede back to his mother when Livli returned, but Rede was hungry. He lunged for her breast greedily once in her arms, and she decided to nurse him immediately.

Perched on a friendship-bench in the passageway outside the row of parlors, she listened to Mimmi babble: how sweet, how precious, a joy, let me do it again.

Livli chuckled. "You need a baby of your own," she said.

Mimmi flushed. "I'm hoping," she answered. "You know I'm linking with Votan this Long-dark."

No, Livli hadn't known. One of the older brothers. Interesting. Perhaps Votan no longer pined for his departed longtime partner, then. He'd certainly be a better choice than Lavrras or Issat.

"Joyous linking," Livli wished Mimmi politely.

"Thanks. I'm eager to welcome a son or a daughter this Mother's Bounty."

Outside the calling-hall next morning, before the start of the linking-rite, Livli knew some discontent.

If it weren't for Thoivra, I'd be a postulant myself, approaching this ceremony with Malaka-degg.

Once the worship service started, her regret faded. The novitiates were excited and nervous. The postulants, Mimmi among them, were excited and ardent. But the publicity attendant on Hammarleeding linking, once a prod toward exaltation, no longer appealed. Maybe it's a good thing that Thoivra succeeded with that ban. *I don't think*

I want this after all. But she did want Malaka-degg. Would Sarvet consent to a private ceremony? Did Livli want any ceremony? After all, she *had* Malaka-degg. How would he feel about linking without formality?

She knew his answer as though he'd just spoken it. *He's always ready to meet me where I am.*

Did that mean he would always say yes to her? No. That wasn't the same thing at all. *He'll always say yes to* me, *even when he says no to something I do or say,* she realized. *That* was her trust.

Livli had planned to delve into *aeros-energea* (as the Siajotti-scroll named air-duoja) with serious focus after Long-dark, but Malaka-degg's brother turned up at long last, although not in the way anyone would have hoped.

She was lingering in the lodge-foyer one evening in Sombry, wondering whether she would sleep in the spa bednook with Malaka-degg or in her own, when a furious clamor on the clapper of the outside bell preceded the abrupt opening of the front door.

A snow-covered brother slammed the door behind him, yelling, "The lodge-mother! Get me your lodge-mother, right now!"

Then he saw Livli, recognized her.

"Healer! Livli! Is anyone missing from Kaunis-lodge?"

It was Steffi Sundin-spring, the young hunter she'd helped treat last winter. Whatever was he doing here? Now?

"What has happened?" she asked him.

Two sisters paused on the stairs, waiting to hear what he would say. Three others turned back from the passage to the parlors.

"Is anyone missing?" he repeated. "That frost leopard was already wounded! Somebody tussled with it and lost before I got it! Are your sisters all within? Metsasta's backtracking and Hirvie went to Tukeva to check on the brothers." His voice was tense, anguished.

Livli tried to think who she'd seen in the refecting-hall. Kaunis was too big to do an easy head count, and Steffi's anxiety was infectious.

"I don't know," she started to say.

Then she did know. "Oh! Mother Divine! Niyena's not back from gathering ice-plant."

She whirled away from him – tossing over her shoulder, "I'll be right back! I'm coming with you!" – and dashed for the back of the lodge, the fastest way to the spa-hall.

Ulla reopened the front door to clang the bell in a continuous peal.

Livli fled for Malaka-degg.

"Will you watch Rede? Niyena's been attacked by the *onderneming*! I have to go! Will you take him?" She was yanking the sling over her head, thrusting the bundled baby – wailing at her abrupt handling – into Malaka-degg's arms.

He accepted Rede without losing his calm. "Ssh, ssh, little *nebbishon*, there now."

Rede hiccuped once, blinked, then quieted. Malaka-degg looked up as Livli started away, his expression lacking his usual humor.

"Ask friend Mimmi to care for Rede," he told her.

"You won't?" She was astounded.

"I come with you, of course."

"No!"

"Livli." His fingers circled her elbow. "Yes. Now go to Mimmi!"

He placed Rede gently in her arms, pulled his boots from the cupboard beside his bednook, unlaced them, and inserted his feet into the leather coverings.

Livli went.

Mimmi took Rede, Ulla handed Livli a filled rucksack and a packet for Malaka-degg to add to his; then they followed Steffi into the night. The snowpack reflected what little light glimmered from the dark, turgid sky. A steady flurry of flakes chilled their cheekbones. Steffi held a lit lantern on a staff, its glow illuminating the footsteps from his journey to Kaunis-lodge.

✤ ✤ ✤

The frost leopard lay where Steffi and his fellow hunter had slain it, its rosette-spattered pelt of silver gray beautiful, the length of its feline fangs intimidating, the welter of its blood . . . messy.

"This is the big one I was tracking last year," Steffi told them. "Same unusual size to the paw, see, and one digital pad askew. Wish I'd got him before he got your friend."

He urged them to hurry, retracing the leopard's track through the forest clearing.

They'd descended all the way to the floor of the valley below Kaunis and still had some way to go before they arrived where the hunters first encountered their prey. This was where the real uncertainty of the night began.

Metsasta was ahead of them. How far? Could they catch him? Could they find Niyena in time?

Metsasta's footprints in the snow were easy to see – he was not trying to be sneaky – and the snowpack at this lower elevation was scant. They hadn't bothered with snowshoes and they moved fast.

How was Malaka-degg's hip holding up?

Livli glanced back, but he was too close for her to assess his gait, and she needed to watch her own step. His face was intent, but showed no pain. Like her, he focused on speed and footing.

The frost leopard's tracks wound through the pines, then along the edge of the forest and over a low saddle of land. As they came over the ridge, Steffi increased the pace.

Did he see something?

The tree boles loomed black out of the falling snowflakes; everything beyond a few strides away was shrouded in white.

A whistle, bird-like, sounded ahead of them.

Steffi answered with a sharper trill.

A moment later they rounded a juniper thicket to find Metsasta awaiting them.

"We're close, brother!" he told Steffi.

They didn't stay to chat, but trotted close on Metsasta's heels. Down a slight slope, across a frozen rivulet, along the edge of another meadow, and then around the mass of a granite outcropping.

The figure at its base, dark against the snow, kneeling and bending, winked into existence from the curtain of flakes.

"Niyena!" called Livli, brushing past Steffi and Metsasta and running forward.

Her friend looked up, eyes haunted. "I'm going to lose him!" she cried.

Livli plumped down on her own knees, her attention transferred to . . . a man, a man of the Reindeer People, lying flaccid and bloody under Niyena's frantic hands. His wooly hair gleamed golden in the light from Steffi's lantern. His face, dark and congested, resembled all too closely Malaka-degg's when he'd first arrived at Kaunis-spa.

Abruptly, Livli knew who he was.

Malaka-degg was lifting her rucksack from her shoulders, dumping his own down beside it, seating himself behind her.

"I anchor. You wield paglunas. This be Kanya-degg," he added.

"Yes."

Her eyelids closed as she sought the balance point from which all healing began. She didn't have much time.

Breathe . . . breathe . . . there!

The silver network of her own energy pattern sparked into being. She opened, let the energy rise, and channeled it out through her phalanges into Kanya-degg, probing the wound at the back of his neck, reaching for the point of mortal vulnerability.

Ah, a raggedness, a breach within a conduit where no breach should be.

She stretched for water-duoja – remembered: *I'm on land* – and strained toward air instead, missed.

Malaka-degg's presence arrived and bore her up.

Then she felt it: feathery, insubstantial, a breeze caught only by *energea*.

She stretched again, snagged it, and spun it to fit her need. Delicately, lightly, a web to close that breach. Fluttering, flexing, then adhered. Yes!

Livli opened her eyes, sagged in Malaka-degg's arms, then gathered herself. She wasn't done.

Or was she? Niyena was taking up where she'd left off, winding bandage around their patient's neck to hold the wad of coagulant herbs against the wound, checking his breathing and his pulse, pulling a blanket over him.

Malaka-degg offered Livli a sip of water from his canteen, took another himself.

Steffi came up from somewhere – what had he been doing? – and wedged his lantern staff into a cranny of the granite bluff.

"Are we camping here? I've checked our perimeter. No wolves in the area, nor any other *onderneming*," he said.

Livli looked at Niyena.

"I think we need to get him back to Kaunis-spa, don't you?"

Niyena nodded. "He's lost a lot of blood, and he's chilled. He needs . . . more than we can do here. Than *you* can do. Isn't that right?"

"I'm not sure the spring will help me with what I must do next," Livli confessed.

She'd repaired the perforation in the artery, but something was far wrong with the spinal *styrke*. Was it severed? She feared it was severed. And if that were so . . . healing might not be possible.

"But . . . yah, let's get him back," she said.

Steffi and Metsasta conferred quietly. Malaka-degg pressed dried pears and nut biscuits on everyone and urged them to drink. Niyena stared at the ground while she chewed. Questions about the fight between Kanya-degg and the frost leopard felt inappropriate.

As they unrolled the stretcher cached in Livli's rucksack – *thank you Ulla* – Niyena muttered: "He saved me."

The trek back to Kaunis was harder than the outward bound journey.

Steffi and Metsasta went first, holding the stretcher handles at Kanya-degg's head. Livli took one middle handle, Malaka-degg, the other. Niyena managed both at the foot.

No longer needing to follow the frost leopard's track, they traversed the connected meadows of the Vrea-vale, avoiding the brambles and branches of the forest, but Kanya-degg's weight pulled at their arms.

Livli and Malaka-degg switched sides often.

The climb up the mountain took the last of their strength. The switchback at the valley-rock almost defeated them. *We should have brought a larger rescue party.* They had to lay Kanya-degg down in the snow while they rested.

Risten arrived, posted as lookout, when they hauled Kanya-degg upward once more. She took one of Niyena's stretcher handles and almost pushed the lot of them past the obstacle with her fresh vigor.

Crossing the spa terrace, Livli felt fatigue overwhelm her.

We're here. We did it.

Inside, Thoivra awaited them.

She was a dumpy matron in colorful tunic and skirt, the tapestried result of expert knitting, featuring green vines laden with fruit and flowers. Her smooth hair circled her head in a braided coronet. Her brown eyes and round face lacked joviality. That was reserved for friends.

"I knew it!" she exclaimed as his bearers eased Kanya-degg through the doors of the spa-hall. "You'll seize any excuse to get more men and foreigners into Kaunis. And I'm not having it, Livli Sarvet-spring! Turn yourselves around and walk back out that door!"

Steffi and Metsasta faltered, and the whole party came to a halt.

"Move aside, Thoivra," Livli replied. Her arms trembled with the effort of keeping Kanya-degg off the floor.

Thoivra drew herself up and advanced a step.

"You've tainted the sister-lodge enough. Get out! Now!"

"Steffi, Metsasta, we need to get our patient to treatment." Livli wasn't sure if her voice was calm out of authority or just because she was so tired. "Second door on the right."

The brothers moved forward.

Thoivra braced herself, but to no avail. With his free arm (a burly one), Metsasta simply set her aside as he might slide a chair astray from its wall.

"Sorry, mother," he murmured.

And then they were laying Kanya-degg on the very table that had received Malaka-degg eleven months before. Thoivra attempted to follow them, protesting and spluttering. Then Gaddja arrived and banished her.

"You can walk out on your feet, or you can land on your backside, but out you will go. You choose!"

Thoivra chose to walk.

A nurse-sister ushered the Sundin-lodgers away to baths, clean clothes, hot drinks, and rest. Malaka-degg refused the same, leaning against the closet wall. The healers closed in on Kanya-degg. His lungs still moved and his pulse was strong, but the muscle tension in his limbs was absent.

"Gaddja, his spinal *styrke* is severed." Livli struggled to suppress a sob. "We can't let Malaka-degg's sweet-brother be crippled!"

Gaddja shot a sharp look his way. "You share a birth-mother?"

"And father," he said.

Gaddja's intake of breath hissed. "I am sorry. The *styrke* of the spinal column do not mend, but let me see if his is divided fully or partially."

Livli did not follow the mother-healer with duoja-sight to view the injury. She was so tired. And she was entertaining a notion: duoja-gift could not stimulate the spinal *styrke* to knit together; water-duoja felt . . . too . . . dense for the job. But what of air-duoja? *Aeros-energea* had touched Tresta's duoja-branches in a way the other duojas could not.

I'm going to try it!

Mother Gaddja was shaking her head. "It's partial, but the connection remaining is so slender . . . it might as well be full." She sighed. "We need to get these wet clothes off him, keep him warm . . . and wait."

Malaka-degg's face set.

"No!" Livli protested.

Niyena slid Kanya-degg's blanket away; a nurse-sister started unlacing his boots.

Livli stayed their hands. "No. Any movement could worsen the damage. Let me try something first."

"You think the new duoja might affect the *styrke*? Not just the grosser flesh? Not just the duoja-branches?" Gaddja's eyes brightened, and she answered her own question. "Worth a try, yah. What do you need?"

"Just . . . two stools." If Livli had to stand a moment longer, she'd drop, and Malaka-degg couldn't be much better.

Seated at Kanya-degg's head with his sweet-brother behind her, Livli could not open her duoja-sight. "Shun it!"

"Ssh, ssh," came Malaka-degg's response. "Draw on me. Draw on me now."

There was a possibility. She'd always waited until she was actively spinning the air. What if she reached for him sooner. Now.

Breathe.

And breathe again.

She . . . opened something, and felt his strength flow in.

Her own branches and roots sparkled into a winking tracery, energy already flowing through her phalanges. She coaxed a tendril of *aeros* into a coil. No, it wasn't fine enough. What about *that* one? Oh! Another wisp, so gossamer gauzy it was hardly there, wafted by.

She snagged it, spun it, spun it.

Still too gross.

What if? She opened deeper, and deeper again; the current from Malaka-degg intensified. *What would this cost him?*

Soundless sound echoed in her being.

She spun the *aeros* tighter still.

It was thinner than a split hair, finer than a strand of starlight. It was pattern alone, all matter pressed from it.

She went in.

It was fire, it was ice, it was pain.

Spinning still, winding and winding from agony to agony,

through bruised seas. Touch pain and double back. Touch pain and back again through swollen hurt. She swam in Kanya-degg's *styrke*, becoming Duoja herself, healing personified. Dragging *aeros* in her wake, she braided a *styrke*.

And dove upward, out, done.

Then blackness claimed her.

❧ ❧ ❧

A baby was crying.

"There now. There, there, little *nebbishon*," came a man's voice.

"He's just hungry." A woman's voice, lowered. "Is she going to be alright? She looks so pale."

"Just tired. She come out of faint soon." The sound of soft pats on the baby's back. "Sh, sh." The infant wails did not diminish.

Livli's eyes flew open. "Rede!"

Mimmi was hovering over her, a cup of something in her hand.

"Give me Rede!" Livli demanded.

"Moment. In a moment," Mimmi answered. "He can wait until you've drunk your beet kvass."

Ugh! *Beet* kvass.

If only it were kraut whey instead. She'd never favored beets in any form. But . . . they'd be good for her. Livli hitched herself up on the pillows at her head, accepted the mug, and gulped valiantly.

Beety, very beety.

Malaka-degg handed Rede into the bednook – his bednook, she realized – and Livli put her son to the breast.

Instant silence.

"I think he's begun teething pains," babbled Mimmi, "poor little brother. Rubbing his gums with an icicle helped at first, but them he started to miss his mother. And then –"

Livli felt a renewal of her old fear, the fear of losing her son.

None of that! I'll never let him go.

Except her culture assumed her consent to such a parting. And she had yet to devise her way to breaking with tradition. *But I will.* And she would. The kernel of confidence planted under Nial's aegis remained strong.

"Mimmi," interrupted Malaka-degg, "I think Livli sleep, if you go."

"Oh! Yah, of course." Mimmi grew briskly efficient. "If you'll come with me, brother, I'll get you settled in a corridor nook. There's plenty of extra blankets. Do you think I should stay in case Livli needs help in the night? The little one might wake, and then –"

Malaka-degg smothered a chuckle, but he followed Mimmi obediently to the door of his room.

Livli shook her head. This was ridiculous.

"Mimmi! He doesn't need another nook. There's plenty of room in this one."

"What!" gasped her friend, stopping in the doorway, turning. "Livli! You'll never sleep with–"

Oh, that was not discreet. Livli bit her lip.

"Um! Malaka-degg often helps me with Rede in the evenings, and . . ."

Making excuses was just as ridiculous as clothing an unneeded mattress. Livli sighed. "Yah. I'm linked with Malaka-degg. We'd have joined the Long-dark rite, if it weren't for Thoivra."

"Oh! Oh, of course." Mimmi recovered her poise. "In that case" – her dimples flashed – "I'll bid you dream deep! Or not!" And she whisked herself away.

Livli felt herself flushing. "Oh, Malaka-degg! Why didn't I hold my tongue?"

"You weary, Livli. Hard to remember secrets, when thoughts slow. And . . . we be secret, yes?"

"Yah," she agreed, yawning. Rede nursing was rapidly turning her fatigue to slumber, but she wanted to know how Kanya-degg faired before she surrendered. "Your sweet-brother?"

"Toes still limp, but he wriggle fingers before he sleep."

"He's awake?" That news dashed some of her drowsiness. "Did you speak to him?"

Malaka-degg nodded. "He wake short time, see me, tell me" – a chortle – "Minmahal joke. We save his spine, Livli."

"I'm so glad."

All that stress and strain – rushing to get to the frost leopard's victim, pushing to get him back to Kaunis, stretching her limits to use air-duoja on the edge of fatigue – was worth it. Kanya-degg would walk because of them. On that thought, she let sleep take her.

Kanya-degg was teasing the nurse-sisters next morning, demanding larger servings of breakfast, and telling Malaka-degg, "You be idiot to hike along bottom of slope in Nerich," upon learning his brother's story.

"You know so much about snow slip last circuit," Malaka-degg rebutted.

Kanya-degg wasn't the sort to look abashed. He laughed and retorted, "No, but I learn fast. More fast than you! Snow slip catch you! Ha, ha!"

Malaka-degg's eyes crinkled. "But frost leopard catch you! Ha!"

Kanya-degg roared. Apparently he found the reminder of his tussle with the leopard hilarious.

Livli shook her head. Brothers!

She glanced aside to Niyena, but Niyena was flushing and looking down, rather than joining in her friend's mock exasperation.

What was that about?

The herbalist made an excuse to leave the closet, missing the rest of Kanya-degg's tale.

He confessed to lingering at Kessel-lodge, where he landed after being separated from Malaka-degg in the blizzard. The brothers there had the best curling sheet in the Fiordhammars and Kanya-degg finished out the match tournament with them, before heading south in search of his errant elder sibling. En route to Kaunis, he encountered a party of Hammar-brothers trekking north in search of the fabled sky-drake of Visserstroud.

He turned aside toward this irresistible lure.

"No worry for a *ritwal-pakain* caught by snow slip, eh?" heckled Malaka-degg.

"Like you worry for me!" Kanya-degg dug back.

They were both smiling, as much delighted as relieved in their safe reunion.

The expedition into Mersstrand took longer than planned – *why am I not surprised*, thought Livli, *I bet most things Kanya-degg does both stray from the plan and also work brilliantly* – and thus Kaunis-lodge was making his acquaintance this Sombry instead of last Labresse.

"But we see drake, Malaka-degg! We *see* it!"

Kanya-degg's Aidinkieli was more fluent than his brother's. He'd probably bantered the whole of every mile north and back with the Hallinta-folk, gaining more language practice than any three other men in his place.

"What was it like?" asked Livli.

Kanya-degg fell uncharacteristically silent. "Icy mist . . . shimmering rainbow . . . breath of ice scour . . . eyes . . . old . . . powerful . . . dangerous. We watch from far away, but it kill all, if it want. Not want."

The swelling in Kanya-degg's neck and upper back took several days to subside, and his control over his lower body returned in pace with the release of the pinched spinal *styrke*.

Once he was on his feet again, he was impossible to keep pent up in the spa.

He explored the sheltered Vyssa-grove, the branching-hall, and the spring-house. He was moving on to the lodge – wouldn't Thoivra have a field day with that – when a dinner stopped him.

Kanya-degg proved allergic to sour-fruit. He broke out in a rash covering his entire body, his joints bruised, and he developed a raging fever.

Livli thought they were going to lose him, after all that beautiful success on his broken back. Healing-duoja, water-duoja, and air-duoja did nothing for him. But Niyena's herbal remedies turned the tide.

The fever ebbed. The rash faded. And the bruises turned green, then yellow, then gone. Kanya-degg was more subdued following this travail than he'd been after the leopard injury.

Niyena, despite her heroic retrieval of him, returned to avoiding her patient.

Livli detained her on a friendship-bench near the kitchens. "Kanya-degg needs you," she said bluntly.

"It's my fault he's in the spa at all," Niyena moaned. "Some healer I am. My patients get worse, not better."

"Niyena!"

The herbalist seemed immovably stuck on this idea. Nothing Livli could say comforted her. Was the running of someone else into danger the real problem? Maybe . . .

"Niyena, this isn't about healing, is it? This is about *your* experience. The cat's snarl in *your* ear. The sight of its bared fangs and wrinkled lip, its extended claws, its lethal leap –"

"Don't!"

Niyena's face went down, her palms came up, and she burst into loud sobs.

"I was so scared, so scared. I was going to die, and then he saved me. He just shoved me off my feet and stepped in front of its pounce from that bluff. It was awful, awful! The blood burst from his neck, but somehow he managed to stab it as he fell, and it ran off. But I didn't know how to save him. He saved me, but I couldn't save him!" Her ribs shuddered with the violence of her grief. "He'd have died, if you hadn't come!"

"But I did come. Malaka-degg and I." Livli touched Niyena's far shoulder in a sideways hug. "Ssh, ssh. It's alright now. Everyone's alright. And you did save him. We'd have lost him to the sour-fruit without you."

Niyena sat abruptly. "Oh."

"What, hadn't you noticed?"

Niyena gave a watery giggle. "Actually, I hadn't."

Livli shook her head. *I should have gotten her to talk before now.* Of course it would haunt her. It would haunt anyone. "Well, notice now."

A reverberating clang and a shout – *yiy!* – much louder than the background clatter of utensils and chatter of the cooks, rang out from the kitchens. Had someone dropped the massive fermentation vat or something?

Rede woke from his nap babbling and struggling to free his arms. "Gah gah gah, boh! Boh!" He meant he wanted down on the floor.

She disentangled him from the sling and lowered him.

"Boh! Boh!" he crowed, pushing against the skirt of the bench.

"Boh!" And he toppled over on his back, having shoved too hard in an attempt to reach sitting.

Niyena laughed again, no water in it this time. "Oh, he's so sweet! *Can* he sit yet?"

"Not yet. But soon, I think."

"Gah boh! Ooo boh!"

"Yah, you're a clever one!" Livli told him and poked his stomach. Rede squealed and rolled, kicking his heels in glee.

"Did you realize that Kanya-degg is a hunter? Back amongst Minmahal-tribe?"

"No." Niyena sounded surprised. "*Is* he?"

"He protects the reindeer herds from wolf packs and from the ice-panthers. He wasn't just being a gallant idiot when he jumped for you. He knew what he was doing."

"Oh!" Niyena looked pensive. "That . . . makes a difference, somehow. I think."

And it did.

After avoiding him for an eight-day, Niyena now glued herself to her patient's side. And because she wanted him roaming Kaunis-lodge as little as did Livli, she took him herb-gathering with her.

That might have worked better, if the pair hadn't departed each morning and returned each evening in full view of the front veranda, but it was an improvement over the verbal contest that would surely erupt between him and Thoivra otherwise.

But there were murmurs among the sisters.

The littlest ones, largely unaware of Malaka-degg's presence through all the months, commented on Kanya-degg's strange clothes (green tunic of boiled wool adorned with bright yellow and white beads) and speculated that he would give good bear-back rides. The novitiates from Falnary's linking rite giggled whenever he strode into sight on the slope. The old crones smiled, either in worry or with an indulgent look in their eyes. But Thoivra's cronies sniffed, tossed their heads, and muttered phrases such as: *disgusting* or *our privacy gone* or *modesty under attack*.

Interestingly, no one was talking about Kanya-degg's brother or about *Livli* and Malaka-degg together. The ice-panther hunter had rather stolen the show. And clearly Mimmi was being more discreet about Livli than had been Livli herself in revealing her connection to the Reindeer man.

Mimmi *was* continuing to talk about the importance of healing being accessible to anyone who needed it and about the wonderful skill of the Kaunis healers. The crowd around her in the refecting-hall and the calling-hall, the number who sought her in the parlors after supper, was definitively larger than it had been before Mimmi espoused this cause.

Livli exerted herself to match her friend's good work, but found it difficult. She preferred evenings spent with Malaka-degg in the spa to those in the lodge parlors. And for every one sister Livli convinced to question Thoivra's ideas, Mimmi convinced three. Still . . . Mimmi's chatty style would never have moved stiff Vilhelma or skeptical Selen.

I must do my part too.

Thoivra's progress was also noticeable. Quite a few sisters turned away when Livli passed by them in the corridor. What would they do if they knew she'd linked with a foreigner?

She shivered.

Nothing good, for sure.

Malaka-degg was fast reaching the point at which he truly would no longer need Livli's guidance for his full recovery. Kanya-degg, also performing strengthening exercises, was fixed for discharge.

Were it not that the brothers surely intended to return to Minmahal-tribe together, he would have been long gone.

Or would he?

Niyena no longer invited him on her expeditions. He simply came along . . . was it eagerly? Yes, eagerly. Kanya-degg sought the herbalist's company. And Niyena . . . glowed in his presence. *Hmm.* Where was Niyena spending nights? Livli had her suspicions.

Falnary segued into Nerich.

Just a year ago I was planting aegis-foil. It seems longer than that.

Nerich gave way to Thyaril, and Thyaril to Ponce.

The black looks Thoivra and her friends gave Livli in the corridors increased in both intensity and frequency. Livli skipped Other-joy and the spring herd-luring (in further futile protest over Malaka-degg's exclusion).

Why does Thoivra have to be so adamant? So rigid? So resistant to change?

Sitting in Sarvet's parlor, the murmur of the Other-joy ceremony down the hall forming a backdrop to her thoughts, Livli remembered a time when she herself had displayed a similar intransigence. It had been Other-joy, and an Iloiset-sister petitioned Kaunis-lodge for sisterhood.

I was so indignant that she would switch mother-lodges just to be with a man.

"A sister's allegiance to her home should be heart-deep, not merely a matter of convenience and practicality," I declaimed.

Agata had fallen in love with a Tukeva-brother when both were present at the spa for treatment. Kaunis granted her request, and she celebrated a linking-rite with her beloved that very Other-joy.

I wasn't wrong, Livli mused. Lightly abandoning one's center, one's own priorities, invited a loss of integrity. But she and her coterie of like-minded friends felt differently by the close of that Other-joy. There had been nothing light about Agata's vows to Eaddji. Or her oath of allegiance to Kaunis.

The breach of tradition disturbed me, just like the changes I want now disturb Thoivra.

And she's no more wrong than I was wrong. But a choice must be made. Either men are allowed to be present in Kaunis or they are not. The rituals of that Other-joy seven years ago helped me and my friends accept change. *I wonder if Thoivra might be similarly eased?*

But the matron's demeanor displayed no signs of softening by either day's close or after.

Livli didn't skip the next fete-day following herd-luring. She couldn't bring herself to deprive Rede of the bell-ringing given to all infants old enough to participate in the Birth-joy fete. Rede was creeping, and was thrilled to discover that the faster he pumped his limbs the more furiously rang the bells circling his wrists and ankles.

"Gah gah boh kah!" he cried, scuttling around the candle-laden altar.

He was difficult to catch when the rite of young chimes ended, and he sobbed as his bells were removed.

Livli still debated her participation in the Long-light festival when Joiesse arrived. She loved the garland-dance, the dawn-branching, and the pageant of legends. But she wanted to dance with Malaka-degg, not Mahde. And Seagga (upheld by Thoivra) remained firm in her ban on foreigners.

As it happened, Livli's choice proved irrelevant.

No one had told Kanya-degg he wasn't welcome.

He'd missed Other-joy, because his injury hadn't yet healed enough to permit him to walk. The day of the spring herd-luring,

Niyena took him on an overnight trek to Kivea-terrrace – for a rare spike-moss that grew there, she said.

At Long-light, Kanya-degg simply joined the fun unasked, partnering Niyena with exuberant panache in all the pair rituals. And when Thoivra screeched that he was profaning sacred ground, he glanced around, saw as many faces for him as against, and burst out laughing.

"Ah, Mother, I be strong for two!" he vowed, kissing her cheek and sweeping her off into the grand hand figure. Poor Thoivra was so astounded she went meekly and made no further protest to the Reindeer-man's presence. Lacking Thoivra's vehemence, Seagga tacitly acquiesced as well.

But Livli saw none of it.

Jorgan returned from his wanderyar that very morning, in the darkness preceding sunrise, hiking directly to Kaunis-lodge, rather than home to Tukeva.

"Did you remember it was Long-light, then?" Livli asked him.

"No. I want to talk with you about something. Something wonderful!" His eyes shone.

Leaving Rede in the bednook with Malaka-degg, she'd risen early herself, hoping to decide her course for the day before it started, and perched on the valley-rock to think. The sky was light above the mountains, but the sloping ground remained dim. She espied motion beyond the brother-camp, someone approaching from the Vrea-vale. A latecomer?

He neared to ten paces before they recognized one another.

"Livli!"

"Jorgan!"

She scrambled to her feet, retreated along the peninsula of the out-thrust rock, and jumped onto the path. He met her right at the steepest bit, hugged her, kissed her, and demanded, "Where can we go to talk? I have so much to tell you!"

Mother Divine, but he'd changed!

The wooly strands of his hair reached past his waist, a neat mustache graced his upper lip, and he was taller than she. Much taller. Even the shape of his face was different, leaner, less round. But his green eyes, just like their father's, and his energetic enthusiasm were his own. He was her sweet-brother, Jorgan indeed, just a little more . . . concentrated.

She grabbed food from the refecting-hall sideboard and guided him to the upper edge of the low meadows.

"Livli!" he burst out. "I'm a healer like you! And I want you to sponsor me at Kaunis-spa."

"Duoja in Dwimmerholdt!" she exclaimed.

They spent the entire day discussing it.

He'd followed their birth-mother's trace south, visiting the island realms of the Merovessic Sea en route to the mainland and fixing in Imsterfeldt for more than a year. Like Sarvet, he learned of flower essences from Maittresse Saussen. Then he moved on through Cambers to Fresange, working on the great rose plantations and combining rose-lore with that of lavender, spice-grass, anemone, and cleavers.

His return to the Fiordhammars took him circling through Tromme-land and an encounter with a Trummor shamanic healer.

He stayed another year.

No wonder he'd changed!

Jorgan argued that since there were brother patients year round in the spa, having a brother healer shouldn't make that much difference. "Let me work under you for a month, so you can test my skills," he urged. "I'm good, I promise you. Crompe-fadar said I achieved miracles like those rumored of the lady-chapels of Fiorish, but I don't want you to take my word for it. I'll *earn* my place at Kaunis."

Sias Divine! How to answer him?

Even after she'd explained about Malaka-degg and Kanya-degg and Thoivra, and Thoivra again, she wasn't sure he understood. Brothers and sisters coming home after a wanderyar tended to forget the constraints of their origins. New ways seemed logical, appealing . . . desirable.

Demon-spawn!

She'd never left home, but his ideas dovetailed with her own developed over this past year. But . . . there was Thoivra. And Seagga. And Thoivra's conservative cohort.

"Look, I don't see my way now," she told him. "And I don't want to risk Malaka-degg's tenure here without an actual strategy. I like your proposal. Let's both do some thinking on the best way to proceed."

Jorgan three years ago would have been impatient of her caution. This older Jorgan nodded decisively, grinned, and agreed.

"But, why," he asked, "is this Reindeer-man so important? You said his hip is fully healed, his shoulder entirely mobile, and his strength nearly restored. And you've learned most of what he has to teach about *aeros-energea*. It's just practice from now on. No harm if we shake things up and he gets pitched out a month early, is there?"

Oh. She'd explained her professional development, she'd mentioned that Malaka-degg was her friend, and she'd detailed the growing conservative sentiment in Kaunis-lodge. She hadn't revealed that Malaka-degg was her . . . lover, as the Silmarish termed it. *I haven't even told him I'm a mother now.* Rede's presence seemed to complicate everything, when she contemplated Jorgan's "shaking things up."

She managed to give him news of her son, but laying bald the essence of her relationship with Malaka-degg eluded her.

"I'm a *mapah*," Jorgan murmured, awe leaking into his eyes. "Livli, that's beautiful. I'm so happy for you." His arm circled her shoulders, and he laid his cheek on the top of her head a moment. "No wonder you're shy of tumult. New mothers usually are."

That didn't sit well.

"Don't dismiss my concerns as hormonal vulnerability," she snapped. "I've lived here all the years you've been at Tukeva and then gone on wanderyar, and my intuition is a good bit more informed than yours!"

He looked startled. "Of course. I'm sorry."

She could see he really meant it and nodded forgiveness.

They rejoined their lodge-mates for supper, agreed to wait and think until Labresse at least.

The hoorah generated by Jorgan's appearance in the refecting-hall was considerable.

The Tukeva-brothers shouted and stamped. Nial gave an impromptu speech. And Sarvet flew out of her ceremonial sun-chair to embrace him and cry actual tears of joy.

Had her calm all those years ago at the son-parting been a mask? Maybe.

Livli felt her own eyes tearing up. She clutched Rede hard enough that he squawked. His reunion with her had been almost as noisy as Jorgan's welcome. This was the first time he'd gone more than a half day without nursing. "Manga monga gah!" he'd screamed from Mimmi's arms. But now he was settling for sleep.

She nuzzled the top of his fuzzy head. He still had that sweet baby smell. *Mmm.*

Livli looked around the refecting-hall. The brothers had settled in for tall tales mixed with singing – and likely a few stories from Jorgan about his adventures – but the sisters were drifting out. Thoivra had stayed only long enough to gobble her food, no doubt embarrassed by Kanya-degg's presumption. Where was Seagga? Niyena, seated beside Livli, was scanning the tables too.

"Livli, we have to do something." Niyena shifted to meet Livli's eyes directly. "*You* have to do something." Her voice was tight and strained.

"*I* have to? Why not you? He's your patient."

Niyena just stared at her.

"Niyena, what is it?"

"Don't you know? You feel the same about his sweet-brother."

Ah. So my suspicions were correct.

"I wasn't sure," she admitted. "You've been . . . very discreet."

Niyena choked back a laugh. "Yah. The herb walks are . . . convenient. I'm not so bold as you.

Did she mean . . . ?

"Suoina or Rahkel would be sure to notice, if I abandoned my own bednook for even one night, let alone many."

Yah, she did mean that. "How did you know?"

"Oh, Livli, don't be silly. I've seen you coming away from the spa-hall at dawn many a time. Besides you and Malaka-degg . . . are too alive and easy in one another's company. It's obvious."

"Surely not!" Startlement clenched her stomach. "Did Mimmi tell you? Does everyone know?"

"Obvious to me," Niyena amended. "You told Mimmi? Why? She's rather a chatterbox, isn't she?"

"It was an accident. And . . . I don't think she's chattered about it." She paused. "Are you happy?"

The worry cleared from Niyena's face.

"He's amazing, Livli. Each herb I introduce him to is miracle in his eyes, and yet . . . he treats me as miraculous beyond even the most amazing of plants."

Livli kept the chuckle seeking escape to a mere widening of her eyes. Niyena was a wilding-sister and a brilliant one at that. Of course she would compare precious things to her beloved plants.

"What of you?" returned the brilliant wilding-sister.

Malaka-degg's face smiled in Livli's memory. That relaxed quirk at the edge of his lips made her want to run to him right now to kiss it. "Yah, I'm happy. If only . . ."

"If only?"

"I'd better bolt to Seagga's cabinet right now, if we don't want our menfolk tossed out on their ears in the morning."

"Can you manage without me?" Niyena flushed. "I know I'd just end up screaming and crying, which wouldn't help."

"No." Would Niyena really rant and sob? Her friend was usually the more controlled of the two of them. Livli couldn't imagine it. "I mean, yes. I'll manage."

Thoivra was amidst a rant of her own in Seagga's parlor, just as Livli had predicted.

"Did you see him? Did you see him?" she spluttered, shaking a knitting needle at their lodge-mother. "He dared touch his filthy foreign lips to *this* cheek! He's got to go, Seagga. Go, I say!" Then she noticed Livli's quiet arrival. "This is your fault, you hussy! I've seen how you look at that Reindeer refuse!"

Seagga interposed. She might have no moral fiber, but she didn't tolerate rudeness. "Come sit, Livli. I imagine you know your patient was causing trouble this afternoon."

Livli checked Rede – fast asleep – and pulled a flap of the sling across his eyes. Seagga had the oil lamps turned up bright.

She accepted a cup of tea from Ulvve before answering, "Well, he's Niyena's patient, but, yah, I heard he joined the Long-light celebrations."

"Which was forbidden as of a year ago," reminded Seagga.

"I still don't think that was right."

"Kanya-degg proved it was right today," shrilled Thoivra.

Seagga demonstrated more unexpected backbone. "Thoivra, you brought it on yourself with your discourtesy. A little quieter way of dealing with it would have eased him right out without fuss, don't you think?"

Thoivra sniffed, dabbed at her eyes with a crumpled kerchief.

Seagga turned back to Livli. "Niyena reports Kanya-degg as fully recovered from his ordeal. But I do understand that he and his sweet-brother wish to travel home together. Besides, he saved our most skilled herbalist from the *onderneming*. We owe him some favor. When will Malaka-degg be ready for discharge?"

Livli had been expecting this question, but hearing it dismayed her nonetheless. She answered with the truth. "By the fall-evener."

"So." Seagga nodded. "Very good."

She looked at Thoivra. "There is your answer, Sister. You must bear him until the equinox."

Thoivra opened her mouth to argue, shut it, then heaved up from her chair. Her glare at Livli could have burnt ice itself. "Admit I'm right," she demanded.

Breathe, Livli told herself.

Her words came out calm, without underlying strain: "No. You're not right." Her own calmness brought more calm in its wake along with inspiration. "You've gotten what you want despite its wrongness, but now I shall receive something I want. Malaka-degg and Kanya-degg shall attend any fete-day to which the Tukeva-brothers are bidden. You shall bear with the Reindeer-men fully in the quarter before their departure."

She did not raise her voice, straighten her body, or tense her face. She sat at her ease. And yet both Seagga and Thoivra bent before her.

"Say it!" she demanded in her turn.

Thoivra bowed her head. "Yah, duoja-healer," she muttered, passing out of the room.

Seagga nodded. "It is as you wish, Livli. But prepare them. There will be no reprieve this time."

Indeed, there would not. In three months Malaka-degg was going. She went to tell him.

He was oiling his boots, almost as if he knew the need to prepare for travel, but not so absorbed that he failed to look up with a smile when Livli entered their room with an air of urgency.

"Kanya-degg out on ear in morning?" He raised an eyebrow.

Her lips twitched. "You saw it then?"

"I think no one mind if they not see me watching fete. Hammarleeding custom interesting." He set his boots aside, wiped his hands on a clean cloth, and rose to take Livli in his arms. "My brother be . . . himself, yes. I not surprised."

"Angry?" she wondered. He didn't seem so. That was one of the things she loved about him. He tended toward amused.

"I have wager with self. How many eight-days before Kanya-degg ruffle sisters' feathers. He last longer than I guess." Malaka-degg smoothed her cheek, peeked into the baby sling, smoothed Rede's sleeping cheek. "So. When we depart?"

"At the fall-evener." She leaned into his chest. "Malaka-degg, I still don't know what to do. Why do I feel any confidence at all? This seems an insoluble situation."

"We wait, Livli. With patience, with hope. Thing often go well in time."

"I don't see how this can."

"Maybe I return home to find eager candidate awaiting *me*. I train and return to Kaunis."

Livli sighed. There was an appealing vision.

"Maybe you visit. Maybe I visit. Maybe we go on Hammarleeding wanderyar together."

That made her laugh. He wasn't proposing serious solutions, just spinning possibilities to prove his point.

"We not know what might turn up unless we keep looking, expecting good things."

"Yah." That was it; why she wasn't despondent. But envisioning Malaka-degg trekking off to the Minmahal remained a displeasing prospect.

He tipped her face up, brushed her lips with his. "I love. Always. I pledge to you."

She nodded, feeling warm inside. He'd not actually said that before, even though he'd demonstrated it every day.

"I also father and *ritwal-pakain* to Minmahal-clan. Sacred trust to make clan strong against demon. Pass to another, yes; abandon, never."

"I know that, Malaka-degg." And she did. "I feel the same about Kaunis-spa. My Hammarleeding sisters and brothers need my healing when they fall sick or injured."

"So we wait; stay true to trust. Both trust."

That felt right, good. Better than the clandestine linking-rite they'd contemplated in Bricember for the summer. This was a private commitment, but no less strong for its privacy.

Livli didn't see Mahde before he left for Tukeva, but Mimmi reported that he'd taken Rede under his supervision all afternoon and done pretty well – not nearly so bumbly and twitchy as before. Livli missed her linking-brother again on Lodge-day, although this time Oaja made sure Rede saw his father.

Third time's the charm, she thought on the morning of Mother's Bounty.

She hadn't been deliberately eluding Mahde. It just worked out that way. And she'd better *not* let it work out that way a third time. Babies did better when their birth-parents collaborated.

She went in search of him as the sun cleared the east range and discovered him climbing the path around the valley-rock, seeking her.

"Livli! You're looking well!"

"Pah pah pah pah!" shrieked Rede, lurching from his seat in the baby sling and stretching out his arms.

Livli laughed and handed the one-year-old over.

"I am well. You?" Were Mahde's shoulders a bit broader? He looked different somehow, older. Although . . . that hangdog air of his still clung to his gaze.

"Yah, I'm fine, but . . . I wanted to tell you ahead that I'm going to participate in the parade of wishes today."

She turned to accompany him back up the slope. "With Thoivra as the Mother's avatar? Uhg! I'll wait until next year."

"She's a ninny," he agreed. "Lucky my wish is simple enough that she can't mess it up." He grinned. "Do you have a wish? This year?"

Was he delaying?

"Oh, I have lots of wishes." She kept her tone light. Telling Mahde her problems would merely burden him without helping her in the least. "But nothing my sisters can help me with." Except that wasn't really true. Making Malaka-degg and Rede recognized denizens of Kaunis-lodge was something *only* her sisters could do. But wouldn't. "What's your wish?" she asked. "Or would you rather not say?"

"Actually I want to say. Not fair to surprise you with it."

"What?"

He squared his shoulders. They really did look broader. "I'm going on a second wanderyar."

"But you can't!"

He flicked a shamefaced glance at her. "I know I won't get back in time for Rede's passing moons, but I thought you could keep him a little longer. You'd like to, wouldn't you? That was why you wanted him to be a girl, after all."

Livli felt . . . aghast?

She'd never been truly frank about the issue with Mahde. How did he know? She'd not meant him to know.

Rede started wriggling in Mahde's grip. "Pah pah pah doh!"

Mahde took firmer hold of him. "Not yet, lil bro! Wait till we get to the steps." He looked at Livli, his eyes steadier this time. "I figured you'd be happy to have him an extra half year. I'll be back by Nerich, and we could do the passing moons then. Or, if I'm not, Nial said he'd be happy to."

"Nial said!" So that's how Mahde knew so much.

"He suggested it, actually."

"Mahde, this is crazy!"

"No, really. I was telling Nial about how I wished I could have another wanderyar. I . . . Livli, you know I still feel like a boy most of the time. Not a man."

No, she didn't know, but she could guess. He still *acted* like a boy.

"I think I took my wanderyar too young. I didn't leave the Fiordhammars, and I tagged on Uddi's heels the entire time. I came back . . . not much different than I left. I need . . . to do something hard on my own."

That . . . made sense. "But Mahde, it's not fair to Rede."

"Or you," he agreed. "But you both need me to grow up, and I can't do it at Tukeva. And Nial agreed I needed to go. He would, of course; the brother of more wanderyars than he can count. He'll be a better *mapah* than me anyway." Mahde's lips compressed. "I'm going, Livli. If the brothers will sponsor me in my bounty-wish. I'm sorry."

They'd reached the lodge steps. Livli sank onto the lowest one. Mahde set Rede on the ground.

"Doh! Doh! Doh!" Rede was excited. His favorite activity was standing, and a step provided a great balancer. He placed his chubby hands on the tread, pushed up to his feet, lifted his hands and teetered, and then plopped back down. "Doh!"

Livli laughed. Then sobered.

"This really is all my doing, isn't it. *You* wouldn't have asked to link with *me*."

Mahde flushed. "I wanted to," he answered, "but, no, I wouldn't have asked. I . . . was thinking about another wanderyar even then."

"Mahde! I wish you'd told me."

His face reddened again. "I wish I had. But that's just it. Not able to hold to my own view against yours."

"Will you be? When you come back?"

"I'm not coming back. Unless I can."

"Thus Nial for Rede's passing moons . . . and ever after."

He nodded.

Rede did another push, teeter, plop. "Ghi ghi doh!"

"Hey, lil bro!" Mahde rubbed his son's head. "Can you forgive me, Livli?"

She sighed. "Honestly, I should be asking you to forgive me."

"No. I may feel a boy, but I'm not. There's fault here for me. Don't take mine for yours."

Livli looked out across the Vrea-vale, the grasses turning golden and the wild pears laden with fruit. Mother's Bounty, indeed. She turned back to Mahde.

"Thanks for warning me. When will you go?"

"Almost immediately, if Tukeva-lodge sponsors me. Perhaps an eight-day. I'll need to gather supplies."

"Then I will have a wish for this year. Thoivra and all. I'm going to ask for Nial to be recognized as Rede's sweet-father, instead of waiting for you to be declared *en palauta*."

"I think that's good. I was hoping you would." He paused. "I'll speak first, if you want to look reasonable. Or second, if you want to look prescient."

"I don't really care." She smiled. "This takes courage, Mahde. Moral courage. I'm proud of you."

"Even though you'd prefer I not go."

"I'm not sure I do prefer that." She reached for her own store of courage. "Because you were right. I don't want to give Rede up. To you, or anyone. And I'm going to find a way to keep him with me until he's grown. Somehow."

Mahde was smiling. "Nial warned me you would."

"Really?"

"Sarvet was just as stubborn. He said."

Laughter bubbled out of her. "Oh, oh, oh! Why did I think I had any secrets? We all know each other too well!"

"Well, yah!"

Later, approaching the Mother-throne, her temporary calm waned under the nibble of nerves. Should she state her wish publicly as planned? Or ask Seagga privately? Or simply wait for Mahde to be declared unreturning? Mahde was near the head of the queue. With Kanya-degg right behind him, and then Niyena. Livli, some way back, figured looking reasonable was probably more important than *not* looking like a victim.

My dignity can take it.

Malaka-degg was not in the queue. He'd enjoyed participating in the panoply of the garlands, marching among the Kaunis-sisters and Tukeva-brothers through the Vyssa-grove with fronds of finger millet and wolfberry to decorate the Mother-throne, then dancing in the half-circle of grass to consecrate the amphitheater. Now he perched on the highest curving tier, seated next to Paiam on its grassy step, one leg dangling over a splintering wooden riser. Rede practiced standing – up, then down, then up – between them.

The Mother-throne stood vacant on the orchestra terrace. A milling press of Hammarleedings surged around it, as some sought the end of the wishing-queue and others climbed to their places on the earthen steps cut into the slope of the mountain. There wouldn't be enough seating for everyone – the Kaunis-cirque was small, intimate – and the remnants would cluster on the edges of the terrace. It didn't matter. The audience would come and go throughout the parade of wishes. What happened on the stage was formal and governed by ritual. What happened in the stands was not.

Sarvet emerged from the pines and started pulling order out of confusion. Her tasseled head dress showed every color of the rainbow, as did the stole over her shoulders. Her directions were quiet, but firm. She gestured the alpenhorn players to arrange themselves to one side as soon as there was space enough, and then they were ready to begin.

Livli's attention wandered. The summoning, anointing, and investing of the Mother's avatar was more compelling when the sister so honored was a friend. And Thoivra's round face bore an annoyingly self-satisfied smirk. *She's savoring queening it over us, not contemplating the service she offers us. Ugh!* Had she been chosen this year because her estranged son was away on his wanderyar? He would never have consented to occupy the bench of the throne with his birth-mother. Thoivra's daughter was more meek, a young girl approaching linking-age.

Finally the preliminaries were done, and Sarvet announced: "Let the parade of wishes begin!"

Jorgan advanced to the throne.

Mother Divine! Livli hadn't noticed he was first of all, and she had a bad feeling about it. He wouldn't ask, *surely* he wouldn't ask for a place as healer in Kaunis?

That was exactly what he asked.

"Sias in sanctuary, a great gift has come to me on my wanderyar. I wield the *aeros-energea* of old Giralliya, and I wish to heal with it in Kaunis-spa as my rightful haven."

Thoivra's daughter looked shocked. Thoivra herself looked furious. She drew breath in rage, but Sarvet touched her shoulder and murmured something. Reminding her that the Mother's avatar merely repeated each petitioner's wish to the community? The decisions for allocating resources (or permission) were not now and not Thoivra's to make. She settled back and spoke the required syllables: "Jorgan Nial-spring wields the air-duoja and begs a place as healer in Kaunis-spa."

Jorgan bent his head to Thoivra and passed off the terrace.

He should have consulted me! Except . . . when would a better time arrive? Livli certainly didn't know, but *now* seemed especially bad.

The queue ahead of her loosed the next petitioner and then the next. Their desires were conventional, safe: a sabbatical at Siajotti and a new assistant in the kitchens. Thoivra recovered her equanimity, grew gracious, signaling her approval of these modest requests. The audience relaxed. Had the earlier tension marked their disapproval or merely their surprise?

Several children came next, and Thoivra grew positively jovial. Queening it, indeed, but the tykes longing for fruit tartlets and visits to Iloiset-lake beamed under her nods.

Mahde walked to stand before the Mother-throne.

"Boyhood lingers upon me, and I wish a second wanderyar to clear my way to manhood." He held his shoulders very straight. Livli, closer to the arena now, could see him swallow, could see the faint distaste crossing Thoivra's features. Was everything and everyone connected with Livli tainted in Thoivra's mind? Probably, but the avatar-sister restrained herself and pronounced Mahde's wish without editorial.

Another stream of children crossed the stage.

Then it was Kanya-degg's turn.

Livli felt her stomach tighten and start to churn. How did she know this was going to be worse than Jorgan's wish. Oh, come on! This was Kanya-degg! How could it not be worse?

"Niyena teach me herb-lore and herb-healing." He sounded delighted with himself. "I wish learn more. More herb-lore, more healing, more Kaunis" – he gestured with a sweep of his arm – "Hammarleeding culture *maganda*" – beautiful – "Niyena *maganda!*"

He grinned, eyes alight.

"I wish learn more Niyena. Be linking-brother Niyena. Be Hammarleeding. Live in Kaunis. Heal in Kaunis. This be my wish." He bowed, then stood smiling.

Did he realize the tumult he'd just loosed?

Yes, he realized. His posture was relaxed, but cynicism touched his lips, contempt for Thoivra, his glance. He knew. And did it anyway.

Livli sighed.

Thoivra bolted upward from her throne, face red, then white, with fury. "You dare!" she hissed.

Sarvet reached an arm toward the avatar-sister, then let it fall with a slight shake of her head. Thoivra would do and say as Thoivra wished.

"Hammarleeding brothers don't live in sister-lodges, and you know it!" she snarled. "I've seen how you look at her. If you think you'll be permitted to foul her purity, to pollute the sanctity of Kaunis-home, you've got another think coming." She drew in a sharp breath through pinched nostrils. Her eyes went flat and cold, and she reseated herself. "Sisters of Kaunis, this outlander Kanya-degg –"

Sarvet leaned in with soft correction.

Thoivra glared, but restarted. "This outlander Parangaian Kanya-degg anak na lalaki ng Pataya-liga at Gishyan-degg" – honored Kanya-degg, son of Pataya-liga and Gishyan-degg – "wishes residence in Kaunis as healer and linking-brother." Her tone would have scoured the dirtiest fleece snow white, but she confined herself to the ritual words. Her daughter leaned away toward the far side of their bench, eyes wide and scared.

Kanya-degg bowed again and strolled off the terrace.

Niyena strode onto it.

More trouble coming. Livli's friend didn't employ her lover's commanding relaxation; she looked militant. She faced away from the Mother-avatar, defying tradition, addressing the sisters and brothers seated on the amphitheater steps.

"Kaunis and Tukeva, Kanya-degg is worthy. He saved my life. He's learning herb-lore as though inspired by Duoja herself. And I love him."

A mutter of sotto voce comment lapped her audience. Niyena stood taller still.

"If he has no place here, I will seek a place with Minmahal-tribe. But he has earned such a place; he brings honor and courage to us." She lifted her chin. "I ask that Kanya-degg be made healer in Kaunis-spa and linking-brother to me in the morrow's rite."

No mere wishing for Niyena. She was asking – no demanding – what she wanted.

A woman's voice rang out – "Kaunis is a sister-lodge!" – echoed by a spatter of agreeing "yah's." The low growl from the brothers never rose to articulate words.

Sarvet stepped forward. "Let the Mother speak."

Thoivra started. Had she forgotten her role? Lapsed into mere listening?

"Niyena Eija-spring wishes" – she paused, delving into memory – "Parangaian Kanya-degg anak na lalaki ng Pataya-liga at Gishyan-degg be granted sponsorship as Kaunis-healer and linking-brother." Thoivra uttered the formal phrases as though they tasted of turpentine.

Niyena nodded, back yet to the Mother-avatar, a faint smile crossing her face. Her slow passage to the terrace edge recalled that of her nominee's. Livli grew rapt under a sudden vision of Niyena in three years: relaxed, confidant, powerful. *Yes, he's right for her.*

But could this work? Surely Kaunis would never grant what Niyena (and Kanya-degg) requested.

Livli studied the women and men on the amphitheater steps. The next petitioners across the stage garnered little of their attention. Brothers gestured and shook their heads. Sisters pursed their lips and fell mute, or argued in shrill whispers. It didn't look promising. Where were Gaddja and Oaja, Risten and Rahkel?

Mimmi's friends, clustered to one side, were among the

unspeaking. Mimmi herself changed her seat, climbing to join Paiam and offering Rede a helping hand for his pull-ups.

"Livli?" Sarvet's voice recalled Livli's scrutiny to the stage.

She stood at the head of the queue.

My turn.

But her feet stayed still.

Why am I here?

There was no need to humiliate Mahde with a public request that his fatherhood pass to Nial.

I refuse.

Yet there was a wish she had to voice. It wasn't sensible. It wasn't prudent. It wasn't wise. But keeping silence would betray . . . too much. She crossed the spongy turf to stand before Thoivra, then spun to face the other way, following Niyena's example.

Let the disgusted features of the Mother-avatar convey her loathing to my back.

Livli lifted her arms. "My sisters! My brothers!" She paused, weighing her tactics, and returned her hands to her sides.

"How many of you have visited Siajotti?"

No one answered, but the hum of murmured conversation ebbed.

"The scroll-hall is an amazing place. It holds stories of the first Hammarleedings to inhabit these mountains. Tales of forgotten heroes who upheld the sanctity of Duoja's spring. And lists of healing lore that hold hope for even the very ill."

She glanced up at Malaka-degg. He was appreciative, expectant, at ease. Next to him, Paiam tilted her head to one side, alert but knowing. *Did* she know? Mimmi had lifted Rede to her knees, steadying the baby while he bounced.

"Siajotti is wonderful, and the reason I can find whatever bit of knowledge I need there is because it is organized. Each scroll rests in its own pigeonhole in its proper cabinet. It's a great system." She stood quiet a heartbeat. "For scrolls."

Behind her, Thoivra hissed wordlessly.

Livli ignored her.

"But, sisters and brothers, what's great for scrolls isn't so great for people. I'm not just a daughter; I'm also a mother. I'm not just a healer; I'm also a friend. I don't fit neatly into one tidy category. And you don't either!"

A hushed mutter passed through her listeners.

"We've grown too narrow. If you're a brother, you can't be here or do that. If you're a sister, you can't be there or do this. If you're a lowlander, you can't be anywhere in our mountains or do anything in our lodges.

"So I have wishes: one wish for all of us and one wish for me.

"Let's meet people as people, and treat them as people. Let's be kind and generous and responsive. If a foreign man loves a Hammar-woman, and she loves him, let them link. If a Hammar-brother contracts the gift to heal" – the mutter of the crowd grew louder, now they knew where she was leading them – "let him heal. Why say no, when we could say yes?"

"There's a time for no!" boomed a man's voice. "And I'd say this is that time."

The rest of his message, if there were one, drowned amidst an outbreak of shouting.

Sarvet moved to Livli's side and raised her sheaf of grain.

The cacophony died.

The Holy Caller spoke: "You may choose not to listen. You may choose not to grant. But you must honor an interval in which your sister speaks her wish." Sarvet fixed her stare on one restive brother, until he quieted. Then she lowered her millet-sheaf.

Livli swallowed. Could she project her next words as clearly as her earlier ones?

"My wish for myself is that you grant me Malaka-degg as my linking-brother and as Rede's sweet-father."

She lifted her gaze to the top corner of the amphitheater. Malaka-degg smiled, straightened his propped leg, and began descending through the multitude, touching a shoulder here, gripping a reaching hand there, as easy as his brother, yet without Kanya-degg's bravado.

He stepped to Livli's side, clasped her hand, and took Thoivra's role. "Livli Sarvet-spring wishes your sanction for Parangaian Malaka-degg anak na lalaki ng Pataya-liga at Gishyan-degg as her linking-brother and as her son's father."

Sarvet lifted the millet-sheaf before anyone started shouting.

"All wishes may be spoken," she reminded them again. The crowd allowed her restraint, but the Mother-avatar didn't.

Thoivra bounced off her throne, stepped around Livli, and commanded: "You will hear me first. Even the avatar speaks her wish at Bounty!"

That was true. Most avatars uttered a prayer for others: health through the winter, prosperity from the autumn lodge-trading, or a specific bequest for a needy friend. But serving as avatar didn't deprive a sister of her personal wish, if she had one. And the choice of when to speak it was hers.

Thoivra stood silent a moment. Regaining her poise? She straightened her shoulders, set her jaw. When she spoke at last, her voice was level.

"Sisters. Brothers. Our traditions are our haven, tested by time, and yielding happiness for all. Following the ways of our forebears, we ensure our health and our prosperity. When we depart from those customs that make us Hammarleedings, we risk everything.

New ways may have merit, but often they do not. Why suffer their disadvantages when we already know what works?"

Thoivra drew a deep breath, then let it go.

"Kaunis-lodge has been testing new and strange methods, and testing them wildly, without safeguards, at the whim of one rebellious and foolish sister."

Livli stilled the protest rising in her. Let Thoivra have her say. Better to refute her thoroughly in one concerted speech than to devolve into a shouting match. The pressure of Malaka-degg's hand on hers confirmed his agreement. But Ulla and Suoinen in the audience looked outraged. Livli shook her head ever so slightly. *Not now, not yet.*

Thoivra continued her speech. How long had she been honing it?

"I've seen our innocent and precious novitiates ogling the outland men who have remained so inappropriately long at Kaunis-spa. I seek protection for these young sisters.

"I've learned that one misguided sister has foresworn the linking-rite and linked without ceremony. I seek her redemption." Thoivra looked sternly toward where Niyena had walked into the Vyssa-grove with Kanya-degg.

A few shocked gasps floated from Thoivra's cronies, seated front and center. Juudet, between her two agog daughters, positively glared.

"I've discovered, along with you, that our renegade" – Thoivra finally glanced at Livli – "intends to deprive her blameless baby of his rightful heritage, refting him from father, father-lodge, and the fatherly rearing proper to boys."

Above them, Paiam tilted her head and rested her knuckles under her chin. *Mistake,* she seemed to convey. Belaboring Livli's revelation wouldn't gain Thoivra points.

"I stand against these perverse and unwarranted experiments," Thoivra declared. "My wish is that Kaunis-lodge return to our ancient legacy, nourishing her sisters in the sacred sanctuary of feminine purity. My wish is a unity, but the steps to achieve it are multiple.

"First, these foreign men must go, and go immediately. They are well. They don't belong here."

"They don't!" called two sisters, breaking the silence holding the crowd. "Send them home!" echoed someone else. Livli gritted her teeth. It was getting harder to stand listening.

"In addition, Kessel or Mirski-lodge must found a brother's spa. Bringing sick and injured men to Kaunis will always lead to the kind of problems we have now."

"Kessel! Kessel!" yelled a brother.

Thoivra nodded. "Next, our defiled sister, Niyena Eija-spring, requires a cleansing-vigil and retreat in solitude."

"That's ridiculous!" Livli burst out. "She's no more defiled than you are!"

Sarvet brandished her grain sheaf; then Niyena stepped out from the Vyssa-grove, Kanya-degg on her heels. They lounged against a pine bole, fingers intertwined, unaware of what was going forward.

"Look at her!" Thoivra exclaimed, losing her dignity. "She's disgusting!"

Niyena's left eyebrow lifted, but she continued to loll at her ease. Kanya-degg shifted his weight forward, then leaned back against the tree trunk, deliberately more relaxed than before. The Reindeer brothers knew how to fight with assurance instead of bluster, no question.

"No contumely, please," Sarvet admonished. "Finish your list."

Thoivra sniffed, as if to convey: *you'll wish I hadn't.*

"Lastly, little Rede must be protected."

Livli stiffened.

Thoivra harassing her rival? Only to be expected. Insulting her rival's friend? Nasty, but shrewd.

Threatening my son? You'll wish you hadn't.

She glanced upward. Rede was asleep, his head snuggled into Mimmi's shoulder. Paiam, composed despite Thoivra's drama, leaned over her great grandson and stroked his cheek, then gestured Mimmi to shift into the shade creeping out from the western trees. Keep the sun from shining into the baby's closed eyes.

Thoivra's voice strengthened.

"Rede's birth-mother is not competent. The boy *must* be removed from her warped purview. I'd suggest he begin his moon-transfer immediately, but his sweet-father is departing." Thoivra's voice oozed scorn. "That still seems the best solution. I propose we name Uddi his moon-father and proceed with it."

Livli's heart felt abruptly cold. This had been her fear from the moment she knew she was with child.

What if I lose my baby?

The scheme to be sure her child was a girl had been mere diversion, something she *could* control (maybe) amidst a sea of things she could not: ill fortune, injury, illness, death. And now loss loomed.

I thought I'd have more time, more ideas, more chances. I thought I could win. Against fate, against foe, against fundamental convention. *I thought my resource could prevail.*

Thoivra's round face reddened in triumph. Her eyes narrowed with malice.

Livli's time was now. And a sense of lack was all she had.

Malaka-degg stepped behind her, transferring her left hand to his left, taking her right hand in his right.

Yes.

And no. She possessed more than dearth and deficit. Much more.

She had the assets of a Reindeer *ritwal-pakain*. She had the confidence Ivvar revealed to her. She had the power of *aeros-energea* and duoja-gift. She knew what to do.

"You're wrong," she told Thoivra.

And then to Paiam – serene Paiam – and waiting Niyena and worried Mimmi: "She's wrong."

Then declared to her gathered sisters and brothers: "Thoivra's wrong, and I'll show you why!"

She reached for air-duoja.

The centering from that moment of certainty was enough.

The current of strength flowing from Malaka-degg was more than enough.

We've practiced this.

Spun threads of duoja streamed through her phalanges and out. Malaka-degg lifted their joined hands, and healing fountained from them, spilling into the amphitheater like a sacred spring, gliding through the roots and branches of all gathered on and around the steps.

There was some darkness there. Congested, cloying, cold. Narrowed branches, misshapen roots.

Livli pushed.

Her own energy – radiant, golden, and sparkling – gushed fiercely, warming chilled constriction, laving detritus, turning gelid shadow to liquid light. Rigid branches grew supple; they flexed, rippled. Scarred roots softened, opened, healed. The duoja-essence that *was* the sisters and brothers glimmered in its flow: translucent, transformed.

A knot of darkness congealed beneath the living currents. Stubborn, dense, resisting. *Thoivra.*

Would gentleness serve?

Livli poured herself through blindly, was bounced aside, back into more welcoming waters. She circled, rushed forward again, skimmed blackness.

More force?

No. *I will be still, I will embrace, I will accept.*

She curled herself around the knot, patient, waiting, kind.

And waited.

All is well, all is sacred, all is yours. Good things lie ahead.

She felt hardness dissolve, melt. She cupped it, patient still, waiting for the flutter of impulse, life ready to move. *There!* She opened, and a glittering silt sifted down, glided away on a dulcet bottom current.

Thoivra's dusk touched dawn. The duoja-pool was cleansed.

Livli felt limpid as sun-warmed water, soothing as ice-cooled mist, gentle as loving touch. Her gift swirled, she swirled: in motion and at peace together, brimming, bubbling, cascading through lagoons and channels made for her, transforming through liquid into breeze, mounting skyward in dizzying sweeps as though she had wings.

The sun dazzled her.

Within its streaming rays the phantom shapes of winged horses took form, soaring through the air, galloping as though cloud were mountain meadow.

They were three.

Chase with us, sweet sister! We glory in thy freedom. Be free!

Why did Livli picture honey, tree apples, and rain? The mare's voice was merry, mellow, like her birth-mother's, and yet not.

Spread thy wings! The stallion's joy might drown a listener with its strength, and yet he conveyed strength enough to Livli that she did spread her wings. What wings were these? She had none. She flew, swooping and climbing, laughter trailing her galloping hooves.

Catch the sun, little sister! Delicate, blithesome, and glad fluted the other mare's behest.

Livli climbed, through light so clear it sang, into light so bright it blinded, beyond into light so magnificent she needed her wings no more and flew without them. Up and up she soared, the pegasi beside her, below her, above her. Into light more than light: light that was joy, beauty, love. She melted and merged.

I am joy. I am beauty. I am love.

A deep tone, rung from the gong of the world, vibrated through her being.

Yes.

Then she was falling. Down and down, without fear. Diving with the pegasi. Down to earth, return to earth, return home.

Standing, she felt Malaka-degg's hands still on hers, lowered now. Felt the heat of his chest at her back.

Loosing her fingers, she spun in his arms, opened her eyes. "Were you there?" she gasped. "Did you hear them?"

His gaze smiled into hers.

"I ride *pakpak kabayo*" – winged horse – "deep into earth, gliding on stream of breath that turn to flame, deeper, always deeper, to the fire-heart of world." Awe transfigured his face. "I feel you with me, bear you up, and fierce *kabayo* speak. Wonders and rapture."

He bent to kiss her brow, breathed: "Believe."

"I do," she whispered. "Oh, I do."

His cheek against hers, she rested in the haven of his creation, a moment of quietude welcome after transcendent flight.

Then the sobs of someone near her ankles recalled her to the mundane. Thoivra was weeping in huddled disarray on the ground. Nor was she the only one so afflicted. Livli scanned the amphitheater, getting her bearings. Sisters crying, sisters exalted. Brothers groaning, brothers reverential. There were Hammarleedings in all states of feeling.

Paiam arrived from the steps, bending to help Thoivra to her feet. Sarvet went to the most shattered of the brothers. Livli looked toward Mimmi. Was she alright? What of Rede?

Her son had slept through it all.

Livli stifled a watery chuckle. Had he dreamed baby dreams of bold steeds? She'd never know. Mimmi looked like she treasured a secret; delightful, private, special. *I'll leave her be, let her enjoy her bliss in peace.* Neither she nor Rede had taken harm.

Others did require her care. Livli went among them, listening, soothing, caring, and listening. Most wanted to talk, although briefly, a word, a phrase, no more.

"... flight through a night of stars ..."

"I came home."

"The father-heart heard my prayer."

"... a ringing neigh of triumph ..."

"Love knew me."

"... from despair to hope to joy ..." That was Risten, welcoming faith.

"... borne on horseback to truth."

They'd received gift and vision, terrible in its power, freeing and frightening. Each withstood it according to his or her nature. Livli was humbled by their respect for her as the catalyst to their revelation.

One sister had reveled in it: mystic Oaja. "Fever burns out contagion, does it not?"

Some while later, Sarvet began reassembling them for the completion of the parade of wishes. Thoivra remained too shaken to resume her role as avatar. Before the Holy Caller could ask those assembled to choose another, their chant coalesced: "Livli! Livli! Livli!"

Smiling, Sarvet led her daughter to the mother-throne. Mimmi brought her Rede. He woke in the transfer, hungry and cranky. Livli sat nursing him as the wishers filed past. Their wishes were very different than they'd planned.

"Let me remember."

"Might Oaja forgive me?"

"I pledge a garland of honor to Eija henceforth each Bounty."

"I give thanks."

"I am sorry." That was Juudet.

"I am healed."

Penultimate, Seagga reached the throne.

"I wish to resign my trust. Let the mothering of the lodge be given to another." She looked sad and happy. And whole. "Thank you, Livli," she breathed.

Very last was Thoivra. She'd rallied enough to stop crying and grow impatient with the friends urging her to go rest. "I wished as the Mother," she pleaded. "Now let me wish as a sister."

Sarvet declared this permissible, but Paiam's intervention was necessary to staunch the importunities of Thoivra's anxious attendants. Paiam herself guided Thoivra into the half-circle, now striped with the reaching shadows of trees, and supported her tottery steps to the throne.

"I was right," she whispered, "but I was also wrong. Old ways are blessing, and new ways, too." Her voice strengthened. "We need a mother who will guide us to a healing blend of both old and new. I wish the mothering of Kaunis to descend to Sarvet Paiam-spring."

Livli was so surprised she said nothing, just as Thoivra had when Niyena requested a place for Kanya-degg in the spa and at the morrow's linking-rite.

"Speak!" the former avatar urged her.

Livli took Thoivra's hand, gentle in her clasp, and addressed their community.

"Thoivra Ohtta-spring wishes our election of Sarvet Paiam-spring as lodge-mother, to befriend us and guide us and judge us. Blessed be."

∗ ∗ ∗

Livli lingered with Malaka-degg in the amphitheater, reluctant to leave the scene of their ecstatic venture. The sun had swung far to the west and lowered, casting the terrace and most of the stepped tiers into shadow. One patch of brightness remained on the topmost corner where Malaka-degg had perched. Lolling against him, Livli tipped her face to the sky's arch, blue as madderfoil petals. The evening air was cooling; the sun's warmth, comforting.

She and slumbering Rede and Malaka-degg were alone. Nial had stayed with them while the Kaunis community filed out of the gathering space toward supper in the lodge. He didn't say much, just gazed contentedly at his daughter, proud and amazed and brimful of gratitude.

"Your mother changed the lives of all dwelling in the Fiordhammars," he told her when he rose to follow the last Tukeva-brother exiting the clearing. "You will change the world." He touched her cheek in parting. "I love you."

She felt loved.

Mimmi returned briefly bringing a picnic meal for them, but stayed only long enough to unpack and serve it. Rede woke as Livli took her last succulent bite of wild pear. He demanded a nibble of the fruit before consenting to nurse.

"Will your brother like living in Kaunis?" Livli asked Malaka-degg.

"Oh, yes. I was surprised he stayed in Minmahal so many year. He more Hammarleeding than Reindeer-man in his soul. Don't you think?"

A faint chuckle lifted her ribs. "Yah. He'd fit right in at Tukeva. Kaunis . . . well, he'll be fine, won't he. It's the sisters who will have some adjusting to do."

"Kanya-degg be the least of that. Healer-brothers living year round in spa and birth-mothers owning choice for rearing of sons, that be change."

Livli sighed. "I'm almost sad," she confessed, "to see the old Kaunis becoming new."

"Of course. The gain worth price, but the price be paid. Loss be real."

"Niyena's so happy she can't walk straight."

Malaka-degg laughed. "Lucky Kanya-degg always walk straight."

They sat in silence for a time. Rede hiccupped, and Livli raised him to her shoulder for burping, then started him on the other breast. He fell asleep before he'd half finished. The day had been long.

Livli was wondering if it were time to seek their bednook in the spa when Sarvet emerged from the Vyssa-grove. Her birth-mother had exchanged her ceremonial garb for ordinary clothing, knee-length tunic and leg coverings. She waved, crossed the stage terrace, and climbed up to them.

"Mahde's gone," she announced, seating herself next to Livli. "I've just seen him off."

"Already? He said he'd need an eight-day for final preparations."

"He was so eager to be gone. Ulla and Ulletta roped in some of the sisters to help gather supplies, so that there need be no delay. He could hardly stand still for the excitement in him, now he knows that fulfillment awaits." Sarvet paused to scan the west sky, just visible over the trees, turning golden. "He told me that he didn't know what waited for him, but that he sensed it was every bit as marvelous as Jorgan's gift of healing. 'The pegasi told me so,' he said, 'and I believe.'"

Sarvet looked at Livli, curiosity in her glance. "I think it's wonderful he's going in hope and inspiration rather than desperation." Another pause. "I was surprised you weren't there to bid him farewell. I know the link between you is severed, but he's an old friend, a cradle friend."

Livli shook her head. "It's alright, Mother. Truly. I bade him farewell this morning. There is no ill feeling between us."

It felt odd calling Sarvet mother. The title had always meant birth-mother before. Now it meant that, and also lodge-mother.

Sarvet's shoulders relaxed. Had she been so worried? Then her shoulders tensed again. "I wish *you* would stay."

Livli smiled.

"Why not?" Sarvet probed. "You could be a healing couple just like Niyena and Kanya-degg." She nodded to Malaka-degg. "And your favorite sweet-brother will be in Kaunis-spa as well. You've always wished Jorgan never left for Tukeva. Now your wish has come true."

"Most of the boy babies will still go to Tukeva. Who will Rede play with? Change won't come that fast." That wasn't her real reason, but it was a factor.

"He'll be a pioneer. Like his birth-mother. Like his *maghra*."

Livli laughed. "I know. And that isn't really it."

Now she paused.

"Mother, do you realize, did you see . . . ?"

"See what?"

"When the pegasi brought you back to Kaunis, the stallion's hooves smote the ground as he returned to the sky, creating our healing spring."

Sarvet lifted an eyebrow.

Livli continued: "The water-duoja I wield is born of that hoof blow."

"Yes." Sarvet didn't question that conclusion, nor did she question where Livli was going. Her spurt of motherly worry had ebbed, swallowed by a holy caller's and a lodge-mother's anchored equanimity.

"The air-duoja comes from the pegasi as well."

Both Sarvet's eyebrows went up.

"It's the breezes driven by their wing-claps!"

"Ah! Yah, that makes sense."

"But, Mother, the Reindeer People have no sacred spring for extraordinary healing. And if I go to them, they will. All the sky is a fount of wellness where I am present."

Sarvet considered her.

"Then, blessed be, daughter. If it feels right to you, then it's right."

"I think so."

"You were always too big for Kaunis to hold." Sarvet drew Livli close, pressed her cheek to Livli's hair, released her. "I'm proud of you. Amazed by you. Inspired by you." She chuckled. "You do know that Minmahal may not be big enough for you either?"

Malaka-degg echoed Sarvet's chuckle. "They will grow bigger. Just as Kaunis grow."

Sarvet's eyes softened. "Yah, she's a world-changer, our Livli." Sarvet sighed. "I'll miss you."

Livli laughed again. "You'll visit, of course!"

And she did.

THE END

Months of the Year

Sombry winter

Falnary late winter

Nerich early spring

Thyaril spring

Ponce late spring

Joiesse early summer

Labresse summer

Jubiante late summer

Sanember early autumn

Ionaber autumn

Noulember late autumn

Bricember early winter

Glossary

Brother A Hammarleeding man or boy.

Brother-lodge Hammarleeding men and boys live in all-male communities apart from Hammarleeding women. The term brother-lodge refers both to a community of males and to the large wooden chalet they inhabit.

Duoja A hero out of Hammarleeding myth, said to guard a sacred spring and to have vanquished warring demons. Her name is also used for the spiritual powers granted the Hammarleedings for healing, luring wild sheep down from the mountain peaks, and other purposes.

Father-lodge Brother-lodges are referred to as father-lodges when the speaker emphasizes the social and spiritual structures underpinning the community.

Linking The Hammarleeding form of marriage is a celebration of their Mother Goddess, and the commitment to deity is emphasized over the commitment between the woman and the man. A couple might remain committed to one another for merely the duration of the ceremony, for a number of months or years, or for life. The bond between each parent and any offspring is permanent.

Linking-brother A woman's mate in the linking ceremony.

Linking-sister A man's mate in the linking ceremony.

Mother-lodge Sister-lodges are referred to as mother-lodges when the speaker emphasizes the social and spiritual structures underpinning the community.

Sister A Hammarleeding woman or girl.

Sister-lodge Hammarleeding women and girls live in all-female communities apart from Hammarleeding men. The term sister-lodge refers both to a community of females and to the large wooden chalet they inhabit.

Sweet-brother A sibling with whom one shares both father and birth-mother.

Sweet-moon After a linking rite, some couples spend an entire month living together in a secluded moon-hut before parting to their separate homes.

Sweet-sister A sibling with whom one shares both father and birth-mother.

J.M. Ney-Grimm lives with her husband and children in Virginia, just east of the Blue Ridge Mountains. She's learning about permaculture gardening, post-carbon preparation, and debunking popular myths about food. The rest of the time she reads Robin McKinley and Lois McMaster Bujold, plays boardgames like Settlers of Catan, rears her twins, and writes stories set in her troll-infested North-lands.

Look for her novels and novellas at your favorite bookstore – online or on Main Street.

J.M. Ney-Grimm maintains a blog featuring flash fiction from her North-lands and other tidbits unearthed by her ever-active curiosity.

Visit her at http://JMNey-Grimm.com.